SHADOWS OF ECSTASY

by the same author

★

WAR IN HEAVEN
MANY DIMENSIONS
THE PLACE OF THE LION
THE GREATER TRUMPS
DESCENT INTO HELL
ALL HALLOWS' EVE

★

THE DESCENT OF THE DOVE
HE CAME DOWN FROM HEAVEN
and THE FORGIVENESS OF SINS
THE FIGURE OF BEATRICE:
A Study in Dante

SHADOWS OF ECSTASY

by

CHARLES WILLIAMS

WILLIAM B. EERDMANS PUBLISHING COMPANY
Grand Rapids, Michigan

ISBN 0-8028-1223-6

Reprinted, March 1980

PHOTOLITHOPRINTED BY EERDMANS PRINTING COMPANY
GRAND RAPIDS, MICHIGAN, UNITED STATES OF AMERICA

CONTENTS

Chapter One

ENCOUNTERING DARKNESS

Roger Ingram's peroration broke over the silent dining hall: "He and such as he are one with the great conquerors, the great scientists, the great poets; they have all of them cried of the unknown:

> *I will encounter darkness as a bride*
> *And hug it in mine arms.*"

He sat down amid applause, directed not to him but to the subject of his speech. It was at a dinner given by the Geographical Faculty of the University of London to a distinguished explorer just back from South America. The explorer's health had been proposed by the Dean of the Faculty, and the Professor of Tropical Geography had been intended to second it. Unfortunately the Professor had gone down with influenza that very day, and Roger had been hastily made to take his place. The other geographical professors, though vocationally more suitable, were both learned and low-voiced, as also were their public addresses. The Dean had refused to subject his distinguished guests, including the explorer, to their instructive whispers. Roger might not be a geographer, but he could make a better speech, and he belonged to the University if to a different faculty, being Professor of Applied Literature. This was a new Chair, endowed beneficently by a rich Canadian who desired at once to benefit the Mother Country and to recall her from the by-ways of pure art to the highroad of art as related to action. Roger had been invited from a post in a Northern University to fill the Chair, largely on the strength of his last book, which was called *Persuasive Serpents:*

7

studies in English Criticism, and had been read with admiration
by twenty-seven persons and with complete misunderstanding
by four hundred and eighty-two. Its theme, briefly, was that
most English critics had at all times been wholly and entirely
wrong in their methods and aims, and that criticism was an
almost undiscovered art, being a final austere harmony produced by the purification of literature from everything alien,
which must still exist in the subjects of most prose and poetry.
However, the salary of the Chair of Applied Literature had
decided him to give an example of it in his own person, and
he had accepted.

He lent an ear, when the toast had been drunk, to his wife's
"Beautiful, Roger: he loved it", and to Sir Bernard Travers'
murmured *"Hug?"*

"I know," he said; "you wouldn't hug it. You'd ask it to a
light but good dinner and send it away all pale and comfortable. I was good, wasn't I, Isabel? A little purple, but pleasing
purple. Pleasing purple for pleased people—that's me after
dinner." He composed himself to listen.

The explorer, returning thanks, was not indisposed to accept literally the compliments which had been offered him.
He touched on ordinary lives, on the conditions of ordinary
lives, on the ordinary office clerk, and on the difference
between such a man and himself. He painted a picture of
South America in black and scarlet; Roger remarked to his
wife in a whisper that crude scarlet was the worst colour to
put beside rich purple. He enlarged on the heroism of his
companions with an under-lying suggestion that it was largely
maintained by his own. He made a joke at the expense of
Roger's quotation, saying that he would never apply "for a
divorce or even a judicial separation from the bride Mr.
Ingram has found me." Roger gnashed his teeth and smiled
back politely, muttering "He isn't worth Macaulay and I gave
him Shakespeare." He would, in short, have been a bore, had
he not been himself.

At last he sat down. Sir Bernard, politely applauding, said: "Roger, why are the English no good at oratory?"

"Because—to do the fool justice—they prefer to explore," Roger said. "You can't be a poet and an orator too: it needs a different kind of consciousness."

Sir Bernard left off applauding; he said: "Roger why are the English so good at oratory?"

"No," Roger said, "anything in reason, but not that. They aren't, you know."

"Need that prevent you finding a reason why they are?" Sir Bernard asked.

"Certainly not," Roger answered, "but it'd prevent you believing it. I wish I were making all the speeches to-night; I'm going to be bored. Isabel, shall we go?"

"Rather not," Isabel said. "They're going to propose the health of the guests. I'm a guest. Mr. Nigel Considine will reply. Who's Mr. Nigel Considine?"

"A rich man, that's all I know," said her husband. "He gave a collection of African images to the anthropological school, and endowed a lectureship on—what was it?—on *Ritual Transmutations of Energy*. As a matter of fact, I fancy there was some trouble about it, because he wanted one man in it and the University wanted another. They didn't know anything about his man."

"And what did they know of their own?" Sir Bernard put in.

"They knew he'd been at Birmingham or Leeds or somewhere—all quite proper," Roger answered, "and had written a book on the marriage rites of the indigenous Caribs or some such people. He wasn't married himself, and he'd never been a Carib—at least not so far as was known. Considine's man was a native of Africa, so the Dean was afraid he might start ritually transmuting energy in the lecture-room."

"Was Mr. Considine annoyed?" Isabel asked.

"Apparently not, as he's here to-night," Roger answered. "Unless he's going to get his own back now. But I never met

9

him, and never got nearer to him than his collection of images." His voice became more serious, "They were frightfully impressive."

"The adjective being emphatic or colloquial?" Sir Bernard asked, and was interrupted by the health of the guests. He was a little startled to find that he himself was still considered important enough to be mentioned by name in the speech that proposed it. He had, in fact, been a distinguished figure in the medical world of his day: he had written a book on the digestive organs which had become a classic, in spite of the ironic humour with which he always spoke of it. He had attended the stomachs of High Personages, and had retired from active life only the year before, after accepting a knighthood with an equally serious irony.

Mr. Nigel Considine, on behalf of the guests, thanked their hosts. The chief of those guests, the guest of honour, of honour in actual truth, had already spoken. The intellectual value of the journey which they had celebrated was certainly very high, and very valuable to the scientific knowledge of the world which was so rapidly growing. "Yet," the full voice went on, "yet, if I hesitated at all at the view which the most prominent guest to-night took of his own fine achievement"—Roger's eyes flashed up and down again—"it would have been over one implication which he seemed to make. He set before us the wonder and terror of those remote parts of the world which he has been instrumental in helping to map out. Birds and beasts, trees and flowers, all kinds of non-human life, he admirably described. But the human life he appeared to regard as negligible. There is, it seems, nothing for us of Europe to learn from them, except perhaps how to starve on a few roots or to weave boughs into a shelter. It may be so. But I think we should not be too certain of it. He spoke of some of these peoples as being like children; he will pardon me if I dreamed of an old man wandering among children. For the children are growing, and the old man is dying. We who are here to-night are here as the servants and the guests of a great University, a University of knowledge, scholarship, and intellect. You do well to be proud of it. But I have wondered whether there may not be colleges and faculties of other experiences than yours, and whether even now in the far corners of other continents powers not yours are being brought to fruition. I have myself been something of a traveller, and every time I return to England I wonder whether the games of those children do not hold a more intense life than the talk of your learned men—a more intense passion for discovery, a greater power of exploration, new raptures, unknown paths of glorious knowledge; whether you may not yet sit at the feet of the natives of the Amazon or the Zambesi: whether the fakirs, the herdsmen, the witch-doctors may not enter the kingdom of man before you. But, however this may be, it is not——" He turned gracefully to renewed thanks and compliments, and sat down.

"Dotty," said Roger, "but unusual. The transmutation of energy must have been biting him pretty badly. I suppose all that was a get-back."

"It sounded awfully thrilling," Isabel said. "What did he mean?"

"My good child, how should I know?" her husband asked plaintively. "The witch-doctors may. Fancy a witch-doctor entering the kingdom of man before Sir Bernard! Rude of him. Sir Bernard, what did you think of it?"

Sir Bernard turned thoughtful eyes on Roger. "I can't remember," he said, "where I've seen your Mr. Considine before."

"Perhaps you haven't," Roger answered, "in which case you naturally wouldn't remember."

"O but I have," Sir Bernard said positively. "I have; just lately. I remember the way he curved his fingers. I can't think where."

"An unknown path of glorious knowledge," Isabel murmured. "The Dean of Geography looks quite annoyed."

"He's thinking of the other things that are being brought to fruition," Roger said, "all about South America. And of the old man who is dying. D'you think Considine meant any one special? or just as a whole?"

"I don't think it was very nice of him," Isabel said. "People might take it the wrong way."

"Well, if you know how to take it the right way . . ." her husband protested. "I suppose he meant something? O heavens, they're beginning again."

They were, but also they were approaching the end. The dinner hovered over the point at which empty chairs begin to appear, and people misjudge their moment and tiptoe out at the beginning of a speech, and others reckon the chances of catching their distant friends before they are gone. At this point every dinner contends with destiny, and if it is fortunate concludes in a rapid and ecstatic climax; if it is unfortunate it drags out a lingering death, and enters afterwards a shuddering oblivion. This dinner was fortunate. The National Anthem implored Diety on behalf of royalty, and dismissed many incredulous of both. Sir Bernard accompanied Isabel from the room. Ingram, buttonholed by a colleague or two, was delayed till most of those present had gone, and when he reached the cloak-room counter, he found it, but for himself, deserted. He was waiting a little impatiently for his things when a voice behind him spoke. "And with what passion, Mr. Ingram," it said, "do you yourself encounter darkness?"

Roger turned and saw Nigel Considine. They had been some distance apart at the dinner, and on the same side of the same table, so that Considine's personality had not been in play except through his rather obscure words. Now, as they stood so near, Roger was surprised to find himself taken aback by the other's face and bearing. He was not as a rule easily impressed by those he met; he had far too good an opinion of himself. But here . . . He saw a man of apparently about fifty, tall, well-proportioned, clean-shaven, with a good forehead and a good chin. But it was neither forehead nor chin that held Ingram; it was the eyes. He thought of the word "smouldering," and almost as quickly cursed himself for thinking of it; it was such a hateful word, only it was the most accurate. Something, repressed and controlled but vivid, was living in them; they corresponded, in their flickering intensity, to a voice that vibrated with some similar controlled ardour. The word "darkness" as it was uttered called to him as it did in the lines he had quoted; he felt as if he were looking at the thing itself. He began to speak, stammered on a syllable, and at last said helplessly: "I? darkness?"

"You spoke of it familiarly," the other said. "You used her language."

Roger pulled himself together; he answered with a slight hostility. "If you mean my one Shakespearean quotation——"

"Isn't that just darkness making itself known?" Considine asked. "Or do you use apposite quotation merely as a social convenience?"

Roger felt ridiculously helpless, as if a believer accustomed to infidels were suddenly confronted by a fanatic of his own creed. But the implied sneer stung him, and he said sharply, "I don't quote."

"I believe that—because of your voice," the other answered. "You must forgive me if I was offensive; could I help wondering if you really made that rapturous cry your own?"

He allowed the attendant to help him on with his coat as he spoke. Roger's own things lay neglected on the counter, and the other attendant waited by them. Roger himself was absurdly conscious of the presence of those two auditors. He had often talked highly in similar circumstances before, not theatrically certainly but with a sardonic consciousness that the subservient listeners probably thought him a little mad, with the slight enjoyment of being too much for them, with an equally slight but equally definite and continuous despair that words which meant so much to him meant so little to others. But Considine was speaking perfectly naturally, only always with that sounding depth of significance in his voice.

"I am glad you liked it," Roger said foolishly.

Considine said nothing at all to this, and Roger became instantly conscious of the fatuity of the words. "Rapturous cry" . . ."glad you liked it." Ass! "No, really," he said very hastily, "I mean . . . I did really mean it. I mean I do like poetry. Good God!" he thought to himself, "if my classes could hear me now."

Hatted and gloved, Considine turned to him. "You are a little afraid of it, I think," he said. "Or else you have spoken your beliefs very little."

"Nobody cares about it," Roger said, "and I mock at my-. self, God forgive me, because there's nothing else to do."

They were moving together out of the cloakroom.

"There's much else to do," Considine answered, "and I think you believe that; I think you dare encounter darkness."

He raised his hand in salutation. Isabel was ready waiting with Sir Bernard, but before he joined them Roger stood still watching Considine going towards the door, and when at last he came to them he was still troubled.

"Darling, what's the matter?" Isabel said. "You're looking very gloomy."

"Mr. Considine's been talking of the fakirs," Sir Bernard said, "and Roger's wondering if he's one."

Roger regarded them for a moment and then made an effort to recover himself. "I don't mind telling you," he answered, "that Mr. Considine has played me entirely off my own stage in my own play, and I didn't think there was a man living who could do that."

"Elucidate," Sir Bernard said.

"I shan't elucidate," Ingram answered. "I don't see why I should be the only fellow to encounter darkness. D'you want a taxi, Sir Bernard?"

Sir Bernard did, and after having parted from the Ingrams and entered it, he lay back and tried once more to remember where he had seen Considine. It was quite recently, and yet he had a vague feeling that it wasn't recently. An idea of yesterday and an idea of many years ago conflicted in his mind—a man with his hand a little lifted, almost as if it contained and controlled power, a hand of energy in rest. Perhaps, he thought, it was the theme of the speeches which had misled him; they had been listening to talk about distant places, and perhaps his mind had transferred that distance to time. It must have been yesterday or he wouldn't remember so clearly. It couldn't have been long ago or Considine, who was obviously younger than his own sixty odd years, would have changed. His gesture mightn't have changed, all the same—well, it didn't matter. As he got out at his Kensington house he reflected that it would come back, of course; sooner or later the pattern of his knowledge would bring that little detail to his mind. The intellect hardly ever failed one eventually, if one fulfilled the conditions it imposed. But it did perhaps rather ignore the immediate necessities of ordinary life; in its own pure life it overlooked the "Now and here" of one's daily wishes. Still, his own was very good to him; with a happy gratitude to it he came into the library, where he found his son reading letters.

"Hullo, Philip!" he said. "Had a good evening? How's Rosamond?"

"Very fit, thanks," Philip answered. "Did you have a good time?"

Sir Bernard nodded, and sat down leisurely. "Roger told us how he liked poetry," he said, "and the explorer told us how he liked himself, and Mr. Nigel Considine told us how he disliked the University."

"Not in so many words?" Philip asked.

"Contrapuntal," Sir Bernard said. "When you've heard as many speeches as I have, you'll find that's the only interest in them: the intermingling of the theme proposed and the theme actual."

"I can never make out whether Roger's serious," Philip said. "He seems to be getting at one the whole time. Rosamond feels it too."

Sir Bernard thought it very likely. Rosamond Murchison was Isabel's sister and Roger's sister-in-law, but only in law. Rosamond privately felt that Roger was conceited and not quite nice; Roger, less privately, felt that Rosamond was stuck-up and not quite intelligent. When, as at present, she was staying with the Ingrams in Hampstead, it was only by Isabel's embracing sympathy that tolerable relations were maintained. Sir Bernard almost wished that Philip could have got engaged to someone else. He was very fond of his son, and he was afraid that the approaching marriage would make, at the times when he visited them, an atmosphere in which, but for brief intervals, he would find it impossible to breathe. Philip's mind by itself was at present earnest and persevering, if a trifle slow. But Philip's mind surrounded and closed in by Rosamond's promised, so far as he could see, to become merely static. He looked over at his son.

"Roger's serious enough," he said. "But he still expects to get direct results instead of indirect. He never realizes that the real result of anything is always round the corner."

"What corner?" Philip asked.

"The universal corner", Sir Bernard said, "around which we are always on the point of turning—into a street where there are all the numbers except that of the house we're looking for. Good heavens, I'm becoming philosophical. That's the result of University dinners."

"I don't think I quite follow you," Philip said.

"It doesn't at all matter," Sir Bernard answered. "I only meant that I should like you to believe that Roger's quite serious, and a little unhappy."

"Unhappy!" Philip exclaimed. "Roger!"

"Certainly unhappy," Sir Bernard said. "He's fanatic enough to believe passionately and not sufficiently fanatical to believe that other people ought to believe. Naturally also, being young, he thinks his own belief is the only real way of salvation, though he'd deny that if you asked him. So he's in a continual unsuccessful emotional conflict, and therefore he's unhappy."

"But I don't understand," Philip said. "Roger never goes to church. What does he believe in?"

"Poetry," Sir Bernard answered, and "O—poetry!" Philip exclaimed; "I thought you meant something religious. I don't see why poetry should make him unhappy."

"Try living in a world where everyone says to you, quite insincerely, 'O isn't Miss Murchison *charming*!'" his father said drily. "Or alternatively, 'I can't think what you see in her.' And then——"

He was interrupted by the entrance of a third person.

"Hullo, Ian," he broke off; "how's the Archbishop?"

Ian Caithness was the vicar of a Yorkshire parish and Philip's godfather. He was a tall man of about Sir Bernard's age and looked like an ascetic priest, which was more by good luck than by merit, for he practised no extreme austerities. But he took life seriously, and (as often happens) attributed his temperament to his religion. He was therefore not entirely comfortable with other people of different temperaments who did the same thing, and a lifelong friendship with Sir Bernard had probably survived because the other remained delicately poised in a philosophy outside the Church. As a Christian Sir Bernard would have probably irritated his friend intolerably; he soothed him as a—it was difficult to say what; Sir Bernard occasionally alluded to himself as a neo-Christian, "meaning," he said, "like most neos, one who takes the advantages without the disadvantages. As Neo-Platonist, neo-Thomist, and neolithic too, for all I know." On the rare occasions when Caithness came to London he always stopped in Kensington; on the still rarer when Sir Bernard went to Yorkshire he always went to church.

"Rather bothered," Caithness said in answer to his friend's greeting. "The Government papers are making capital out of the massacres of the missions, and demanding expeditions."

"What massacres?" Philip asked in surprise. "Being down in Dorset for a couple of weeks has cut away the papers."

"There've been a number of simultaneous native risings in the interior of Africa," Caithness answered absently, "and so far as we can hear the Christian missionaries have been killed. The Archbishop's very anxious that the Government shan't use that as a reason for military operations."

"Why ever not?" Philip said staring.

Caithness made an abrupt gesture with his hand. "Because it is their duty, their honour, to die, if necessary," he said; "it is a condition of their calling. Because the martyrs of the Church must not be avenged by secular arms."

"A very unusual view for the Church to take," Sir Bernard murmured. "Normally. . . . It's a curious business altogether. I was told this afternoon that the Khedive has left Cairo for a British warship. Roger's anthropological idols getting active, I suppose."

"The pressure on Egypt must be pretty bad, then," Caithness said. "Well, that isn't our business. We can't, of course, object to any steps the Government think it wise to take in their own interests, so long as they don't use the missions as a reason. The Archbishop has intimated to the Societies who sent them out that no material ought to be given to the papers —photographs or what not."

"Photographs!" Sir Bernard exclaimed suddenly. "It was— of course, it was. My mind would have done it, Ian, but thank you for helping it." He got up and went across the room to a drawer in the lower part of one of the bookcases, whence he returned carrying a number of old yellowish photographic prints. Out of these as he turned them over he selected one, and sat down again.

"Of course," he said, "I was looking through these a day or

two ago: that was what fidgeted me all the time Considine was telling us about old men and children. And if that isn't Considine . . . he's got his fingers curved in exactly the same way that he had to-night."

Philip moved round and looked over his father's shoulder. The photograph showed two men, one of about seventy, the other some twenty years or so younger, sitting in basket chairs on a lawn with the corner of a verandah showing behind them. The clothes were late Victorian; the whole picture was Victorianly idyllic. Philip saw nothing surprising about it.

"Which is your Mr. Considine?" he asked.

"The one on the right," Sir Bernard answered. "It's an an exact likeness. When he was speaking to-night he had his head up and his fingers out and coiled just like that. And he wasn't a day older."

"Who's the other man?" Philip asked.

"The other man", Sir Bernard answered, leaning back in his chair and looking thoughtfully at the photograph, "is my grandfather. My grandfather died in 1886."

"Um!" said Philip. "Then of course it can't be your Mr. Considine. He looks about fifty there, which would make him over a hundred now. His father, I suppose."

"It's the most unusual likeness I ever saw, if it's his father, or his grandfather, or his great-uncle, or his first, second, third or fourth cousin," Sir Bernard protested.

"But it must be," Philip said. "You don't suggest that this *is* Considine, do you?"

"The probabilities against it are heavy," his father allowed. "But aren't the probabilities against two men looking so much alike also heavy?"

Philip smiled. "But where one thing's impossible the other must be true," he said.

"And which is impossible?" Sir Bernard asked perversely.

"O come," Philip protested. "If the other figure here is your grandfather this photograph must have been taken before

1886. So it's impossible—or very, very unlikely that the other man is still alive, and he certainly wouldn't be speaking at a dinner. Is it likely? Do you know who took the photograph, by the way?"

"I took it myself," the other said. "With my own little camera. Given me on my twelfth birthday. By my grandfather. I was staying with him for the summer."

"You don't remember who this other man was?"

Sir Bernard shook his head. "I remember being very pleased with the camera. And I remember that various people stayed at the house. And I photographed every one I could. But what he called himself then I couldn't say."

"But if it was Considine then he'd be a hundred or more by now! Did he look it?"

"If he looked it," said Sir Bernard, "I shouldn't be staring at this photograph. No, Philip, you're right of course. But it's unusual."

"It must have been," Philip agreed.

"Though if a man's nerves and stomach were sound," his father went on, "and if he kept himself fit, and had no accidents—on my word, *mightn't* he look fifty when he was really a hundred? Perhaps he's found the elixir of life in the swamps of the Zambesi."

Philip felt the conversation was becoming absurd. "If you take it that it's his father and that there's a strong family likeness, I don't see that there's any difficulty," he said.

"I know," Sir Bernard answered. "But I want there to be a difficulty. So I want that photograph to be a photograph of him and not of his wife's maiden aunt or whatever you suggested. You needn't look superior. It's exactly the way most people come to believe in religion. And if most people think like that, there must be something in it, Cogitatio populi, cogitatio Dei——, and so forth. O well, I shall go to bed. Perhaps I shall meet Mr. Considine again one day and be able to ask him. Good-night, Philip, good-night, Ian. Wake me if the Africans come."

Chapter Two

SUICIDE WHILE OF UNSOUND MIND

Philip was down the next morning before his father or his godfather, urged by a very strong anxiety to see the papers. Trouble in Africa, as it happened, was possibly going to affect not merely high national and political affairs but his own personal arrangements. Africa, of course, was a large place, and the Christian missions had been established, he had gathered, somewhere in the centre; he wasn't much disturbed over them. But what his father had called "the pressure on Egypt" was another matter. Philip's own job was engineering, and he had not long before come to an arrangement with a business company known as "The North African Rivers Development Syndicate," by which he was to go out to whatever North African Rivers were to be developed as assistant constructing engineer. His chief, a man named Munro, was already out there, somewhere in Nigeria, and in a couple of months Philip was to join him. Meanwhile he was putting in some time at the London offices of the Syndicate, which was run by two brothers named Stuyvesant. But though these were the official heads it was generally understood in the City that the real force behind the company was a much richer man, a certain Simon Rosenberg, who, among his interests in railways and periodicals and fisheries and dye-works, in South African diamonds and Persian oils and Chinese silks, in textiles and cereals and patent-medicines, rubber and coffee and wool, among all these had cast a careless eye on African rivers. In that side of the business Philip wasn't very interested. Sir Bernard had satisfied himself that the company was as sound as could reasonably be expected, and a year's work—or perhaps even two years—would give Philip a start in his profession. Then he would, all being well, come home and marry Rosamond, and see what jobs were going at home. Munro was a fairly big man and if Munro gave him a good word. . . .

It was consequently something of a shock to him, when he opened the paper, to find two huge headlines competing. On the left a three-column space announced "Multi-millionaire Found Dead; Rosenberg Shot"; "Terrible Discovery in Rich Man's Library." On the right a similar space was filled with: "Africans Still Advancing"; "Hordes in Nile Valley"; "Rumours of Trouble in South Africa"; "French Defeat in Tangier." Philip goggled at the thick type, and instinctively tried to read both accounts at once. He was still immersed when Caithness came in, just preceding Sir Bernard.

"I say," Philip cried to them, "Rosenberg's shot himself."

"Rosenberg!" Sir Bernard exclaimed. "Whatever for?"

"It doesn't say," Philip answered. "He was found in the study of his house late last night by the butler, who thought he heard a noise and went to see."

"And found he had," Sir Bernard said. "Nasty for the butler." He picked up his own paper, and opened it so that he and Caithness could look at it together. But the priest's eyes went first to the columns of African news, and after his first glance Sir Bernard's followed them. They read the brief obscure telegrams, the explanatory comments, the geographical addenda. It seemed that something very unusual was happening in Africa. To begin with, all communication with the interior had completely ceased. Telegraphs had ceased to function, railways had been cut, roads had been blocked. By such roads as had not been blocked there were emerging against all the outer districts hostile bodies of natives, some so small as to be less than a raid, some so large as to mean an invasion, and at that, wherever they appeared, a victorious invasion. The Egyptian army, which had for some weeks been moving leisurely south in order to suppress trouble in the south-east, was now retiring in considerable disorder and even more considerable haste. The French had "suffered a set-back"; the Spaniards had fallen back towards the coast. Communications with Kenya, with Nigeria, with Abyssinia, with Zanzibar, had ceased. Raids had taken place on the English territories in the South. Air-investigation was being undertaken. The Powers were in touch and were taking necessary steps.

"But what", Caithness said, "has happened to the air-investigation of the last month?"

"It hasn't come back," Sir Bernard answered. "I was talking to a man in the War Office the other night, and he told me that they've sent out aeroplanes by the score, and hardly any have returned. Some have, I suppose, but what they reported is being kept dark. Philip, I think the African Rivers look like being in too much spate for your engineering."

"But what about Rosenberg?" Philip asked. "Do you suppose that's what made him kill himself?"

"Did he kill himself?" Sir Bernard said, turning to the other columns. " 'Butler hears shot. . . letter for the Coroner . . . police satisfied. Financial comment on page 10'; yes, well, we can wait till after breakfast for that. Curious, I wonder what decided him. Let's just see whether the Archbishop said anything."

It appeared that the previous day had been agitated in both Houses. In the Commons the Prime Minister had announced that forces were being dispatched immediately to punish the various tribes guilty of the abominable massacres at the mission stations. Asked by half a dozen members of the Opposition at once whether he could promise that these expeditions should not develop into costly Imperialistic wars, and whether the action taken was by request of the ecclesiastical authorities, the Prime Minister said that the Archbishop had naturally deprecated further bloodshed but that he and other ecclesiastical authorities had recognized the right of the State to protect its citizens. Asked whether he would undertake that no further territory would be seized, he said that no annexations would be made except by mandate from the League of Nations. Asked whether other Governments were taking action, he said that the House should have all information as soon as he received it.

This had been in the afternoon. In the evening the Archbishop had asked the Lord Chancellor for permission to make a statement, and had then said that—in consultation with such other Bishops as happened to be in London—he had written at once that morning to the Prime Minister, definitely stating that the ecclesiastical authorities were entirely opposed to the dispatch of punitive expeditions, and begging that none should be sent. The Bishops were of the opinion that no secular action should be taken to avenge the martyrdom of the slaughtered missionaries and converts, and wished to dissociate themselves from any such action. A noble and indignant peer—a lately returned Governor-General—asked the Archbishop whether he realized that natives understood nothing but force, and whether he meant that war and the use of force was a sin; whether in short the Archbishop were disloyal or merely stupid. The Archbishop had referred the noble peer to the theologians for discussions and determinations of the use of force. The use of force was an act which was neither good nor evil in itself; the use of force in circumstances like the present appeared to himself and his colleagues a breach of Christian principles. Another peer demanded whether, if the Government were to dispatch punitive expeditions, the Archbishop would seriously accuse them of acting in an unchristian manner? The Archbishop said that the noble peer would remember that Christianity assumed a readiness for martyrdom as a mere preliminary to any serious work, and that he was sure no noble lord who happened to hear him and was a Christian would be unwilling to suffer tortures and death

24

without wishing a moment's pain to his enemies. He apologized to the House for reminding them of what might be called the first steps in a religion of which many of his hearers were distinguished professors. The House rose at nine minutes past seven.

"Dear me," said Sir Bernard, putting down his paper.

Philip looked up from his own with a faint but perplexed smile. "Is this you, sir?" he said to Caithness.

"No", Caithness answered, "I don't think so. It seems pretty obvious, after all."

"I had no idea the Archbishop was so venomous," Sir Bernard said: "I think he certainly must believe in God. Mythology always heightens the style."

Caithness said, rather sombrely, "Of course the Prime Minister will win in the end."

"I should think it most likely," Sir Bernard said. "What was it Gibbon said—'all religions are equally useful to the statesman'!—Still, you've done your best. What do you want to do to-day?"

"I may as well go back to Yorkshire," Caithness answered doubtfully. "I've been all the use I can be."

"O nonsense," Sir Bernard said. "Stay a little, Ian; we see precious little of you anyhow. Stay till the African army lands at Dover, and then we'll all go to Yorkshire together—you and I, and Philip and Rosamond, and Roger and Isabel."

Philip winced. His father's remark struck him as merely being in bad taste. It was too remote even to be a joke. He said coldly "I suppose I'd better go to the office?"

"I think you should," Sir Bernard assented. "You'll be perfectly useless, of course. If it's a case of Africa for the Africans, they'll want to develop their own rivers, and as the Syndicate depended on Rosenberg it may not be able to develop itself. But you can find out the immediate prospects. The inquest will be to-morrow. What about coming to the inquest?"

"Why, are you going?" Philip asked.

"Certainly I am going," Sir Bernard answered. "I met Rosenberg quite a number of times, and I've always wondered about him. His wife died a couple of years ago, and I fancy he's been going to pieces ever since. No, Ian, *not* because of monogamy; no, Philip, *not* because of love. I'm sorry; I apologize to both of you, but it wasn't. It was because he'd developed a mania for making, for her, the most wonderful collection of jewels in the world. He had them too—marvellous! Tiaras and bracelets and necklaces and pendants and earrings and so on. I met *her* occasionally—not so often as him, but sometimes, and she looked not merely like the sun, the moon, and the eleven stars, but like the other eleven million that Joseph didn't know about. She was a magnificent creature, tall and rather large and dark, and she carried them off magnificently. In fact, she was a creation in terms of jewellery, the New Jerusalem turned upside down so that the foundations showed. And then she died."

"Couldn't he have still gone on collecting jewels?" Caithness asked scornfully.

"Apparently not," Sir Bernard said mildly. "He saw them *on* her, you see; they existed in relation to her. And when she died they fell apart—he couldn't find a centre for them. They were useless, and so he was useless. At least I suspect that's what happened. You didn't see her, so you won't understand."

Caithness gave a short laugh. "A noble aim," he said.

"Well, it was his," Sir Bernard remonstrated, still mildly. "And really, Ian, if it comes to comparisons, I don't know that it was worse than collecting poems, like Roger, or events, like me. I might say, or souls like you, because you do collect souls for the Church just as Rosenberg collected jewels for his wife, don't you?"

"The Church doesn't die," Caithness said.

"I know, I know," Sir Bernard answered. "But that only means you're more fortunate than Rosenberg in preferring a hypothesis to a person. At least, perhaps you are: it's difficult to say. I've a good mind to ask Roger to come to the inquest too."

"It seems rather gruesome," Philip said, hesitating.

"O my dear boy," Sir Bernard protested, "don't let's be adjectival. Here's a rich man shot himself because of a difficulty with life. Is it really gruesome to want to know what that difficulty is and how much like the rest of our difficulties it was? But at your age you daren't trust your own motives, and you're probably right. At mine one has to trust them or one couldn't enjoy them, and there's not much opportunity to do anything else."

Persuaded either by such maxims or from motives of equal potency both Philip and Roger did actually accompany Sir Bernard the next day, though Caithness refused. The court was certainly crowded but they managed, through some diplomatic work by Sir Bernard, to get in. The coroner, a short hairy official, dealt with everyone in the same sympathetic manner.

The evidence was brief and explicit. The butler who had found the body and summoned the police was called. His master (he said) had had one visitor that evening, a Mr. Considine (Sir Bernard looked at Roger, who sat up sharply). After Mr. Considine's departure, about twelve, his master had called him in to witness his signature to a document, and had then dismissed him. It had been about a quarter of an hour later when he had thought he heard the sound of a shot in the study. He had gone there . . . and so on through the difficult time that followed. The police described their arrival, their examination. Doctors described the nature of the wound.

Mr. Considine was called.

Sir Bernard lay back in his seat and studied the witness, mentally comparing him to the photograph. It was absurd that they should be so much alike, he thought, when they must of course, be different. He gazed at him with an inexplicable curiosity that seemed strangely to become even more vivid when by chance Considine's eyes, passing over the court, as he moved to the witness-box, met his. Roger was leaning eagerly forward, and a glance of recognition went between him and Considine. Philip felt and showed no particular interest.

Considine explained the reason for his visit. He had been on his way home after a dinner and had passed the deceased's house; on an impulse he had determined to call, chiefly because he had been for some time . . . disturbed . . . about his state of mind. Deceased had, as people said, "lost hold"; he had no hope and no desire. He had lost interest alike in his business and in his amusements.

"Can you suggest what caused this breakdown?" the coroner interrupted. "His health—the doctor has told us—was quite good?"

"His health was good," Considine answered, "but his health had no purpose, or rather that purpose had been destroyed. He had made for himself an image, and that image had been removed. His wife while she lived had been the centre of that image; the jewels in which he clothed her completed it. She died; he had no children, and he had not enough energy to discover some other woman whom he could display in a like manner. He had externalized in that adorned figure all his power and possession; it was his visible power, his acknowledged possession. The jewels themselves, magnificent as they were, were not sufficient. Also I think there returned on him something of a childish fear; he was terrified of the destruction that haunts life."

"You tried to cheer him up?" the coroner said.

Considine paused for a moment. "I tried," he said slowly, "to persuade him to live by his own power rather than by what could be at best only properties of it. I tried to persuade him to live from the depth of his wound rather than to pine away in the pain of it; to make the extent of his desolation the extent of his kingdom. But I failed."

"I see—yes," said the coroner vaguely. "You thought he needed bringing out of himself?"

Considine considered again, a longer pause. "I thought he needed to find himself," he said at last, "and all of which himself was capable. But I could not work on him."

"Quite, quite," said the coroner. "I'm sure the sympathy of the Court is with you, Mr. Considine, in your regrets that your efforts were unavailing. I've no doubt that you did all that you could, but there it is—if a man won't or can't bestir himself, mere talk won't help him. Thank you, Mr. Considine."

"Good heavens!" Sir Bernard said to Roger in a smothered voice, 'mere talk'! Mere——"

The letter for the coroner was now produced, but carried things little further. It stated simply that Simon Rosenberg took all responsibility for the act of suicide, to which he had been driven by the full realization of the entire worthlessness of human existence. "We may, I think," the coroner interrupted himself to say, "mark that sentence as evidence of a very abnormal state of mind." Unconscious of the lowering glare which Roger turned on him, he went on: "There is enclosed with this brief letter another document which purports to be the deceased's last will and testament. I have had the opportunity of submitting it to the deceased's solicitors, Messrs. Patton & Fotheringay, and in order that you may have all the evidence possible on deceased's state of mind before you I shall now read it."

He proceeded to do so. It began normally enough, followed up this opening with a few legacies to servants, clerks, and acquaintances, and then in one magnificent clause left the whole of the rest of the estate, real and personal, shares, jewels, houses, lands, and everything else from the smallest salt-cellar in the farthest shooting-lodge to the largest folio in the London library, to two second cousins, Ezekiel and Nehemiah Rosenberg, defined with all necessary exactitude as the grandchildren of the deceased's grandfather's younger brother Jacob Rosenberg.

"And I do this," the strange document ran on, "because

they have followed in the way of our fathers, and kept the Law of the Lord God of Israel, and because though I do not know whether there is any such God to be invoked or any such way to be trodden, yet I know that everything else is despair. If this wealth belongs to their God let him take it, and if not let them do what they choose and let it die." Nigel Considine and the Grand Rabbi were named as executors, with a hope that though they had not been consulted they would not refuse to act.

There was a prolonged silence in court. Roger Ingram thought of several verses in Deuteronomy, a line or two of Milton, and a poem of Mangan's. Sir Bernard wished he knew Nehemiah and Ezekiel Rosenberg. Philip thought it was a very peculiar way of making a will. The coroner proceeded to explain to the jury the difference between felo-de-se and suicide while of unsound mind, with a definite leaning towards the second, of which (he suggested) "despair— to use the word chosen by the deceased—was, anyhow when carried to such an abnormal extent as the letter and will together seem to indicate, perhaps in no small measure a proof." The jury, after a merely formal consultation, in the rather uncertain voice of their foreman agreed. The court rose.

On the steps outside, Sir Bernard and Roger instinctively delayed a little and were rewarded by seeing Considine come out. He was listening to a round-faced man who was probably either Mr. Patton or Mr. Fotheringay, but in a moment he noticed Roger, waved to him, and presently, parting from his companion, came across.

"So, Mr. Ingram," he said, as he shook hands, "I didn't expect to see you here."

"No," Roger answered; "as a matter of fact I came with——" he completed an explanation with an introduction.

"But, of course I know Sir Bernard's name," Considine said. "Isn't it he who explained the stomach?"

"Temporarily only," Sir Bernard answered.

Considine shrugged. "While man needs stomachs," he said, "which may not be for so very much longer. A very ramshackle affair at present, don't you think?"

"In default of a better", Sir Bernard protested, "what would you have us do?"

"But are we in default of a better?" Considine asked. "Surely we're not like that poor wretch Rosenberg who couldn't live by his imagination, but died starved, for all his stomach and his mind."

"So far," Sir Bernard said, "both the stomach and the mind seem normally necessary to man."

"O so far!" Considine answered, "and normally! But it's the farther and the abnormal to which we must look. When men are in love, when they are in the midst of creating, when they are in a religious flame, what do they need then either with the stomach or the mind?"

"Those", Sir Bernard said, "are abnormal states from which they return."

"More's the pity," Roger said suddenly. "It's true, you know. In the real states of exaltation one doesn't seem to need food."

"So," said Considine, smiling at him. "The poets have taught you something, Mr. Ingram."

"*But* one returns," Sir Bernard protested plaintively, "and then one does need food. And reason," he added, almost as an afterthought.

Considine was looking at Roger. "Will *you* say that one must?" he asked in a lower voice; and "O how the devil do I know?" Roger said impatiently. "I say that one does, but I daren't say that one must. And it's folly either way."

"Don't believe it," Considine answered, his voice low and vibrating. "There's more to it than that."

The words left a silence behind them for a moment, as if they were a summons. Roger kicked the pavement. Philip waited patiently. Presently Sir Bernard said, "Do you know the legatees by any chance, Mr. Considine?"

Considine's eyes glowed. "Now there," he said, "if you like irony you have it. Yes, I know them—at least I know of them. I knew the family very well once. They are strict Jews, living in London because they are too poor to return to Jerusalem. They live in London and they abominate the Gentiles of London. They are fanatically—insanely, you would say—devoted to the tradition of Israel. They live, almost without food, Sir Bernard, studying the Law and nourished by the Law. They are the children of a second birth indeed, and they exist in the other life to which they were born. What do you think they will do with Simon Rosenberg's fortune and Simon Rosenberg's jewels?"

"They could, I suppose, refuse it," Sir Bernard said.

"Couldn't they use it to improve conditions in Palestine?" Philip asked, willing to appear interested.

Considine looked at Roger, who said, "I don't know the tradition of Israel. Are jewels and fortunes any use to it?"

"Or will they think so?" Considine answered. "I do not know. But it was a Jew who saw the foundations of the Holy City splendid with a beauty for which the names of jewels were the only comparison. We think of jewels chiefly as wealth, but I doubt if the John of the Apocalypse did, and I doubt if the Rosenbergs will. Perhaps he saw them as mirrors and shells of original colour. However, I suppose, as one of the executors, it will be my business to find out soon."

"It's extraordinarily interesting," Sir Bernard said. "Do, my dear Mr. Considine, let us know. Come and dine with me one day. I've something else I want to ask you."

On the point of making his farewells Considine paused.

"Something you want to ask *me*?" he said.

"A mere nothing," Sir Bernard answered. "I should like to know what relation you are to a photograph of you that I took fifty years ago."

Roger stared. Philip moved uneasily; his father did put things in the most ridiculous way.

"A photograph of me," Considine repeated softly, "that you took fifty years ago . . . ?"

"I do beg your pardon," Sir Bernard said. "But that's what it looks like, though (unless you've improved the stomach out of all knowledge) it probably isn't. I wouldn't have bothered you if other subjects for discussion—jewels, digestion, and the tradition of Israel—hadn't cropped up. But unless you take that unfortunate coroner's view of 'mere talk', do be kind and come."

Considine smiled brilliantly. "I do a little," he said, "but I allow it is a purification, a ritual and actual purification of the energies. I'm rather uncertain how much longer I shall be in England for the present, but if it's at all possible . . . Will you write or telephone or something in a day or two? My address is 29, Rutherford Gardens, Hampstead."

"Hallo," Roger said, "we're up that way. My embalming workshop's there," he added sardonically.

Sir Bernard turned his head, a little surprised. Roger caught his eyes and nodded towards Considine.

"*He* knows," he said. "I embalm poetry there—with the most popular and best-smelling unguents and so on, but I embalm it all right. I then exhibit the embalmed body to visitors at so much a head. They like it much better than the live thing, and I live by it, so I suppose it's all right. No doubt the embalmers of Pharaoh were pleasant enough creatures. They weren't called to any nonsense of following a pillar of fire between the piled waters of the Nile."

"It's burning in you now," Considine said, "and you are on the threshold of a doorway that the Angel of Death went in—not yours."

"If I could believe it——" Roger said. "Ask me to dine too, Sir Bernard. I want to ask Mr. Considine questions about *Paradise Regained*."

33

Chapter Three

THE PROCLAMATION OF THE
HIGH EXECUTIVE

By the time that Philip arrived home that evening the wildest rumours about Africa were being spread. At the office things had been during the last few days as bad as he had feared they might be, and he had been as useless as Sir Bernard had expected. Nothing had been heard from or of Munro for some weeks. Rosenberg's suicide and, even more distressingly, his will, had startled and bothered the Stuyvesants to an indescribable degree. The motive power behind them, the object of motion in front, had both disappeared in blood; and no-one had the least idea what would happen. The Rosenberg legatees had been traced by mid-day; they were living in small upper rooms in Houndsditch, served by an old woman of their race. Extraordinary efforts had been made to procure interviews with them; unsuccessfully, since they merely refused to speak. There were, certainly, in the afternoon papers, sketches of them, but that was hardly the same thing. Even Governments were by way of being interested; high personages gazed at the reproductions dubiously. The two brothers looked as if they might be incapable of realizing the responsibilities of their present position. Two old, bearded, and violent faces stared out at England from journalistic pages. England stared back at them, and for the most part, quite reasonably, abandoned its interest. The Chief Rabbi also refused to be interviewed. Mr. Considine was interviewed, very unsatisfactorily, since he in effect refused to foreshadow, forestall, or foretell anybody's intention. Philip read certainly that Mr. Considine had said that he was sure that there was no need for any public anxiety, that good sense (a quality which the Jews, he was reported to have declared, possessed to a marked degree) would distinguish the actions of the Rosenberg brothers, and that in the present critical times all minor racial prejudices must be set aside. By which Philip understood him to mean that racial prejudice in regard to Africa must swallow up the rest, as the serpent of Moses swallowed the others. He didn't feel quite convinced that Considine who on the steps of the coroner's court had exclaimed to Roger that a pillar of fire was burning in him had said all that. In the other columns of the papers racial prejudice was getting a firm hold.

There were articles by anthropologists, with diagrams of negro heads; articles by explorers, with photographs of kraals; articles by statisticians, with columns of figures; articles by historians, with reproductions of paintings of Vasco da Gama, Thotmes III, Chaka, and others; articles by bishops and famous preachers on missions, with photographs of Christian negroes, converted and clothed; articles by politicians on the balance of power in Africa with maps curiously tinted; articles by military experts on possible strategy, with maps lined and blobbed. There were letters from peace champions and war invalids. There were, in short, all the signs of the interest which the public was believed to feel. Philip at last abandoned them and fell back on consideration.

Except for that one remark on the pillar of fire, and the mysterious allusion to the foundations of the New Jerusalem, he hadn't noticed anything special in Considine's conversation, but those two did rather stand out. If Considine had not obviously been a . . . well, a gentleman, Philip would have suspected him of belonging to the Salvation Army. Of course, he had been talking to Roger, and Roger's own language was apt to be unbalanced. There were moments when Philip, what with his father and Roger, and even his godfather, with his refusal to allow martyrs to be avenged, felt that he was surrounded by eccentrics. He thought with relief and delight of Rosamond; Rosamond wasn't eccentric. She was so right, so peaceful, so beautifully the thing. She was a kind of centre, and all the others vibrated in peculiar poses on the circumference. She herself had no circumference, Philip thought, ignorant of how closely he was striving after St. Augustine's definition: "God is a circle, whose centre is everywhere and His circumference nowhere." She was small and dainty and she moved, as it were, in little pounces. And yet she was so strong; it was as if strength pretended to be weak. No, it wasn't that, for after all, she did need protection—his protection; she was strong enough to need no other and weak enough to need his. Philip took that decision quite seriously; in the economy of the universe he was not perhaps finally wrong. For he was very innocent in love, and the awful paradoxes which exist in that high passion and are an outrage to rational argument were natural to him rather because of his innocence than because of his egotism. That innocence might turn to egotism; that candid belief of his heart be hardened by his pride and turned from a simplicity to a stupidity. But at the moment he was very much in love, and in love he had not yet reached an age capable of sin. He was still a child of the new birth; maturity of intellect as of morals was far distant.

Such a childhood he owed partly, surprised as he would have been to hear it, to his father. The placid irony of Sir Bernard's contemplation of life distilled itself over the wisdom of this world equally with that of every other. Dante was to him no more ridiculous than Voltaire; disillusion was as much an illusion as illusion itself. A thing that seemed had at least the truth of its seeming. Sir Bernard's mind refused to allow it more but it also refused to allow it less. It was for each man to determine how urgent the truth of each seeming was. Philip had not been discouraged from accepting the seemings of his own world, of school, University, and business; but he had been subtly encouraged to give free play to his own individual phenomena. A thing might not be true because it appeared so to him, but it was no less likely to be true because everyone else denied it. The eyes of Rosamond might or might not hold the secret origin of day and night, but if they apparently did then they apparently did, and it would be silly to deny it and equally silly not to relish it. Sir Bernard had never said this in so many words. But the atmosphere which he created was one in which such spiritual truths could thrive unhindered, and their growth depended upon their own instinctive strength.

Serenely unconscious of what he owed, Philip felt his own serious growth wiser than that cool air of gracious scepticism. He thought his passion was hidden from it as from the sun, when in fact it throve in it as in the soft rains. He said nothing of Rosamond's eyes—which certainly were not, to Sir Bernard, anything remarkable—to his father, and supposed that the unformulated gospel they taught him was also a secret. He said nothing of them to anyone indeed, not having, nor caring to have, that tendency towards talk which marked his future brother-in-law. Roger, out of sheer interest, had given him every opportunity, and was rather disappointed that not one was taken. "I'm sure I talked enough about you," he complained to Isabel.

"You're more interested in metaphysics," she said. "Philip's just a believer; you're a theologian."

"I've a more complex matter to study," he said. "If I were a poet I would make the Matter of Isabel equal to the Matter of France and the Matter of Britain."

"My honour wars with my credulity," she answered. "I'm not really more interesting than Rosamond but I like to think I am."

"I don't think Sir Bernard approves of Rosamond," Roger said meditatively. "Why not, do you suppose? Can he really not think her good enough? Does he secretly adore Philip? My son, my son, and all that?"

37

Isabel was silent for a minute; then she said: "I'm awfully tempted to tell you, Roger, but perhaps I won't. I do think I know what he feels, but it'd be rather hard on Rosamond to talk of it, wouldn't it?"

"Devil!" said Roger. "You'd see your husband die of an insatiable curiosity rather than sully your integrity by giving him a crust of fact. You're as bad as the other Isabella—the one in *Measure for Measure*; you're avaricious of chastity. I don't want to be nice; I want to be malign and malevolent— and omniscient. Very well; have it your own way. I shall now go and lecture on Pure Women in Literature, with sub-sardonic allusions to you, Shakespeare's Isabella, and Mr. Richardson's Pamela. And I shall be back, in a bad temper, to tea."

It was to tea on the same day that, when he did return, he found Philip had invited himself, having abandoned the distracted office for an hour with Rosamond. Isabel had come in from an afternoon's walk, and when they all met in the drawing-room it was she who said: "Roger, you're looking very serious. What's the matter, darling? Didn't they remember who Pamela was, or did they think she was nice, or what?"

Ingram stretched himself in an armchair. "Have any of you", he asked, "seen an evening paper?"

"Not since two o'clock," Philip said. "Is there something important?"

"That", Roger answered, "depends on what you think important. There's an African proclamation."

"What!" Philip was so surprised that his eyes left Rosamond's hair to rest on the newspaper that Roger was holding. "Is there really? What does it say?"

"It says that the Socratic method is done for," Roger said seriously. A small frown appeared on Rosamond's face and went away again. Philip, without frowning, conveyed the impression of a frown and said: "Do be serious. It's important to me to know. What *does* it say?"

"It says exactly what I've told you," Roger said, more sardonically. "It says you think too much, Philip, and it says your father is just the last kind of mistake. It's no use blaming me. I didn't write it. I'm not even sure that I know what it means."

Isabel, taking a sandwich, said: "Read it, Roger. The Socratic method doesn't really help one to choose a frock. I know because I tried it once. I said, 'Must not a colour which suits me, and a cut that I admire, be desirable? It would seem so, Socrates.' And yet it wasn't. Do read it."

Philip, having thus been defrauded of his protest, waited in the silence of injured decency to hear more. Rosamond looked at him sympathetically. Roger dropped two of his papers, opened the third, and read.

"Alleged Statement by African Leaders. Document received by Foreign Office and Press. Where is the High Executive? African Aims Reported to be Disclosed. By the mid-day post a document was received at the offices of all the London newspapers which is, with all reserves in regard to its authenticity, given below. The editors of the London papers have been in communication with the Foreign Office, and learn that a precisely similar document has been received there. Not only so, but the Foreign Offices and the Press of other European countries have also been communicated with in the same way. In Paris and Madrid this alleged manifesto has already been published, and the British Government, after consultation with the editors, has raised no objection to its publication here. If it is genuine—a question which is being investigated—it pretends to offer some kind of explanation of the late remarkable events in Africa. The manifesto, or proclamation, as it might be called, is as follows:

" 'In the name of the things that have been and are to be, willed and fated, in the name of the gods many and one, the Allied Supremacies of Africa, acting by the will and speaking

39

by the voice of the High Executive, desire to communicate to the rest of the world the doctrine and purpose of the cause in which they are engaged. They announce their immediate purpose to be the freeing of the African continent from the government and occupation of the white race; their farther purpose to be the restoration to mankind of powers which have been forgotten or neglected, and their direction to ends which have hitherto been unproclaimed. They announce their profound belief that, as to the European peoples in the past, so to themselves in the future the conscious leadership of mankind belongs. It is not an imposed but an emerging leadership, superior to its disciples as to its enemies because of the conscious potentialities which exist in it. The potentialities of that superiority do not attempt to deny the capacities of Europe in their own proper achievements. The High Executive of the African Allies desires, in its first public summons to the creative powers of the world, to honour the immortal finalities of the past. It salutes the intellect, the philosophies, the science, the innumerable patterns of Europe. But it asserts that the great age of intellect is done, nor was the intellect ever that power which its disciples have been encouraged to believe. The prophets of Africa, who are not found only among its own peoples but include many of other races both in the past and in the present—the prophets of Africa have seen that mankind must advance in the future by paths which the white peoples have neglected and to ends which they have not understood. Assured that at this time the whole process of change in mankind, generally known as evolution, is at a higher crisis than any since mankind first emerged from among the great beasts and knew himself; assured that by an equal emergence from intellectual preoccupations, the adepts of the new way have it in their power to lead, and all mankind has it in its power to follow, not certainly by the old habits of reason but by profounder experiments of passion, to the conquest of death in the renewed ecstasy of vivid experience; assured of these things the

Allied Supremacies appeal to the whole world for belief and discipleship and devotion.' ''

Roger paused and looked up. Rosamond, again frowning a little, was eating cake. Philip was listening with his mouth open and his eyes staring. Isabel was attending with a serious and serene care. Roger grinned at her and resumed.

" 'The peoples of Africa appear before the world in arms, in order to claim from the sovereign authorities of Europe that freedom which is their due and their necessity on the one hand; on the other their privilege and opportunity. They will and they are fated to achieve that freedom. But their arms are of defence and not of aggression. They are willing to concede all possible time and convenience to the Powers of Europe. They no more desire to waste their energies and those of their opponents on war than on any other lower exterior imitation of heroic interior conquest. They are not anxious that the discipleship of the European imagination should be made more difficult by the mundane stupidities of dispute and battle. But the administration of Africa by the white race is now a thing of the past—to be remembered only as intellectual sovereignty will be remembered, a necessary moment that was willed and was fated and has ceased.

" 'To those among the peoples of Europe who know that their lives have origin and nourishment in the great moments of the exalted imagination, the High Executive offers salute and recognition' ''—Roger's voice began to linger over the words—" 'to all who owe their devotion to music, to poetry, to painting and sculpture, to the servants of every more than rational energy; greater than those and more numerous, to all who at this present moment exist in the exchanged or unexchanged adoration of love, it calls more especially. There, perhaps more surely and swiftly than in any other state of being outside the transmuting Way, can the labour of exploration be begun; there is the knowledge, the capacity, the

41

herald apprehension of victory. These visionaries are already initiate; they know in themselves the prophecy of the conquest of death. To all such the High Executive appeals, with ardour and conviction. Believe, imagine, live. Know exaltation and feed on it; in the strength of such food man shall enter into his kingdom.

" 'The High Executive permits itself to offer to the Christian Churches its congratulations on the courage and devotion of those their servants who have sustained death by martyrdom. Convinced as it is that the Churches have, almost from the beginning, been misled by an erring principle, it nevertheless honours those martyrs as sublime if misguided instances of that imagination which it is its purpose to make known to mankind and which the rites and dogmas of the Christian religion dimly proclaim. It is assured by its belief in man and by the exalted courage of those martyrs that they would have desired no other end, and it takes full responsibility for having advised its august sovereigns that they could bestow on Christian missionaries no more perfect gift.

" 'The High Executive will be prepared to send representatives at any time to any place fixed by the Powers of Europe or by any of them; or to enter into negotiations in any other way that the Powers may desire. It will assume the fixing of such time and place or the opening of such negotiations to be a guarantee of safe-conduct for its representatives, and it will be prepared to suspend as soon as possible the military, naval, and aerial operations upon which it is engaged.

" 'Given in London, by direction of the High Executive, in the First Year of the Second Evolution of Man.' "

Roger stopped. Almost before his voice had ceased, Rosamond said: "Philip, darling, you haven't eaten anything. Have a cake?" Philip for once took no notice. Roger said: "About a thousand words—a little more. Allowing for recapitulations in its extremely rhetorical style—the High

Executive hasn't studied the best models—say, seven-fifty. Either pure waste or the most important seven-fifty words I've ever read."

"I haven't got the hang of it," Philip said in bewilderment. "What does it mean?"

"It—what did it say?—it calls to you more especially, Philip," Roger went on. "It salutes you, because you have the vision of the conquest of death in the exchanged adoration of love. It expects you to do something about it all at once." His eyes lingered on Isabel, and then became abstracted. He sighed once and got to his feet. "I'll have some more tea," he said. "The cup that cheers but not inebriates after words that inebriate but do not cheer."

Isabel, pouring out the tea, said: "Don't they cheer you, dearest?"

"Not one bit," Roger answered. He leaned gloomily against the mantelpiece, and after a pause said suddenly, "Well, Rosamond, and what do you make of it?"

Rosamond answered coldly. "I wasn't listening, I don't think it's very nice, and really, Roger, I don't see why you need have read it."

"The High Executive of the African peoples asked me to," Roger said perversely. "What don't you like about it—giving up intellect or having the vision of the conquest of death?"

"I think you're simply silly, Roger," Rosamond exclaimed and stood up. "And if it was written by a lot of . . . a lot of Africans, that makes it more disgusting than ever. I don't think it ought to have been printed."

Isabel spoke before Roger, sadistically watching Rosamond, could reply. "Do you think it's authentic, Roger?" she asked.

"My dear, how can I guess?" her husband answered, more placably; then he shifted his position, and added: "It's authentic enough in one way; there is something more."

Isabel smiled at him. "But need we think we didn't know it already?" she asked softly. "It isn't very new, is it?"

He was looking across the room at the high bookcase.

"If they came alive," he murmured, "if they are alive—all shut up in their cases, all nicely shelved—shelved—shelved. We put them in their places in our minds, don't we? If they got out of their bookcases—not the pretty little frontispieces but the things beyond the frontispieces, not the charming lines of type but the things the type means. Dare you look for them, Isabel?" As he still stared at the bookcase his voice altered into the deeper sound of a subdued chant.

> *"He scarce had ceased when the superior fiend*
> *Was moving towards the shore*

> *"Hid in its vacant interlunar cave*
> *"And thus the Filial Godhead answering spake."*

Rosamond said sharply: "Do be quiet, Roger. You know I hate your quoting."

"Quoting!" Roger said, "quoting!" and stopped in despair. He looked at Philip as if asking him whether he couldn't do something.

Philip didn't see the look; he was meditating. But the silence affected him at last; he raised his eyes, and was on the point of speaking when Rosamond interrupted, slipping her hand through his arm. "Don't talk about it any more, darling," she said; "it's too horrid. Look, shall I come as far as the Tube with you?"

He stirred—rather heavily, Roger thought—but as their eyes met he smiled back at her, and only Isabel's hand prevented her husband from again quoting the High Executive on the exchanged adoration of love. It was therefore with a slight but unusual formality that farewells were spoken, and Philip departed for the station.

Roger remained propped against the mantelpiece, but he said, viciously, "She 'wasn't listening'!"

Isabel looked at him a little anxiously. "Don't listen too

44

carefully, darling," she said. "It's not just cowardice—to refuse to hear some sounds."

He pulled himself upright. "I must go and work," he said. "I must exquisitely water the wine so that it may be tolerable for weak heads." By the door he paused. "Do you remember your Yeats?" he asked.

> *"What rough beast, its hour come round at last,*
> *Slouches towards Bethlehem to be born?*

I wonder. Also I wonder where exactly Bethlehem is, and what are the prodigies of the birth."

Chapter Four

THE MAJESTY OF THE KING

In the Tube Philip read the proclamation of the High Executive over again, and, to the best of his ability, considered it. He was uneasily conscious that Rosamond would have disapproved of this, and he couldn't help feeling that it was only by an oversight that she hadn't asked him to please her by leaving it alone. However, she hadn't, so he was morally free. There stirred vaguely in his mind the subtler question of whether he were free by a strict or by an easy interpretation of morals: did exact justice, did a proper honour, demand that he should follow her choice or insist on his own? But the question never got as far as definition; he was aware of a difficulty turning over in its sleep—slouching towards Bethlehem but not reaching it—and almost deliberately refrained from realizing it. Because he did want to know, more accurately, what this alleged declaration had said about love. Unlike Roger and, fortunately for him, like Rosamond, he had no particular use for the masters of verse. He was therefore ignorant of the cloud of testimony that had been borne to the importance and significance of the passion that was growing in him. He had certainly heard of Dante and Beatrice, of Tristram and Iseult, of Lancelot and Guinevere, but there he stopped. He had hardly heard, he had certainly never brooded over, that strange identification of Beatrice with Theology and of Theology with Beatrice by which one great poet has justified centuries of else doubtful minds. But by that secular dispensation of mercy which has moved in the blood of myriads of lovers, he had felt what he did not know and experienced what he could not formularize. And the words which he now

46

read did not so much startle his innocent devotion by their eccentricity as dimly disturb him with a sense of their justice. He had had no use at all for the African peoples except in so far as they gave him an opportunity to follow his European habits in providing Rosamond with a home and a car and anything else she wanted. The prospect of the great age of intellect being done, also left him unmoved; he hadn't realized that any special great age of intellect had existed— except for a vague idea that a period of past history known as the Middle Ages was considerably less intelligent than the present, and that there had been a brief time when Athens, and a rather longer time when Rome, was very intellectual. But when all that seemed to him meaningless had been removed, there still remained the fact that never before, never anywhere, had any words, printed or spoken, come nearer to telling him what he really felt about Rosamond than this paragraph which purported to come from the centre of Africa, and from dark-skinned chiefs pouring up against the guns and rifles of England. He knew it was silly, but he knew it said "adoration," "vision," "apprehension of victory," "conquest of death." He knew it was silly, but he knew also that he had felt through Rosamond, brief and little understood, something which was indeed apprehension of victory and conquest of death.

When he got home he found his godfather alone, and, rather against his own intention, found himself approaching the subject. Caithness had seen the proclamation and was inclined to be a little scornful of it: which may partly have been due to the unrecognized fact that, while Roger and Philip had both found their interior passions divined and applauded, Caithness had had his referred to merely as "a misguided principle." He doubted the authenticity, and went on to add: "Rather bombastic, don't you think? I don't pretend to know what it means."

Philip said, "Roger seemed quite impressed by it."

"O Roger!" the priest said good-humouredly. "I called it bombast but I expect he'd call it poetry. I don't mean that it

47

hasn't a kind of thrill in it, but thrills aren't the only thing—certainly they're not safe things to live by.''

Philip thought this over, and decided that he agreed with it. Only his sensations about Rosamond were not—no, they were not *thrills*: and he wasn't at all clear that they weren't things to live by. He said, shamelessly involving Roger: ''He made fun of me about it—he seemed to think that part of it was meant for me. The paragraph about—O well, some paragraph or other.''

Caithness looked down at the paper. ''This about the exaltation of love, I expect,'' he said, with a rather charming smile. ''Roger would be all in favour of that; the poets are. But perhaps they're more used to living on the hilltops than the rest of us.''

''You don't think it's true then?'' Philip asked, with a slight and irrational feeling of disappointment. Irrational, because he hadn't actually expected Caithness to agree with a gospel, if it was a gospel, out of Africa. Sir Bernard had once remarked that Caithness limited himself to the Near East in the matter of gospels, ''the near East modified by the much nearer West.''

But over the direct question Caithness hesitated. ''I wouldn't care to say it wasn't true,'' he said, ''but all truth is not expedient. It's no use making people expect too much.''

''No,'' Philip said, ''I suppose it isn't.'' Was he expecting too much? was he, in fact, expecting anything at all? Or could whatever he expected or whatever happened alter the terribly important fact of the shape of Rosamond's ear? He also looked again at the paper, and words leapt to his eyes. ''Believe, imagine, live. Know exaltation and feed on it——''

''You don't then,'' he said, unwontedly stirred, ''really think one ought to believe in it too much?''

''Why yes, my dear boy,'' the priest answered. ''Only these things are so often deceptive; they change or they become familiar. One can't trust one's own vision too far; that's where religion comes in.''

Sir Bernard would no doubt have pointed out, what did not occur to either of the others, that this merely meant that Caithness was substituting his own hobby for Philip's. But he wasn't there, and so, vaguely depressed, especially as he couldn't feel that Rosamond's ear would ever change, the young man turned the conversation, and shut away the appeal of the High Executive for the time being in whatever corresponded in his mind to Roger Ingram's bookshelves.

The African trouble, however, displayed, during the next few days, no possibility of being shut away. The steps which the Powers, on the unanimous testimony of their spokesmen, were harmoniously taking produced no effect against the rebels (as the enemy was habitually called). It became clear that the "hordes" consisted, in fact, of highly disciplined and well-supplied armies. In the north of Africa the territory held by the European forces grew daily smaller; all Egypt, except Cairo, was lost; the French were pressed back to the coast of Tangier; the Spaniards were hustled out of Morocco. The Dominion of South Africa was sending out expeditions, of which no news returned—certainly there had not been much time, but there was no news at all, or none that was published. In England an official censorship was attempted, but failed owing to the speedy growth of a party which demanded "Africa for the Africans." Normally the massacre of the Christian missionaries would have been fatal to such a demand, but the recalcitrant attitude of the Archbishop hampered the more violent patriots. Rumours got about of the appearance of hostile aeroplanes over the Mediterranean and the coastline of Southern Europe. Negroes in London and other large towns were mobbed in the streets. Roger reported to Isabel that not only negroes but comparatively harmless Indians had disappeared from his classes. It was evident that the Government would be driven to some measure of internment.

It was so driven, more quickly than had been expected, when the news came of the sinking of a transport crowded

49

with Indian troops which were being rushed to South Africa. That the African armies should be able to operate destructively by sea as well as by land was a shock even to instructed opinion, and, among the uninstructed, crowds began to parade the streets, booing and cheering and chasing any dark-skinned stranger who showed himself. Even one or two Southern Italians had, for a few minutes, an uneasy time. The crowds were of course dissolved by the police, but they came together again like drops of water till the evening's amusement was done and they reluctantly went home.

The reaction of all these events on the money market was considerable, and it was not eased by the uncertainty which still existed on the situation of the late Mr. Rosenberg's affairs. Nothing definite was known, since the Chief Rabbi and Mr. Considine persisted in their silence, as did the two legatees. But an uneasy feeling manifested itself, both in the streets around the brothers' house and in the wider circles of finance. It could not be said that anything unusual was going on, for nothing at all seemed to be going on. But the stillness was alarming. No-one could believe that the two aged and devoted students of Kabbalistic doctrine were fit persons to control the vast interests of the Rosenberg estate. But no-one could prevent their doing whatever they liked with it. Nehemiah and Ezekiel came out to the synagogue and went home again, and went nowhere else, though well-dressed strangers in cars descended on Hounds-ditch, and were engaged with them over long periods. In Houndsditch itself strange tales of the jewels began to spread, following vivid accounts of them in the papers. The thrill of the jewels and the thrill of the Africans contended; hungry eyes followed the Jews as hostile eyes followed such rare negroes as could still be seen in the East End. A sullen excitement began to work around them, a breathless and vulgar imitation of the exalted imagination which the High Executive had declared to be the true path to desirable knowledge.

A more natural excitement, though perhaps equally crude

from the point of view of the High Executive and that other High Executive represented among others by the Archbishops, affected innumerable suburban homes when the selling began. Gradually but steadily the prices of shares in the Rosenberg concerns began to fall. It was said that someone knew something and was standing from under. A shiver of panic touched finance, allied to that other panic which had already touched the extreme villages of Southern Europe. Nervous voices made inquiries over telephones in England as nervous eyes watched aeroplanes over the Mediterranean. From each background of silence a thin mist of fear crept out and was blown over many minds. Something shook civilization, as it had been shaken a hundred times before, but that something loomed now in half-fancied forms of alien powers, of negroes flying through the air and Jews withdrawing their gold. Day by day the tremors quickened. Neglected expositors of the Apocalypse in Tonbridge or Cheltenham, old ladies, retired military men, and an eccentric clergyman or two, began to say boldly that it was the end of the world. At Birmingham a man ran naked through the streets crying that he saw fire from heaven, and leaping on to the railway lines was killed by an express train before the police could catch him."Second Adventist goes mad at Birmingham," said the evening papers. The Churches found that growing crowds attended them. The Government unofficially suggested to the Archbishops that they should discourage people coming to church. The Archbishops issued a Pastoral Letter from which they naturally could not exclude some of their irritation with the Government; and of which therefore the first part, which was addressed to the new converts, tended towards a scornful and minatory tone. This, if anything, made matters worse, the converts naturally arguing that if the Church could afford to use that voice the Church must feel itself very safe indeed; and this feeling was strengthened by the second part which was addressed to the faithful in language that in normal times would have been ordinary enough. "And you, little children, love one another," it began and continued on the same theme, ending with another quotation, "My peace I give unto you; not as the world giveth give I unto you." The idea that these incantations contained a magical safety found more and more believers; and Sir Bernard congratulated Caithness on a greater spread of the Faith in ten days than in ten years previously. On a world already thus agitated fell the second communication of the High Executive. This, after the earlier formal invocation of "things willed and fated," "gods many and one," went on in something of a high style of distress to lament that the Powers of Europe had not thought well even to answer the earlier message, much less apparently to prepare themselves for any negotiations. They had instead, by all means at their command, increased their armies and strengthened the war. "Some check", the message went on, "the African armies have administered to this gathering defiance, but the High Executive has felt compelled to advise its august Sovereigns that mere measures of defence will no longer be sufficient. If the Powers of Europe are determined to force war upon Africa, then Africa will be compelled to open war upon Europe. The gospel which is the birthright of the African peoples and which they offer as a message of hope even to the degraded and outworn nations of the white race carries no maxim which they are unwilling to practise. With a profound but unrecognised truth the Christians of Europe have declared that the blood of the martyrs is the seed of the Church. This maxim Africa knows, understands, obeys. In the high mysteries of birth and death, not only physical generation or physical destruction, but those spiritual experiences of which these are but types, Africa has learnt the secret duties of man. Her peoples offer themselves in exaltation to the bed of death as to the bed of love. With an ecstasy born of their ecstasy, with a communication to its children of that which they first communicated to it, the High Executive summons them to what is at present the final devotion of conscious being. They and it are alike indifferent to the result, if the armies of Europe destroy them they will but find in death a greater thing than their conquerors know. But the armies of Europe will not destroy them, for the Second Evolution of man has begun. Their leaders and prophets, and the High Executive which is their voice and act, address themselves no longer to the children of intellect and science and learning. They turn to their own peoples. Daughters and Sons of Africa, you are called to the everlasting sacrifice. Victim or priest at that altar, it matters not whether you inflict or endure the pang. Come, for the cycles are accomplished and the knowledge that was of old returns. Come, for this is the hour of death that alternates for ever with the hour of love. Come, for without the knowledge of both the knowledge of one shall fail. Come, ye blessed, inherit the things laid up for you from the foundations of the world."

On the evening of the day when this invocation appeared, the crowds in the streets were thicker than ever. The first death was reported in a special edition of the papers; a negro had been literally hunted over Hampstead Heath and afterwards (not quite intentionally, it was thought), killed. Sir Bernard rang up Isabel.

"Nothing," he said, when she answered, "except that you once said that Hampstead was the negro quarter of London, and I thought I'd like to know whether there was any trouble up there."

"Not to say *trouble*," Isabel said. "There was a little friction at the gate, and we've got a coloured gentleman in the house at present."

"Have you indeed?" Sir Bernard exclaimed. "Was it you or Roger who brought him in?"

"Both of us," Isabel explained. "We heard a noise in the street and we looked out, and there was a negro—at least, he was a black man; a negro's something technical, isn't it?— against our gate, and the most unpleasant lot of whites you ever saw all round him, cursing. Roger went out and talked to them, but that was no good. He said something about behaving like Englishmen, and I suppose they did; at least they began to throw stones and hit out with their sticks. So Roger got him through the gate, and I got them through the front door, and here he is."

"You're not hurt, Isabel?" Sir Bernard said sharply. "What about the crowd?"

"O they threw things at the house and smashed a window, and presently the police came and they went away," Isabel answered. "No, thank you, I'm perfectly all right. I'm just going to make coffee. Come and have some."

"Where's your visitor?" Sir Bernard asked.

"Talking African love songs and tribal poetry with Roger in his room," Isabel said. "They agree wonderfully on everything but the effect of the adverb. Roger's evolving a theory that adverbs have no place in great poetry—I don't understand why."

"I should like to hear him," Sir Bernard said. "Thanks, Isabel; I'll come up if I may."

"Do," said Isabel, "and I'll postpone the coffee for half-an-hour. Till then."

For once Sir Bernard took a taxi; as a general rule he avoided them, preferring the more actively contemplative life of buses and tubes, and preferring also never to be in anything like a hurry. When he arrived he found Philip and Rosamond, who had been dining out, sitting side by side on the kitchen table, watching Isabel make the coffee.

"Come in here, Sir Bernard, won't you?" she said when she had let him in, "and you shall see the refugee soon. He's in the only room with a fire, and as Rosamond is terrified to death of him we have to linger in the kitchen to keep comfortably warm. 'October nights are chill,' as someone said. No, don't tell me."

"Isabel," her sister protested, "I'm not terrified of him, but

I don't think it's quite nice of him to stop here. Why doesn't he go home?"

"With mobs prowling round the garden gate?" Isabel asked. "And Roger still making noises to show the union of accent and quantity? My dear Rosamond, when you're married you won't want Philip's friends to go home until he's thoroughly tired out. Otherwise he'll barge into your room at midnight and go on with the conversation with you. And as you're asleep to begin with, and as you don't know what the conversation was about, and as you don't know whether he wants you to agree or disagree though you'd do either for peace, you'll find it very difficult to be nice to him. I have never", Isabel went on, pouring milk into a saucepan, "really quarrelled with Roger. . . ."

"Isabel!" Sir Bernard murmured.

"Not really," Isabel persisted, "except once, and that was when he woke me up by calling out to me very late one night, 'Isabel, what is there in verse which is the equivalent of the principle of the arch?' I really was angry then, but he only kept murmuring lines of poetry and trying to see if they were like an arch. All that because a friend of his who had been to dinner had gone away at half-past eleven instead of half-past one. Always remember, Rosamond my child, that a man needs you to get away from."

"You mean needs to get away from me, don't you?" Rosamond asked, looking possessively at Philip.

"No," Isabel said, "Sir Bernard, the milk's boiling . . . thank you so much. No, Rosamond, I don't. I mean exactly what I said. A man must have you——"

"I wish you wouldn't keep saying 'a man,' Isabel," Philip remonstrated.

"Very well—give me a spoon, Philip—Philip then must have you there in order to be able to get away. If you weren't there he wouldn't be able to get away."

Rosamond looked uninterested. Philip reflected what a curious thing it was that so many people he knew should want to chatter like this. His father did it, Ingram did it, Isabel did it. Sometimes he understood it, sometimes he didn't. But he never understood it as now, suddenly, he understood Rosamond's arm when she leant forward to pass a plate to her sister; somehow that arm always made him think of the Downs against the sky. There was a line, a curved beauty, a thing that spoke to both mind and heart; a thing that was there for ever. And Rosamond? Rosamond was like them, she was there for ever. It occurred to him that, if she was, then her occasional slowness when he was trying to explain something was there for ever. Well, after all, Rosamond was only human; she couldn't be absolutely perfect. And then as she stretched out her arm again he cried out that she was perfect, she was more than perfect; the movement of her arm was something frightfully important, and now it was gone. He had seen the verge of a great conclusion of mortal things and then it had vanished. Over that white curve he had looked into incredible space; abysses of intelligence lay beyond it. And in a moment all that lay beyond it was the bright kitchen, and Sir Bernard standing up to go into the other room. He jumped to his feet and with a movement almost of terror took the loaded coffee tray from Isabel.

"Quietly," Isabel said as they came to the door of the nondescript room where the Ingrams habitually, alone or with their intimates, passed their time. "Quietly; let's hear what the rescued captive and his saviour are talking about."

She opened the door gently, and Ingram's voice came out to them. "O rhythm!" he was saying, "rhythm is the cheap pseudo-metaphysical slang of our day. At least it was; it's dying now. Everyone explained everything by talking about rhythm. It's a curious thing that people who will sneer at a man for doing nothing all his life but making words sound lovely and full of meaning will be quite happy over life so long as they can explain it in words that are almost meaningless. I sometimes think the nearest we can get to meaning is to feel as if there was meaning."

"Yet at least rhythm's distinctly felt," said another voice, a rich strange voice; "so far they attempt to discover a knowledge of the whole."

"O so far!" Ingram said, and jumped off the table on which he was sitting as Isabel pushed the door right open and came into the room. After a table had been found for the tray, introductions took place; at least Ingram began to say, "O Rosamond"—he stopped suddenly; "By God," he said, "I don't know your name."

The stranger, a tall magnificent young creature, darkly bronze, bowed to Rosamond: "My name is Inkamasi," he said. "At least," he added, a trifle scornfully, Sir Bernard thought, "that is the simplest form of it."

"Quite," Roger said brightly. "Miss Murchison, Mr. Travers—hallo, Sir Bernard, I didn't know you were here—Sir Bernard Travers, the Belly-King."

It was a name with which his intimates had teased Sir Bernard in the days of his practice. Philip frowned, forgetting that though the black—if you could strictly call him black—was to him an entirely new and not very desirable acquaintance, the occurrences of the last two hours had put him on terms of intimacy with the Ingrams. Rosamond, rather nervously, kept close to his side. Roger sat down again on top of his large knee-hole writing-table, and took the coffee Philip handed him.

" We were talking——" he began.

"Yes, darling, we heard you," Isabel said. "Don't trouble to repeat it just at once. And I hope that doesn't sound too rude," she added to the stranger, "only when Roger's got more than two people to listen to him he always begins to lecture."

"I ought to have gone long ago," the other said. "But your husband kept me, talking of poetry and song and the principles of being."

"But", Isabel said, "must you go yet? I mean, will it be wise?" She looked at Roger.

57

"O quite," the African said. "The police will have cleared the streets, and I don't live far away."

Roger looked at the clock. "Twenty to ten," he said, "better wait a little. I didn't quite get the hang of what you were saying about Homer. I'll walk round with you presently. Sir Bernard'll be interested in Homer; he had a line from him on the title-page of his book, opposite the peculiarly loathsome diagram that formed the frontispiece."

"I didn't even know you'd looked so far into it," Sir Bernard said.

"I generally give the title-page a fair chance," Roger said. "One can't always judge books merely by the cover. It's a book on the stomach," he explained to Inkamasi, "with nine full-page photographs and about fifty more illustrations, each more abominable than the others. When it was published Sir Bernard gave copies to all his friends, because he knew they wouldn't read it and wanted to hear them explaining why. Brave men cut him afterwards."

"I should like to see it," the African voice said. "I did a little medical work before I took up law."

"Well, it's buried under Rabelais, Swift, and *Ulysses* at the moment," Ingram grinned at Sir Bernard," but I'll get it out for you before you come again. 'Lend it you I will for half a hundred years.' But not give it. I retain it to keep me humble."

"I think I'll go now," Inkamasi said, putting down his cup. "Thank you, Mrs. Ingram, for being so kind."

" O well, if you will," said Roger. " Coming, Philip? "

"Yes, rather," Philip answered, with a momentary private hope that he wouldn't have to help defend this black man against even an unpleasant white.

"Philip," Rosamond whispered to him, with a soft pounce, "don't go. I don't like him."

"Must," he whispered back. "Shan't be long, dearest."

"We'll all go," Sir Bernard said. "The streets aren't too quiet. I'm not at all sure, Mr. Inkamasi, that you wouldn't be wise to take advantage of the Government's offer to remove friendly aliens. If you're living alone——"

The African dilated where he stood. "I will go alone," he said. "They will not attack me twice."

"No, of course not," Roger said. "Never attack the same man twice is a well-known rule of mobs. Nonsense, man, no one knows who's about. I think you ought to stop here; you can, you know. We told you that before."

"Do," Isabel put in.

Inkamasi seemed to hesitate, then he said rather vaguely, "No, I'm sorry, I must go. There are reasons. . . ."

"Are they really vicious, Roger?" Sir Bernard asked.

"Nasty little things," Roger answered. "The usual kind. I believe they'd have bolted before if Inkamasi and I had rushed them. He nearly scattered them by himself but there were just enough to feel safe."

"I know them," the African said disdainfully. "There are others like them in my country—they would run from a lion."

"As bad as that, are they?" Roger asked gravely. "Good heavens, many's the time I've chased a lion or two down Haverstock Hill by just shouting at them. Like you were doing when we came out. By the way, what were you shouting?"

The African drew himself up and his magnificent form seemed to expand before the young man's eyes. He cried out: "They asked me my name and I told them. I am Inkamasi of the Zulus, I am the chief of the sons of Chaka, I am the master of the impis, I am Inkamasi the chieftain and the king."

There was a dead silence; and then suddenly Roger, almost as if some challenge in the other's voice had stirred him to motion and speech, answered in the voice he had for verse. He threw up his right arm; he cried out, "Bayate!"; he held the Zulu rigid by the unexpected salute. And then someone else moved, and Roger dropped his arm and grinned and said: "Rider Haggard. But it's true, isn't it?"

"It is true," the king said. "It is the royal salute that you

59

give, though I've only heard it once or twice in my life before. But I thought in England you'd forgotten royalty."

"Well, in a kind of way we have," Roger said. "And then again in a kind of way we haven't. And anyhow I didn't know you really kept it in Africa."

"There are those among you who would like us to forget," the Zulu answered. "But it isn't easy to forget Chaka. Have you forgotten Cæsar?"

He seemed to expect no answer; he turned again to Isabel, but this time with a greater air. "Good-night, Mrs. Ingram," he said. "Your husband will be back soon. They shan't come far. Good-night, Miss Murchison. Sir Bernard, will you tell me one thing I have always meant to look up about the stomach?"

Isabel came back from the front door to Rosamond with a bewildered air. "Tell me," she said, "are those three taking care of him or is he taking care of them?"

"I think it's perfectly horrible," Rosamond said. "How could you let him come into the house, Isabel?—everything smells of him. The king, indeed! It's almost profane."

Isabel raised her eyebrows. "What, calling himself a king?" she asked.

"It was the way he talked, looking like a god," Rosamond said, almost hysterically. "I hate him to look like that."

Isabel looked at the coffee cups. "Shall I clear them away?" she said, "or shall I leave them for Muriel? Roger won't call her Muriel, he says it makes him feel unclean. So awkward, because he always has to go and find her if he happens to want anything. He can't just call out 'Hi!' Don't worry, Rosamond, I don't suppose you'll see him again."

"I hate him," Rosamond repeated. "Why didn't he stop in Africa?" She walked to the window. "Isabel, they won't come here, will they?"

Isabel looked at the fire, herself a little shaken. In spite of her mockery of her sister she knew quite well what Rosamond had meant by calling Inkamasi "profane." It was a wild protest against the sudden intrusion of a new energy, the making violently real of a thing that had become less than a word. For a few moments royalty—a dark alien royalty—had appeared in the room, imposed upon all of them by the mere intensity of the Zulu chieftain's own strength and conviction. By virtue of that wide reading which both she and her husband loved, she had felt a shadow of it at times; in the superb lines of Marlowe or Shakespeare, in the rolling titles heard on ceremonial occasions at Church or in local celebrations: "The King's Most Excellent Majesty," "His Majesty the King-Emperor," "The Government of His Britannic Majesty." But on Rosamond unprepared by such imaginative experience the sudden consciousness of this energy and richness—believing so greatly in itself and operating so near her— had come with a shock of dismay. Besides, when all had been said, they were all on edge with the African news, and to have an African in your own rooms overwhelming you with himself—— No, she didn't like it, Rosamond was right.

The single bliss and sole felicity,
The sweet fruition of an earthly crown.

The divine lines came riding back into her memory. "It isn't", Roger had said once at one of his "popular" lectures, "what poetry says, it is what poetry is." These lines described kingship, but that wasn't their strength. They invoked kingship, they grew by their very sound into something of the same enormous royalty which the Zulu had for a moment worn; they were the safe possession in themselves of that sense of single bliss and sole felicity which they affected to describe. In them it was apart from her, to be enjoyed and endured only as she chose, it was hers. But if it went abroad, moving in the world not at her decision or the decision of those like her, but in its own right and power, the energy which was royalty and poetry dominating and using her by means of hands and voices and eyes. . . .

Rosamond came back from the window to the fire, and Isabel remembered that she hadn't replied to her sister's question. She said: "No, they won't come here."

Rosamond answered: "You won't see him again?"

"Who—the king?" Isabel asked. "I don't suppose so."

"I don't think you ought to," Rosamond said. "It's not very patriotic, is it? Why ever did you let Roger bring him in?"

Isabel stiffened a little. "My dear little girl," she answered, "I don't 'let' Roger. If there's any letting done," she went on, relaxing, "he does it. But I don't think he quite knows it."

Rosamond's face suggested that Philip would be "let" or not, fairly often. Isabel added: "Would you rather we'd 'let' the crowd get at him?"

"Yes," her sister answered. "You don't know how I hate him. He's . . . abominable."

"Don't be silly, Rosamond," Isabel said. "You let things upset you so, though you do seem such a sedate little creature. I don't suppose you'll see him again, and if you do what difference does it make?"

Rosamond moved uneasily. "Why isn't Philip stronger?" she said. "He needn't have gone tonight."

Isabel broke into a laugh. "You want Philip to be the world's strong man led by a woman's hair," she said. "You can't have it, darling. Philip's no caveman."

"I don't want a caveman," Rosamond cried out. "I hate him anyhow. He looks like Roger does when he quotes that beastly poetry. It isn't decent. It's like those horrible people on the Heath."

"What on earth do you mean? What horrible people?" Isabel asked, really bewildered.

"Disgusting beasts," Rosamond went on. "You know what I mean—all those brutes lying about at night. They make everything so . . . so *loathsome*. Why can't people be nice and behave properly?"

"And not quote poetry or be kings of the Zulus," Isabel murmured. "You do hate a good many things, don't you? You're not going to marry Philip, I hope, because you hate him rather less than the other young men you know? I don't think he'd be entirely satisfied with that."

"Philip!" Rosamond uttered, in a tone so unlike her usual deceitfully soft voice that Isabel looked at her in alarm. There had been in that one word scorn and hate and fear, almost as if Philip rather than the Zulu stood for everything that Rosamond most detested, as if she were aware now for the first time that the world was not simply Rosamond Murchison's oyster, that indeed it was a great deal more like an octopus, the tentacles of which she had seen waving at a distance in the night. The king—Philip—poetry—people on the Heath—African proclamations—certainly there was a huge something whose form lay hidden in the darkness and the distance without; something Rosamond had always avoided, unless occasionally. . . . Isabel remembered how her small sister, who had always carried herself as if she pretended to disdain chocolates, had once secretly and greedily devoured a whole boxful. It had been an unpleasant episode, made worse by an ignored but definite attempt on Rosamond's part to make Isabel herself the culprit; only appalling physical results had made innocence certain. Rosamond perhaps hated an octopus that lay not merely without. Isabel, bending her brows at the fire, and trying to be lucid and loving at once, was not altogether sorry when Rosamond said suddenly: "I'm tired: I'm going to bed. Say good-night to Philip for me," and vanished.

Roger, meanwhile, was walking with the others towards the house where Inkamasi lived, at one end of the line of four, with Philip at the other, and Sir Bernard and the Zulu discussing stomachs in between. It occurred to Ingram with a slight feeling of shame, as he heard the older man explaining and assenting, that although in the past Sir Bernard had always been able and willing to discuss literature, he himself had never been either able or willing to discuss stomachs. He had liked and admired the specialist, but he had assumed as a matter of course that his own specialization was a more public, even a more important, thing. To justify himself he allowed the suggestion to arise that Sir Bernard had been perhaps a little too easy-going, too disinclined to press his own interests. After all, it was in a different way a note of his son's character also. Philip was a nice creature, but he never imposed himself; he was graver and more solemn than his father but equally swept on the current of conversation. That Sir Bernard had now for many years been able unnoticed to direct any conversation to any end he wished, but that all ends seemed to him equally interesting, naturally did not occur to the younger specialist. Ingram was himself so devoted to his own subject and neglectful of others that he inevitably assumed a similar devotion and neglect in his friends, and explained their behaviour on this hypothesis. As he glanced sidelong at the disputants therefore he saw in Sir Bernard an example of a man a little ill-treated by society, and made up his mind to read the famous book at the first opportunity. Nor could he refrain, as his eye caught the Zulu's face in the light of a lamp, from reflecting upon how differently this stranger had dominated their emotions. The sudden crisis had tricked him into what was almost an absurdity. But in fact, he reflected, the sudden crisis was not separate from Inkamasi; it *was* Inkamasi. It was a human force that had overthrown him. His emotions, caught unguarded by his self-attentive mind, had moved him, and his emotions themselves had been moved by a stronger emotion issuing from the stranger. Rhythm had followed rhythm. "God damn and blast rhythm!" he thought angrily, "I will not use their malodorous slang." But the word had started his associations; half a dozen lines leapt into his mind flushed with war and royalty, from "My nightingale, We have beat them to their beds," down to "stunned of heaven or stricken pale Before the face of the King." Perhaps there was something in rhythm after all; perhaps Milton meant something profounder than was usually thought by saying that the great poet should himself be a poem; perhaps——

"Don't you think so, Roger?" Sir Bernard asked.

Ingram came back with a shock. "I beg your pardon," he said, "I wasn't listening. Don't I think what?"

"Don't you think that the king had better not go on living alone?"

"Are you alone in the house?" Ingram asked the Zulu.

"I am the only sub-tenant," Inkamasi said gravely. "There is a landlady."

"Then of course you mustn't," Ingram said. "Is this it?" They had stopped outside a house in one of the smaller apartment-letting roads bordering the Heath. "You could be attacked and done in here quite nicely—from back and front. You'd better come and stop with us as I told you."

Inkamasi shook his head. "That is very kind of you, Mr. Ingram," he answered, "but I couldn't expose Mrs. Ingram to any unpleasantness."

"Nonsense," said Roger. "She won't——"

Sir Bernard laid a hand on his arm. "A moment, Roger," he said. "I speak as a snob, but so did Saint Paul on occasion, I seem to remember, and I also am an Apostle. Or at least I know the Home Secretary. Now in two or three days the Government will be driven to arrest and intern all the Africans in London. No, of course, it won't want to, but it won't be able to let them be done to death one by one. I suggest it will be much more to the point if the king is staying with me, because my word will probably be taken for him. And he can walk in the garden and study digestion theoretically and practically."

"You mean they'll let him alone there?" Roger said. "Yes, I suppose that's true. Well, we'd better look for a taxi then."

"Stop a minute, Mr. Ingram," the Zulu said. "Sir Bernard, this is extraordinarily kind of you. But it would make it a little difficult for me perhaps, if I may say so. If I came to stay with you, I should be committed to neutrality, if not to friendship. And supposing I wanted to help my people?"

A car came softly along the street towards them. Sir Bernard said dubiously, "It would necessitate, I suppose, an implied parole. But would you be worse off? You can't do much for them now; and if you're attacked and killed——"

He paused; behind them the car also stopped. Roger, glancing over his shoulder as he heard the king say, "I mustn't pledge myself; I mustn't be bound," saw Nigel Considine spring out. He gave a quick exclamation and his companions also looked round.

"Why, Mr. Ingram," Considine said, and saluted Sir Bernard and Philip, "this is a happy meeting. I didn't know you were friends of my friend."

"Through the introduction of a London crowd," Roger answered. "So we just strolled home with him."

"I was afraid of that," Considine answered, "so I've come to carry him off." He smiled at Inkamasi, and Philip wondered why he and his father and Roger should suddenly seem so small standing around those two other figures. Sir Bernard said, "I was just suggesting that the king should stay with me." But the African and Considine were gazing at each other, and neither of them answered.

"I must be free," Inkamasi said suddenly. "I must do what I choose."

"You shall be free; you shall do what you choose," the other answered. "But you will come with me now, and presently I will set you free." He broke suddenly into a stream of unrecognizable syllables which the others supposed were Zulu, and still he held Inkamasi's eyes with his own, and the African stammered and began to speak and ceased, and the urgent commanding voice flowed on. Inkamasi put out his hand suddenly towards Sir Bernard, who was next him, and took his arm. He cried out suddenly in English, "But I do not wish —I do not choose——" then his whole figure sagged and his hand drew itself away. Considine said something to him even more sharply; he moved forward, and slowly, almost as if moving in his sleep, got into the car. Considine, following him, paused by the door and turned.

"Sir Bernard," he said, "in a very few days I shall be leaving England. But I've written to you to-day to ask if you will dine with me to-morrow. I apologize for the short notice. If you would—and perhaps these gentlemen too? Let's discuss verse once more, Mr. Ingram, before I go."

"Must you go?" Roger, to his surprise, heard himself saying.

"All that's mine remains," Considine said, "even if embalmed or diluted——" he smiled, and there was victory in his face. He looked back at Sir Bernard, who said only, "Thank you very much!"

"At eight to-morrow then," Considine said. "Good-night." He leapt into the car and at once it slid away. The three stood staring after it. At last—

"Well," Sir Bernard said, "I do want to ask him about the photograph. And lots of people talk rather big. But if Mr. Considine can bully a Zulu prince who could bully us . . ."

"I don't see anything in him particularly," Philip said. "But I was surprised the king let himself be persuaded."

Sir Bernard began to walk away. " 'Persuaded,' Philip? Do you think 'persuaded' was the word?" he said.

"I don't think the king wanted to go," Philip said. "But of course I don't know what Considine said in Zulu, if it was Zulu."

"Nor do I," said Sir Bernard. "But I know what I should say in that tone. I should say, "Come on, you fool! It's me telling you." When I was in practice I kept that voice for telling American millionaires to eat less. There are moments when I wonder whether I really like Mr. Considine."

Chapter Five

THE NEOPHYTE OF DEATH

The five of them were sitting at a round table—Considine at the head, Sir Bernard on his right, Roger on his left, Inkamasi next Roger, and Philip between the king and Sir Bernard. They were served by two men who, Sir Bernard remarked at once, were evidently not of the usual servant type. They were much more like young men of his own class, but they were adept at their work; only they waited with an air of condescension and if they had occasion to speak they never said "sir" except indeed to Considine and the king. Considine's own manner towards them was that of an equal who accepts by right some special service; there existed between them a grave courtesy. Occasionally, while the dinner proceeded, one of these gentlemen in waiting would go to the door in answer to a discreet knock, receive a message, return to whisper it in Considine's ear, and take back a softly murmured answer. But such secret interruptions did not interfere with the general conversation, which turned at first upon the Rosenberg crisis.

"You have talked to the legatees?" Sir Bernard said.

"Why, yes," Considine smiled, "and they have taken a stand which might have been foreseen, which I did foresee. The solicitor and I—you remember Mr. Patton?—met them and the Chief Rabbi, and showed them the will. We had to go to them; they would not come to us. When I saw them I did not wonder at it. Their whole minds were given to other things. They are concerned—as how should they not be?—with one chief matter, the rebuilding of the Temple in Jerusalem."

"Are they though?" Roger said. "And what will they do with the money?"

"What do you think?" Considine said. "What do *you* think, Sir Bernard? Remember that they are fanatical in their vision and desire."

"Take it," Sir Bernard answered, "and spend all that comes from it in Jerusalem."

"Refuse it," Philip said, as Considine lifted friendly eyebrows at him before looking at Roger, who considered, his head on one side.

"I don't know them, of course," he said, "but you encourage me to hope that the others are wrong. Take it—refuse it—something else. Take it and not take it. . . . I know—take it and withdraw it, sell everything, and keep the result."

"Exactly," Considine answered. "They insist on selling out all the Rosenberg properties, and what they have from that—however large or small—they will spend on building the Temple again."

"But the loss——?" Sir Bernard exclaimed. "It will take years, won't it?"

"They are too old to spend years in patience," Considine said. "They will have it done immediately, for fear they should die before the work is begun."

"But can't you stop them?" Philip said.

"Believing what I do believe," Considine answered, "why should I stop them? It is a great act of creation; they prepare for Messias."

"And the jewels?" Roger asked. "Are they to be sold too?"

"No," Considine said; "those they will take as they are, 'an oblation to the Holy of Holies, a recompense for iniquity and for that one of their house who has touched the unclean thing.' I repeat their words."

"If they ever get them to Jerusalem——" Roger suggested.

"That may be part of the executor's business," Considine answered. "I shall do my best for them while I've the time."

"It'll cause a good deal of disturbance," Sir Bernard said thoughtfully. "Rosenberg was interested in a great deal, wasn't he?"

"A great deal," Considine agreed, adding with a faint smile, "Perhaps it was a little unfortunate that Patton, intending the best, pointed out that Rosenberg had religious interests which would be upset by such an action. He instanced a concern called the Anglo-Catholic Church and Home Adornment Society, which manufactured crucifixes and pictures of saints. Somehow Rosenberg was mixed up in it. It didn't placate them."

"Patton, I suppose," Sir Bernard said, "felt that all religions meant the same?"

"I was sorry for him," Considine said, again smiling faintly. "Even the Chief Rabbi could hardly quieten them. Yes, Sir Bernard. I don't say that Patton's wrong, but there remains the question of what religion all the religions mean."

"Perhaps that's what the African proclamations are trying to tell us," Roger said. "Do you believe in them, Mr. Considine?"

"In what sense—believe?" Considine asked.

"D'you think they're authentic?" Roger elaborated. "And if authentic, d'you think they mean anything?"

"Yes and yes," Considine answered. "I see no reason why they shouldn't be authentic—and if they are then I think they mean something definite. It is a gospel, perhaps a crusade, which is approaching."

"Jolly for us," Roger said. He shifted his eyes to Inkamasi, and said, "And what do you think?" thanking his gods that the other was next to him and that vocatives of address could therefore be avoided. How did one speak to a Zulu king?

Inkamasi looked up heavily. The last twenty-four hours, Sir Bernard thought, seemed to have dulled the young African. His eyes went to Considine, who said, "Yes; let the king tell us if he thinks this gospel has meaning."

Why did Considine, he wondered, speak so, with such high gravity in his voice? He waited with interest for Inkamasi's answer but when it came it took them but little farther. He answered the question, but no more. "Yes, I think it has a meaning," he said, and his eyes fell again to his plate.

Sir Bernard looked back at Considine, who was (he noticed) eating very little, a few fragments of each course, a few sips of wine, and that with an air rather of courtesy than of interest or desire. He was behaving as a gracious host should, but what host was this who was waited on by gentlemen, who spoke of gospels and crusades, who seemed to dominate from his seat the visitors he permitted to speak freely? Sir Bernard said: "It's a little cheap, isn't it? 'The conquest of death'?"

"You don't desire the conquest of death?" Considine asked.

"I find a difficulty in understanding it here," Sir Bernard said.

"Why?" Considine asked again.

Sir Bernard hesitated, and Roger broke in swiftly, "Because we've never heard of it happening, and because we've never noticed that reading poetry and being in love led to anything that looked like the conquest of death. At least, I can't think of any other reason. What does it *mean*?"

"There are two things it might mean," Considine said, "living for ever or dying and living again. And will you"— he leaned a little forward—"will *you* tell me, Mr. Ingram, that you haven't felt one or both of these when you deal with great verse?"

Philip saw Roger's face change. He was looking steadily at Considine, and he continued to look for more than a minute before he answered. In that time the sardonic and almost bitter humour which often showed in him, as if he were weary of fighting that stupidity against which "the gods themselves contend in vain", and as if he despised himself both for strife and weariness—that half-angry mockery

71

vanished, and it was with a sudden passionate sincerity that he said, "No, no; you're right. One dies and lives in it, but I can't tell how."

"Only because you haven't looked that way," Considine said, with an illuminating smile. "You handle the stuff of the experiment, the stuff which the poets made, but they made it out of what is common to us all, and there are things which they, even they, never knew. And as for love, is there any one of us, since we are men and have loved, who doesn't know that there is within the first moments of that divine delight some actuality of the conquest of death?"

Half by chance, his eyes rested on Philip, who, as if called by that commanding gaze from his habitual shyness and dislike of speech, stammered out: "Yes, but what is there to do? It's like that, but what can I do?"

"You can know your joy and direct it," Considine answered. "When your manhood's aflame with love you will burn down with it the barriers that separate us from immortality. You waste yourselves, all of you, looking outwards; you give yourselves to the world. But the business of man is to assume the world into himself. He shall draw strength from everything that he may govern everything. But can you do this by doubting and dividing and contemplating? by intellect and official science? It is greater labour than you need."

"Govern?" Sir Bernard put in. "What do you mean by governing the world? Ruling it, like Cæsar?"

"Cæsar", Considine answered, "knew of it. I am sure he did. This man who had so many lovers, who could bear all hardships and use all comfort, who was not athlete or lover or general or statesman or writer, but only those because he was Cæsar, who founded not a dynasty but a civilization, whose children we are, who dreamed of travelling to the sources of the Nile and sailed out to the strange island whither the Gallic boatmen rowed the souls of the dead, who was lord of all minds and natures, didn't he dream of the sources of other

72

waters and set sail living for a land where the spirits of other
men are but helplessly driven? Rule the world? He *was* the
world; he mastered it; the power that is in it burned in him and
he knew it, he was one with it."

"Cæsar died," Sir Bernard said.

"He was killed, he was destroyed, but he was not beaten
and he did not die," Considine answered. "Why does a man
die but because he had not driven strength into the imagination of himself as living?"

Sir Bernard put his hand in the pocket of his dinner jacket,
but he paused before withdrawing it, as the subdued but
powerful voice swept on. "Cæsar had the secret then, and if
Antony had had it too Europe might have been a place of
lordlier knowledge to-day. For he could have destroyed
Octavian and he and the Queen of Egypt in their love could
have presented the capacities of love on a high stage before
the nations. But they wasted themselves and each other on
the lesser delights. And what failed at Alexandria was unknown in Judæa. Ah, if Christ had known love, what a rich
and bounteous Church he could have founded! He almost
conquered death in his own way, but he was slain like Caesar
before he quite achieved. So Christianity has looked for the
resurrection in another world, not here. The Middle Ages
wondered at visions of the truth—alchemy, sorcery, fountains
of youth, these are part of the dream. The Renascence knew
the splendour but lost the meaning, and it was tempted by
learning and scholarship, and ravaged by Calvin and Ignatius
with their systems, and it withered into the eighteenth
century. They did well to call that the Augustan age, for
Cæsar had fallen and Christ was but a celestial consolation.
But the time is come very near now."

Roger said, "But how? but how?"

Considine answered, "By the transmutation of your
energies, evoked by poetry or love or any manner of ecstasy,
into the power of a greater ecstasy."

The photograph in Sir Bernard's hand dropped on to the table; leaning forward, he said, his eyes bright with a great curiosity, "But do you tell us that you have done it?"

"I have done one thing," Considine said. "I think I shall do the other when I have made a place for it on earth. I live, except for accident, as I choose and as long as I choose. It is two hundred years since I was born, and how near am I to-night to any kind of natural death?"

He did not exalt over them or seem to speak boastfully. He leaned back in his chair, and with an exalted certitude his eyes held them motionless, while his voice put to them that serene inquiry. Clear and triumphant, he smiled at them, and his gentlemen stood beside him, and his wine, hardly touched, glowed in its glass, as his own spirit seemed to glow in the purged and consummate flesh that held it. Philip remembered Rosamond's thrice-significant body, and yet this body was more significant even than Rosamond's, for here there arose no lovely and mournful mist of unformulated desire. And Roger's mind, but half-consciously, sought to recall some great verbal wonder that should serve to express this wonder, and failed. Sir Bernard's scepticism, forbidding incredulity, left him to savour the full possession of an un-rivalled and exquisite experience. Only the Zulu king sat with his head on his hand and showed no knowledge of the talk that proclaimed immortality present in the shape of a man.

The minutes seemed to pass as the others gazed, yet they did not seem minutes, for time was lost. Nearer than ever before in their lives to a sense of abandoned discipleship, the two young men trembled before one who might be their predestined lord. It was Sir Bernard's voice that broke the stillness.

"And this other thing?" he said. "What else is there you foresee?"

Considine smiled once more. "This is only a part," he said. "Because I live, men shall live also. But they shall do greater works than I, or perhaps I shall do them—I do not know. To live on—that is well. To live on by the power not of food and drink but of the imagination itself recalling into itself all the powers of desire—that is well too. But to die and live again—that remains to be done, and will be done. The spirit of a man shall go out from his body and return into his body and revivify it. It may be done any day; perhaps one of you shall do it. There have been some who tried it, and though they have failed and are dead we know they were pioneers of man's certain empire. It is what your Christ announced—it is the formula of man divinized—'a little while and I am not with you, and again a little while and I am with you'. He was the herald of the first conqueror of death."

There came at the door one of those discreet knocks, and a gentleman-in-waiting went lightly and returned to murmur a message. Considine listened and looked at his guests; then he added, ending what he had been saying, "and I will show you the intention that shall, one day, succeed."

He murmured a few words to his servant who returned to the door and went out. Considine looked round the table and rose. "Let's go into the other room for our coffee and perhaps you'll be indulgent to me," he said. "I generally have music played after dinner—can you listen for a few minutes without being bored?"

They murmured assurances, and stood up, following him as he moved from the room and on to another door which a servant opened for them. It was a long high room into which they came (to judge from the proportions visible), but a part of it was cut off by hanging curtains of an extraordinarily deep blue, a blue so deep that though it had not the blaze it had the richness of sapphire. Sir Bernard exclaimed when he saw it, and Considine said to him, "You see my travels also have not been in vain."

"Where did you find this, then?" Sir Bernard said. "It beats the best stained glass I've ever seen."

"It was woven for me once," Considine answered, "in a village where they see colour as well as St. John saw it in his vision. Sit down here, won't you?"

There were a group of comfortable chairs at the end of the room farthest from the curtains, and to these the visitors were, half-ceremonially, ushered. The gentleman in attendance offered cigars and cigarettes to all but Considine; when they were settled, he went over to the curtains and at a nod from his master drew them a little back. Beyond, through the opening, they could glimpse similar panelled walls to those between which they sat. Sir Bernard could see at the farther end of the room a group of figures, a cello, and violins. The gentleman in waiting, standing in the opening, made a sign with his hand, withdrew to the door, and remained standing there. The music began.

Both the Travers loved music; it was indeed—besides events—Sir Bernard's only emotional indulgence, and he was therefore more on his guard against it than perhaps even his alert intelligence altogether realized. Philip was not far advanced in its obedience; he, in a despised but correct phrase, "knew what he liked," and was humbly and properly aware that "he didn't know much about it." He prepared to listen, and for the first few minutes was engaged in trying to recognize some of the phrases that floated to him. He seemed to have heard them before, but he couldn't place them; they were followed by other sounds which he knew he couldn't place. It was, he supposed, "modern music"; there was at intervals something very like a discord. But as he listened he began to lose touch with it, and to think more and more of Rosamond. There was nothing surprising in this; he very often did think of Rosamond, with or without music. But he was thinking of her in harmony with the music. A rush and ripple of sound went through him and in his brain it was not so much sound as Rosamond's visible form, the quivering line of her exquisite side; and the violins swept up more quickly and her round full neck grew up in that ·beautiful dream and her chin became visible, and they slowed and sighed, and there between her welcoming arms and her breasts was a something of fullness and satisfaction which invited him, but not to her. For the music that so created her form in his imagination at the same time swept his imagination round and round her form, but its cry drove him from her. She seemed to be there; almost she moved her hands to him, the music moulded itself into her palms, but the force of it kept him from them. More clearly than ever before in his waking thoughts he saw the naked physical beauty that was Rosamond and would have drawn her to his heart, but that, darkly and deeply as never before, the energy of music which was in that beauty invited and adjured him to attend to itself alone. His blood flowed, his breath came heavily, in the growing intoxication of love, but the harmony that caused it summoned him back from its image to its power. He felt himself flowing away from Rosamond, with no less but with greater passion than he had seemed to flow towards it. His passion had reached a point of trembling stillness before, and had closed then, perhaps in a kiss or an uncertain caress, perhaps in a separation and a departure. But now it found no such sweet conclusion, and still as the sources of his strength were opened up, and the currents of masculinity released, still he, or whatever in that music was he, seemed to control and compel them into subterranean torrents towards hidden necessities within him. Flux and reflux existed at once, but he could not name the end to which the reflux turned. It should be dispelled into some purpose, but what? but what? He seemed to cry out, and he heard an answer; he heard Considine saying, "It is two hundred years since I was born, and how near am I to any kind of death?" That might well be; this strength within might well carry him on through two hundred years; time was only its measure, not its limit; its condition, not its control. "Feed; feed and live," he heard a voice crying, and then the voice was itself but music, and the music receded, and he heard it mighty at a distance, and then less mighty but nearer, and at last, trembling all over, he realized how he was sitting, shaken and troubled, in a chair by the fireside, and how beyond the curtains the sound of the violins trembled also and died away. He looked round and met Roger's eyes, and knew that in them also recognition was beginning slowly to return.

Roger never much cared for music, but he had not been sorry when it was proposed to him; imposed upon him, he was inclined to think, would have been a better term, since quite apart from politeness no-one would have dared object to Considine's obvious intention. At least, Sir Bernard might; Sir Bernard could do most things, but Roger was quite clear that neither Philip nor himself would. But he didn't object, even mentally; he rather welcomed the suggestion, since he, not caring for music, would have a little while to order his confused ideas. Considine's conversation—especially with this two-century climax—had got rather beyond them. Besides, he wanted to try and see what he meant by agreeing to the statement that all great art seemed to hold contemporaneous death and new life. He settled himself, glanced indolently towards the distant musicians, and looked for a line to experiment on. It ought to be a good line; he picked out, "And thus the Filial Godhead answering spake." The music, he was aware, had begun. Very well then: now—— The simple analysis, the union of opposites which so often existed in verse, was clear enough. There was the opposition of the Latin "Filial" and the English "God," and of the ideas expressed in those words—Filial, implying subordination and obedience; Godhead—authority, finality. Something similar was true also of "answering" and "spake." That was elementary—but about death . . . the music was getting in his way; bother the music—the words were becoming a kind of guide to it, not to his thoughts. His thoughts showed him the lovely and delicate manipulation of . . . of what? Words; the association of words: "the Filial"—a twist and cry of the violins broke sharply on

him—"Godhead." "Filial"—he was filial to something; filial
—the subordination of himself in the presence of something,
of godhead, the godhead this triumphant sound was speeding
through his consciousness; filial—the smooth vowels and
labials, the word that was he sliding so easily in and through
the energy of the whole line, an energy that broke out in the
explosive consonants of "Godhead." Filial—that was to die,
to be drawn down by this music into reconciliation with something that answering spake. But it was he that answering spake—
answering, answering, answering, what but that which spake?
"Spake, spake," the notes sang out; not saying "spake" but
sounding it; they were speaking. It—the word, the sound, was
itself speaking; "spake" was only an echo of what it said.
"The Filial Godhead answering spake"—and Roger Ingram
was being left behind, even the Roger Ingram that loved the
line, for the line was driving him down to answer it by
dying and living, to be nothing but a filial godhead. Milton
was but a name for a particular form of this immortal energy:
the line was but an opportunity for knowing the everlasting
delight, the ecstasy of all those elements that combined in its
passionate joy, knowing it by being part of it. His intellect had
shown him the marvellous glories of the line, but as he passed
into it and between its glories his intellect revealed itself but
as one of the elements. A moral duty swept him on. This
energy was to be possessed, to possess him, and then—then he
would have time to find yet greater powers even than that.
Power, power—"the Power so-called Through sad incompetence of human speech"; even the great poets were but sad
incompetence; nothing but the transmutation of even the
energy they gave could be an answer to the energy they took
from some source beyond them. He hung, poised, unconscious of
himself repeating words silently and very slowly, opening himself
to them: "sad incompetence of human speech"—"thus the
Filial Godhead answering spake." And the violins descanted
on it, and slowly died away; and as slowly he came to himself

79

and looked up to meet Philip's welcoming and inquiring eyes.

The music ceased. Considine stood up and came over to his guests. "Did you care for it?" he asked.

No-one found it possible to answer immediately; at last Sir Bernard, with a sudden movement, came to his feet. He looked at Considine, and against the other's majestic form his smaller figure seemed to gather itself together. He looked, and said, in a voice not without a note of victory, "Well, I kept my head."

"You are proud of that?" Considine asked disdainfully. Sir Bernard shrugged. "It fulfils its function," he said. "I like to take my music like a gentleman. What was it?"

"It was made by one of my friends," Considine said. "He had overcome all things except music, but that lured him to spend his power and he died. We feed on what he did that we may do more than he."

"But——" Roger began, arrested by something in these words, "but do you mean—is it a waste to make music?"

"Mustn't it be?" the other asked. "If you want more than sound it's a waste to spend power making sound, as it's a waste to spend on the beloved what's meant to discover more than the beloved."

"But this means the death of everything!" Roger exclaimed.

"And if so?" Considine asked. "Yet it isn't so. It's possible to make out of the mere superfluity of power greater things than men now spend all their power on. The dropping flames of that fire are greater than all your pyres of splendour. And when death itself is but passion of ecstasy, we will make music such as you couldn't bear to hear, and we will be the fathers of the children who shall hear it. Listen to the prophecy."

He turned and nodded to the gentleman in waiting, who had after the music ceased again drawn the curtains, and now went out of the room. Considine left his guests together and returned to a small table near the curtains. The only light in the room came from a tall standard near him, so that Sir

Bernard and the others were clustered in the shadows and not clearly to be seen.

Roger glanced at the African, sitting by him almost as if asleep, and then looked back again at Considine. He stood there, an ordinary gentleman in an ordinary dinner-jacket, but the black of the clothes and the tie, the white of the front and the cuffs, gathered into a kind of solemn insignia. Roger saw him, against the immense and universal sapphire of the draperies behind him, a figure in hieratic dress, motionless, expectant, attentive, having power to give or to withhold, as if an Emperor of Byzantium awaited between the East and the West the approach of petitions he only could fulfil. His hands were by his sides, his head was a little thrown back, his eyes were withdrawn as if he meditated, and behind him the vast azure hung as if it were a cloak some attendant had but that moment removed and still held spread out before he folded it. Modern, contemporary—antique, mythical—neither of these were the truth. He stood as something more than either, being both and more than both. It was Man that stood there, man conscious of himself and of his powers, man powerful and victorious, bold and serene, a culmination and a prophecy. Time and space hung behind him, his background and his possession, themselves no more separate but woven in a single vision, the colour of the living background to that living domination. "Death itself but passion of ecstasy"—death itself might well have been lying at those feet in black, shining and pointed gear, as in delicate armour, at the direction of the hands which fell from between the stiff, shining and sacerdotal cuffs. The ritual of a generation was changed into a universal ritual; so for Philip Rosamond had turned her dresses into significance; so always and in all places have the gods when they walked among men changed into their own permanent sacramental habits the accidental raiment of the day.

Phrases of the talk rushed back into Roger's mind—other phrases of the proclamation of the High Executive—"moments

81

of the exalted imagination": here and now was such a moment, here and now that imagination made itself visible before him and overwhelmed him with its epiphany.

The door opened. Considine turned his head. The gentleman in waiting stood aside and said in a low clear voice: "Colonel Mottreux and Herr Nielsen." Two men came into the room. The first was a tall, lean, rather hatchet-faced man, not unlike Roger himself, but with fiercer and more hungry eyes, as Roger's might have been had all the real placability which his love of Isabel and his service of poetry gave him been withdrawn. He looked like a soldier but an ambitious soldier who doubts his future; only as he bowed abruptly to Considine he showed a not merely military subordination; his eyes fell and did not for a moment recover. There came after him a different figure—a man German-built, sunburnt and weather-beaten, but still young, or young anyhow he seemed to those who watched, though in the new spiritual air they breathed they were aware that youth and age might have other meanings than usual in terms of time. He bowed much more deeply than Mottreux, and once well in the room he halted while the other went forward.

"My dear Mottreux," Considine said, not moving, but smiling and holding out his hand. Colonel Mottreux pressed it lightly, almost deferentially; his eyes went to the guests.

"These gentlemen have been dining with me," Considine said. "I've wished them to remain a little. We'll talk of your other business later, Mottreux. Let Herr Nielsen tell me his purpose first."

Mottreux stood aside and motioned to Nielsen who came forward and halted two or three steps away.

Considine stretched out his hand, and the other bowed over it, genuflecting a little at the same time as if he were in a royal or sacerdotal presence. But he came erect again and faced his suzerain with an air almost as august as his own. His face was ardent with a profound resolution; to say that "his soul was in his eyes" was no description but a definition. They burned with a purpose and Considine's looked back at them as if he received that purpose and confirmed it.

"Why have you come to me?" he asked, gently, and as if it were a ritual rather than a necessary interrogation.

"I have come to beg for the permission," the other said.

"The permission is in yourself," Considine answered. "I only hear it, but that it's right that I should do. Are you a child of the Mysteries?"

"Since you showed them to me," Nielsen said.

"That was fifty years ago," Considine answered, and the watchers in the shadow thrilled and trembled as they heard the calm voice, and that which, equally calm, replied, "I've followed them since."

"Tell me a little," Considine said, and the other considering, answered, "I have endured love and transmuted it. I have found, when I was young, that the sensual desires of man can be changed into strength of imagination and a physical burden become the bearer of the burden. I have transmuted masculine sex into human life. I am one of the masters of love. And I've done this with all things—whatever I have loved or hated, I have poured the strength of every love and hate into my own life and what is behind my life, and now I need love and hate no more."

He paused, and Considine said, shooting one swift glance towards his guests: "Is this a greater or lesser thing than hate or love?"

"Sir, it's strength and health beyond describing," Nielsen said. "But it's now that I long to go farther."

Considine turned and faced him full, asking "What will you do now?"

"I will go down to death and come again living," the other said.

Considine's eyes searched him long in silence: then he said slowly, "You may not come again."

"Then let me die in that moment," the other cried out. "That's nothing; it doesn't matter; if I fail, I fail. But it's not by dreaming of failure that the master of death shall come. Haven't you told us that this shall be? and it's in my heart now to raise my body from death. I'm not like you; I'm not necessary in this moment to the freeing of men; let me set free the fire that's in us; let me go to break down the barriers of death."

He flung out his hands and caught Considine's; he poured upon his lord the throbbing triumph of his belief and his desire. Considine's voice, fuller and richer than any of the hearers had known it, answered him: "The will and the right are yours, not mine. I'm here only to purge, not to forbid. There must be those who make the effort and some may never come again, but one at any moment shall. Go, if you will; master corruption and the grave; make mortal imagination more than immortal; die and live."

Nielsen dropped on a knee, but his face was turned upwards to Considine's who, stooping, laid his hands on the other's shoulders. Behind the two exalted figures the deep blue of the curtains seemed to be troubled as if distance itself were shaken with the cry and the command. The splendour of colour quivered with the neighbourhood of the ecstasy of man imagining the truth of his being, and creating colour by the mere movements of his imagination. The two were alone, alone in a profound depth of azure distance, so greatly did their passion communicate itself to the things that had been made out of like passion. The woven colour and the woven music had been made at some similar depth of devotion, and all that mingled intensity swept through and filled the room, so that the imaginations of Roger and Philip felt and moved in it, and Philip, panting almost with terror, felt the music he had heard and the colour he saw and the figures before him gather and lose themselves in one piercing consciousness of Rosamond, which yet was not Rosamond but that of which

Rosamond was a shape and a name; and Roger felt phrases, words, half-lines, pressing on him, and yet not words or lines but that which they defined and conveyed—and before them Considine cried again to the ardent postulant of transmuted energy: "Die then, die, exult and live."

Only the Zulu king lay back as if asleep in his chair, and in his Sir Bernard, freed from the temptation of music, watched and savoured and keenly enjoyed every moment of the incredibly multitudinous and changing fantasy which was mankind. He wouldn't deny that he was looking at a man two hundred years old telling a man of, say, seventy to die and live again; it might be—it was unusual but it might be. He couldn't imagine himself wanting to die and live, because that (it seemed to him) would be to spoil the whole point of death. The worst of death was that it was the kind of experience it was very difficult to appreciate in the detached mood of the spectator, let alone the connoisseur. But he had done his best in his own case by rehearsing to himself—and occasionally to Philip—all the ironies which the approach of death often releases on a man. "I may babble obscenities or make a pious confession to Caithness," he had said. "Or I may just lie about and cry for days. One never knows. Try and enjoy it for me, Philip, if I'm past it. I should like to feel that somebody did, and death so often undoes all one's own hypotheses, even the hypothesis that one isn't important." But he feared that Philip wouldn't find it easy to enjoy.

He thought of this for a moment as he watched Nielsen rising slowly to his feet; he thought of it as he looked at the benediction which Considine's face shed on the new adventurer. They were still speaking to each other but he couldn't hear what was being said; he saw Mottreux come forward, and then he saw the Colonel and Nielsen bowing and going to the door. He drew a deep breath and lay back in his chair, but he was immediately distracted by Philip who said in a low voice, "I can't stand any more of this; I'm going."

On the other side Roger also moved. "It's true," he said. "He's right."

Sir Bernard, a little startled, looked at him. Was Roger becoming a convert to this new gospel? He said, "You believe in him?"

"No," Roger said, "but I believe he knows what poetry is, and I've never met a man before who did."

Before Sir Bernard could answer Considine came over to them, and instinctively, in fear or hostility or homage, they all rose. "You see," he said, "there are those who will try the experiment."

"Must I really believe," Sir Bernard said, "that that friend of yours is going to commit suicide with the idea of animating his body all over again?"

"Exactly that," Considine said.

Sir Bernard sighed a little. "It *is* a religion," he said. "And I hoped that man was becoming sane. I think I should dislike you, Mr. Considine, if dislike were ever really worth while."

"And I should have despised you once, Sir Bernard," Considine answered, "but not now. Before you die you shall know that the world is being made anew."

He had hardly spoken when they heard without, as if it echoed, applauded, and proclaimed his words, a sound distant indeed but recognizable, though for a moment they doubted. It was the noise of guns firing. Faint and certain it reached them. Philip and Roger jumped, and even Sir Bernard turned his head towards the window. Considine, watching them, smiled. "Can it be the African planes?" he asked ironically. "Has intellect failed to guard its capital?"

A shout or two came up to them from without, the noise of running feet, a whistle, several cars passing at great speed. Sir Bernard looked back at Considine. "Are you bombing London then?" he asked politely.

"I," Considine laughed at him. "Am I the High Executive? Ask the Jews who believe in Messias, or Mr. Ingram who

86

believes in poetry, or your son who (I think) believes in love, or the king who believes in kingship, ask them what power threatens London to-night. And ask them if they think glory can be defeated by gunpowder."

"I should think it might, if glory is making use of petrol," Sir Bernard said. "I'm sorry that in the circumstances perhaps we'd better go. If your friend's blown to bits by a bomb he'll find it a trifle difficult to revivify his body, won't he?"

"The Christian Church for a considerable time believed it could be done," Considine said. "But I forget that you're not even a Christian."

Roger broke in. "My God!" he said, harshly, "*are* you bombing London?"

Considine changed in an instant from mockery to seriousness. "Be at ease," he said. "Mrs. Ingram's perfectly safe— except indeed from the mobs whom alone your wise brains have left to be the degraded servants of ecstasy. The only deaths to-night will be sacrifices of devotion."

Sir Bernard walked towards the door; a white and bewildered Philip went along with him. Roger lingered a moment.

"I don't know whether I hate or adore you," he said, "and I don't know whether you're mad or I. But——"

"But either way," Considine interrupted, "there is more in verse than talk about similes and metres, and you know it. Hark, hark, there is triumph speaking to man."

The guns sounded again and Roger ran after his friends.

Chapter Six

THE MASS AT LAMBETH

Before Sir Bernard and Philip reached Colindale Square, peace had again filled the night. The raid, if raid it had been, seemed to have been driven off, although the house, when they reached it, was awake and vocal. Caithness was waiting for them in the library, anxious but not perturbed. He knew nothing more than they did, the guns had been sounding, at intervals and at a distance, for something under an hour, then they had ceased. The police had been hastily instructed to spread the news that all was clear, and (in less loud tones) that no damage whatever had been done. Materially this might be true, but not mentally. The agitation which shook London was as much worse than that which the German raids had caused as the fear of negro barbarism was more fundamental than that of the Prussian. London hid and trembled; the jungles were threatening it and the horrors that dwelled in them. It was but for a few minutes—less than an hour—but it had happened. The morning would perhaps increase the fear when it was uttered; for the moment darkness and separation made it private.

Caithness listened with profound attention to the account Sir Bernard gave him. But he showed a distant tendency to discuss it in language which, though hostile, was far too like Considine's to please his friend or reassure Philip. He seemed to find most difficulty in accepting the possibility of Considine's age—which, as Sir Bernard pointed out, was due to the fact that he disapproved of Considine's ideas. "If you thought he was a saint—your kind of saint—you'd think it might be a miracle," he complained. "You will fall back on the supernatural to explain the unusual. But that doesn't matter: the real problem is whether he's the High Executive."

"You say he talked as if he was," Caithness said.

"Yes, but this magniloquent kind of rhetoric can never be trusted," Sir Bernard said. "He might be merely mad. And if he is there's no sense in talking to the Prime Minister about him. Even if I do he won't be there, of course."

"The man I'm thinking about", Caithness said, "is the Zulu. You told me last night he said he was a Christian."

"In a parenthesis, while we were talking stomach," Sir Bernard said. "To explain the strength of his digestion, no doubt."

"And to-night," Caithness went on, unheeding the last remark, "to-night he was different?"

"My dear Ian, you haven't begun to understand Mr. Considine," Sir Bernard answered. "Every one was different. Roger went off plunged in a reverie, which is very unlike Roger. And——" he glanced at his son and changed the sentence—"and I was quite incapable of connected thought. And the king—as everybody calls him, so let's—the king was comatose."

Caithness began walking up and down the room. "I don't like it," he said. "I don't like the sound of any of it. And especially I don't like a Christian to be under this man's influence or in his power. If he can affect you——"

"What on earth harm——" Sir Bernard began, and was interrupted by the priest.

"He evidently thinks he's got hold of some infernal power," Caithness went on, "and if—if by the wildest possibility he were mixed up with this African delirium—are we to leave one of the Faith exposed to his control? He's done it harm enough already. God knows what he may be doing to him. He may have hypnotized him into obedience."

"Literally", Sir Bernard asked, "or metaphorically?"

"What does it matter which?" Caithness threw back.

"D'you suppose one's worse than the other? Are we to have a Christian spiritually martyred here among us?"

"Certainly not," Sir Bernard said. "St. Iago, and charge, Spain! Where?"

But Caithness took no notice; he stood still and silent for a minute, and Sir Bernard observed, with interest, that he was praying. Caithness, he reflected, had always been a little inclined to call up his own spiritual reserves under such a quite honest pretence of invoking direction, though he was always rather careful to keep the command in his own hands: Sir Bernard couldn't remember that God had ever been known to disagree with Ian, anyhow in ecclesiastical affairs. It was therefore with a sense of gratified accuracy that he heard the priest say, "Well, I'm going up there."

"What, now?" he asked curiously.

"Certainly," Caithness answered. "And if this Zulu is still there I shall insist on seeing him."

"And supposing Mr. Considine refuses?" Sir Bernard asked.

Caithness looked at him abstractedly. "O I don't think he'll refuse," he said. "He either won't care to or he won't dare to. Will you come and show me the house?"

"Anything for a quiet life," his friend answered. "Even to conducting a Christian lion to a Zulu victim. What a world! And Rosenberg found it uninteresting. But I dare say he didn't know many Christians. I warn you, Ian," he went on as they left the room, "that if Considine's there I shall pretend I don't know you, and that I've come back for a cigarette case presented to me by grateful patients. Because if he isn't the High Executive——"

"And if he is?" Caithness asked. "If he *is*?"

"That," Sir Bernard said, "is my only hope of an excuse for driving you. O no, no taxis, thank you. If I have to help abduct a king, let me do it in my own car, so as to have a right to put up a gold plate: 'In this car His Majesty the King of the

Zulus once fled from the conquest of death.' Why don't you like the conquest of death, Ian?''

"That's all been done," Caithness said, and Sir Bernard, as they came to the garage, gave a little moan. "Not in Considine's sense it hasn't," he said. "You're just confused. O well—but I think *you'd* probably like Considine if you could ever get to know him. Get in, and we'll try."

It was a little after midnight when they ran through Hampstead. Sir Bernard stopped the car at the corner of the road, and the two of them walked up it. There were more windows lit up than was usual, owing to the raid, but Considine's house was in darkness. They went up the steps and Caithness rang. In a few minutes he rang again, and again.

"He's probably directing the raid," Sir Bernard said. "Or flying up to meet the planes. Levitation, I think they call it; some of your saints used to do it. Similar to the odour of sanctity."

Caithness said: "We shall have to find a window."

Sir Bernard sighed happily. "What a night we're having!" he said, following his friend. "No, Ian, not that one: it's too near the road. Somewhere away at the back. One takes off one's coat, I believe, and presses it against the glass before striking a sharp blow in the centre. We ought really to have treacle and brown paper. You wouldn't care to wait while I went and knocked up the nearest grocer for some golden syrup? We could use the rest of the tin as an excuse for calling. I wonder if at his age Considine can eat golden syrup without getting himself all sticky? That'd almost be worth living for."

But since at the back of the house there was at least one window a little open there was no need to resort to these more uncertain methods. The two gentlemen pushed it up, very quietly, and entered. Sir Bernard, scrambling in, thought to himself, " 'I will encounter darkness as a bride,' I hope she likes me." Within all was silent. They found their way cautiously along, and emerged at last in the hall, where Sir

Bernard assumed direction. Either the house was for the time empty or everyone was asleep. The second alternative was so unlikely that they permitted themselves to assume the first.

They did not, however, relax their caution until they came at last to the room where they had heard the music and seen Nielsen, and left the king in his sleep and Considine in his triumph. Sir Bernard felt that they were not treading so delicately but that one heard them; he seemed to see Considine standing far off, his head a little turned, listening to them, and he wondered if there would be some sudden interference in some unknown manner. But though the suspense endured it did not increase, and in the light of the room they saw Inkamasi still sitting in his chair.

Caithness went quietly across the room towards the Zulu, Sir Bernard paused by the door, listening for footsteps, and watching what went on. The priest kneeled down by the chair, and, after studying the African's face for a few minutes, said in a low voice of energy, "Inkamasi, what are you doing here?"

The Zulu stirred under that intense regard and intense voice and answered, "Inkamasi waits for him who caused sleep."

Sir Bernard jerked suddenly, for the voice was more like Considine's own than the Zulu's, yet fainter than either, as if from a distance the master of substitution interposed between the priest and the sleeper. Caithness said, "Do you sleep by your own will?"

"I watch by the will of him that rules me," the other answered monotonously. "Inkamasi is hidden within me. It's I yet not I that sleep."

"In the name of the Maker of Inkamasi," Caithness said with superb and deep confidence, "in the Name of the Eternal and Everlasting, in the Name of Immanuel, I bid you awake."

"I do not know them," the sleeper answered, "and I keep their sound from Inkamasi lest he hear."

"By the virtue in created life, by the union of Man with God, by the Mother of God in the world and in the soul, I command you to wake," Caithness said.

"I do not know them, and I keep their sound from Inkamasi lest he hear," the sleeper answered.

"In the Name of the Father, the Son, and the Holy Ghost, be silent and go out of him," Caithness exclaimed, making the sign of the cross over the Zulu. "Inkamasi, Inkamasi, by the faith you hold, by the baptism and the Body of Christ, I bid you wake."

The sleeper did not answer but he did not move. As if some closed powers hung, poised and equal, over or within him he lay silent. Sir Bernard remembered how, but a little before, he had seen Considine standing in front of the azure profundity of the curtain, which still hung there, as in the depth of space, and it seemed to him as if from the spectral image of that figure and from the kneeling priest two separate currents of command impinged upon the king and in the moment of meeting neutralized their strength. The central heart of the Zulu beat beyond those conflicting and equal intensities, in oblivion of the outer world yet perhaps in liberty. He waited to see what more Caithness could do. But though the priest concentrated his will and intention, though he tried once or twice to speak, the stillness was prolonged. He had silenced the speaker in Inkamasi, but the very effort held him also silent. He strove to impose his determination upon the Zulu, but he could not pass beyond the gate which he had succeeded in reaching; he could not call the other back through it. He knelt praying by the chair and the minutes went by.

Sir Bernard thought, "We can't possibly stop here. We don't know where Considine's gone, we don't know whether he's coming back, and I should hate him to have to worry the exalted imagination with such a detail as what to do with us. He might want us for some new experiment in the conquest of death. I wonder whether——" He peered out through the door; nothing was happening. He turned back into the room. "If Ian and Considine are locked in a spiritual chest-to-chest wrestle," he thought, "perhaps it's time for a mere intellectualist to have a word. A timid tentative word."

He went across the room and round the back of the chair. His eyes met the priest, and by the force of old friendship communicated something of his purpose. Caithness, still silent and intent, moved his hands from where they rested on the Zulu's shoulders. Sir Bernard put his hand very gently under an arm, and as gently lifted it forward. It yielded easily to his pressure and when that pressure was removed dropped back again. Fearful of speaking lest some rash word should bring down the balance against him, Sir Bernard went lightly to the front of the chair, and picked up the Zulu's hands. He drew them gently, gently forward and upward, he pulled them towards him till the arms were extended, he pulled with the least little extra firmness, and easily as the hands moved the body moved also. The king rose to his feet, following that physical direction, and Sir Bernard took a step backward towards the door. Inkamasi followed him. Caithness, still caught in spiritual combat, also rose, but he made no movement to assist; he left that visible action to his ally. Sir Bernard, taking another step backward, waited till the Zulu was in movement, then he slipped to one side and, still holding the left hand in his own left, put his right fingers on Inkamasi's back. He pressed gently; as if automatically the Zulu moved on. Slowly they passed to the door, Sir Bernard on one side, Caithness on the other. They went in front of that hanging curtain of blue, and for a moment Sir Bernard could have believed that they were drawing Inkamasi out of its influence and depth, could have wondered whether indeed he were doing well thus to interfere on behalf of one magic against another. "What doest thou here, Gehazi?" he said to himself. "Do I really want to save a jungle-king for Ian's passion? One religion or another, it's all the same—'She comes, she comes, the sable throne behold Of Night primeval and of Chaos old.' I suspect I'm just getting a little of my own back on Considine. Never mind; it's too late to change now. Round the corner—so."

They moved on, that curious mingling of intention directing the passive African, through the still house, down the steps, to the waiting car. Still in silence, Sir Bernard made the other two get in at the back and himself returned to the driving-wheel. Once more they ran through London, and in the cold October night brought the sleeper to Colindale Square. There at last, once in the library, Sir Bernard turned to Caithness. "And now what?" he said. "Because I can't personally conduct this Christian of yours about the world for the rest of my life. And I don't, just at the moment, see what you propose to do."

"I know what I shall do," Caithness said. "Do you notice he moves more of his own will since we brought him out of the house?"

"I wouldn't quite say that," Sir Bernard said, "but he needs less direction. It *is* a kind of hypnotism, I suppose."

"It's like a locking up of the outer faculties in his master's will," Caithness said. "But the others are there, only they can't hear us. They may hear a greater than us. To-morrow a voice shall call to him that no tyrant shall silence."

"Meaning——" Sir Bernard said. "My dear Ian, you've no idea of how like Mr. Considine's conversation yours is."

"To-morrow", Caithness said, "I will offer the soul and mind of this man to our Lord in the operation of the Mass. The Archbishop will let us use the chapel at Lambeth."

"And you think that will help him?" Sir Bernard asked with interest.

"Subject always to the will of God," Caithness answered.

"O quite," Sir Bernard assented. "The will of God, of course. Heads I win, tails you lose. However—— And now do you think we dare go to bed?"

"I shan't myself," Caithness said. "I'll watch by him to-night. But you go on."

Sir Bernard looked dubious. "I don't think I should feel quite comfortable," he said. "Suppose the High Executive suggested to him a little exalted imagination of freedom, I don't know that you could stop him. I think, Ian, we'll both settle down with him. I really don't feel capable of undressing a Zulu king; we haven't the stuff to do the *grand coucher* properly. Why is royalty so impressive?"

"It's the concentration of political energy in a person," Caithness said thoughtfully, "the making visible of hierarchic freedom, a presented moment of obedience and rule."

"I think I prefer the Republic," Sir Bernard said; "it's the more abstract dream. But I'm too tired to discuss it. Let's settle as well as we can. Will you have the divan?"

Neither of them slept much—indeed Caithness remained wakeful in his chair, except when for change of comfort he walked up and down a little. Sir Bernard, having slipped away for a few minutes to change, locked the door, took the key with him, and stretched himself on the divan, but only to feel himself revolving the events of the evening. Once his mind was relaxed it became conscious that it was more distressed than it had known. The impact of these high, strange, and violent ideas, the circumstances of colour, music, and ceremonial with which they had been accompanied, the dim suggestion of vivid personalities accepting and serving them and ringing around Considine's own exalted figure, the dimmer but not negligible possibility that here in London moved the mysterious High Executive of the African declarations, the great intention of Nielsen's voice, the threat and anger of the guns answering some threat hurled from the hidden places of the negro nations, the obedience of Inkamasi to some distant control, the passion of Ian Caithness—all these things shook his sedate and happily ironical brain. This was an irony which his habits found it difficult to bear, for it struck at the root of his own irony. And one nearer thing troubled him yet more closely. There had been five of them at dinner that night, and three of them had gone together, and of those three how many had come away? Roger and Philip had gone with him, but it was not the same Roger that had parted from him afterwards, and Philip was labouring under some unaccustomed burden. He felt obscurely alone—his own house, his own friends, were grown alien to him; nowhere in all the world was there one intimate with whom he could mock at the monstrous apparitions that loomed on the out-skirts of his mind, closing round the slender spires and delicate gardens, in which of late its chosen civilization had moved. Not so much the facts, though they were grotesque enough, but the manner of the facts, disturbed him—the triumph, the fanaticism, the shadows of ecstasy. Other memories forced themselves on him—an insane political hot-gospeller in Hyde Park, Caithness vestmented in an ecclesiastical cere-mony, the antique faces of the Jews in the crude reproductions of the papers, a look in Philip's eyes as he watched Rosamond, the silly raucous voices of the crowd in the streets: where was detachment, where was contemplation there? Amidst all the gracious achievements of the mind what wild rites of self-immolation were again to be practised? the rich blue of those curtains was marvellous in its beauty, but in what depth of rapturous experience had it been woven? and was that rapture, with all that must accompany it of danger and terror, indeed desirable for man? Someone had cried out somewhere lately—"I will encounter darkness as a bride"—"She comes . . . the sable throne behold" . . . to encounter that as a bride; the words meant to him something far beyond his nature. Darkness was to be exiled, not embraced; and when, as in the hour of death, it could no longer be exiled, it should be received with a proud and courteous if constrained hostility. It was Roger who had cried: Roger who loved some mysterious energy that he himself had never found, or finding had mistrusted and banished. He looked from his couch on the shaded room, the dark face of the African chieftain, the pacing figure of the priest of crucifixion; he listened to find if he should again hear the sound of the guns that warned him of a crusade which had spies and devotees in the city where he lay, in the friends by whom he was surrounded, nay, in the very spirit which moved in his obscure self.

Nevertheless, he rose early the next morning with a mind still determined to enjoy its stand against enemies within and without, and gravely put his telephone at Ian's disposal in order that the priest might speak to Lambeth. It seemed to Sir Bernard very unlikely that the Archbishop would be up, but either he was or he was caused to be. After a prolonged conversation Caithness came back to say merely that all had been arranged. Philip, who apparently had also had very little sleep, offered to drive, more for the sake of doing something, his father suspected, than because he was very clear what was supposed to be happening. But it was a perfectly good idea, Sir Bernard thought; he himself had done all, and rather more than all, that could be thought reasonable, and if Caithness's Deity were going to fight Nigel Considine for the soul of the Zulu king, he would himself maintain towards such fantastic spiritual warfare a beautiful neutrality. He liked Inkamasi as an individual; he sympathized with him as an African; he was prepared to be interested in him as a king. But he was certainly not prepared to help decide whether he should turn out a fervent Christian or a submissive Considinian; the powers concerned could settle that between them. He saw the others off, and returned first to have breakfast and then to ring up Roger and urge on him the advisability of removing himself, Isabel and Rosamond to Colindale Square—in case of further air-raids. Roger made some objection about correspondence, but a long discussion conducted between Sir Bernard at one end and sometimes Roger, sometimes Isabel, sometimes both of them at the other, and sometimes merely between themselves, ended in their accepting his offer. "I had thought of leaving London," Sir Bernard said, "but if we decide to go, we can all go together. It'll be kinder to Philip for you to come here, and I have the finest sort of cellar if it's needed."

Meanwhile, Philip at the steering-wheel was trying to order his own distracted mind. He certainly hadn't had much sleep; the evening had shaken him far too much. That curious music, so closely allied to Rosamond yet ever avoiding her, calling and driving him to look for something that seemed to hide in her yet had to be found for its own sake not for hers, that music would by itself have prevented sleep. And when to it was added the obscure talk of Considine's—and talk that meant something. The moment of vision in Isabel's kitchen, when Rosamond's arm had lain like a bar of firmamental power across the whole created universe, dividing and reconciling at once, had stirred in him something more than masculinity, and whatever had been stirred had recognized its own kingdom in Considine's voice when he had spoken of the divine delight which foretells and communicates the conquest of death. Philip was not much concerned with the conquest of death as such in the future, but he was vitally concerned with its immediate presence. He became dimly aware that though Rosamond would die the thing he had seen in Rosamond not merely could not die but had nothing whatever to do with death. Even if it passed—though of course it couldn't pass—but even if it did pass, still its passing had got nothing whatever to do with it. Its presence, he toiled laboriously at an undefined thought, had got nothing to do with its absence. Was it so very surprising then that men could determine *not* to die? He rather wondered whether he could manage to discuss this with Rosamond, only she was always impatient of his slow mind, and he wouldn't be able to find words for it. Also, probably, she wouldn't care about it; she'd feel it was disagreeable and a trifle obscene, and perhaps she was right. She and Considine wouldn't get on very well; only then—far off a single unmistakable note sounded and ceased—only then which of them. . . . Shocked, as such lovers are, by the implied disloyalty, when first some alien fate separates itself from the hitherto universal fate which is the beloved, he put it hastily out of his mind. He had not understood, in his confusion, the accusation which his father had flung at Considine, and Sir Bernard considerately had not pressed it on him. The High Executive was something to do with negroes, and Considine was a man in London with whom he had dined. The conquest of death itself would have been an easier matter to Philip than the union of those two thoughts in a single idea. But the two experiences ran closely parallel in his troubled heart.

At Lambeth he followed the others, Caithness gently guiding the Zulu by a hand on his arm. Philip, without exactly professing and calling himself a Christian, had a general idea that he disagreed with the people who disagreed with Christianity. His father's own disagreement slightly accentuated this, because in the usual reflux of the generations he tended to assume that his father's mind was insufficient. And anyhow any mere mental and argumentative disagreement was past bothering him at the moment. He couldn't possibly have sat in the car while the others went wherever they were going; and if the king had really been put to sleep, he thought the king ought to be wakened. But even the relation of Considine with the king did not cause him to suspect whose determination had challenged England in the strange and piercing notes of the Allied Suzerainties of Africa. So he went on.

One of the Archbishop's chaplains met them and brought them to the private chapel. Caithness led Inkamasi to the rails of the sanctuary and there caused him to kneel, kneeling himself by his side. Philip slipped behind a chair. The Archbishop, vested in the ordinary chasuble, and the chaplain, acting as server, made their entrance. Murmured sentences were exchanged and the Archbishop went up to the altar.

Philip had long ago lost touch with the ritual of the Mysteries, and the opening prayers brought back to him only a confused memory of uninteresting moments in boyhood and youth. The Archbishop, with a swift intense movement, wheeled towards the kneeling four and began the Commandments. Caithness turned his gaze on to Inkamasi, and seemed to concentrate it, as the celebrant uttered, almost as if in an incantation and with his look also fixed on the Zulu, "Thou shalt have none other gods but me." The chaplain answered softly, and the beating series of directions went on. The Archbishop turned again to the altar, murmured a longer prayer, another, and came to the Epistle.

Of the Epistle and Gospel Philip, unused to the phrasing and tone, understood very little. A phrase here and there struck him. "Greater is he that is in you than he that is in the world." "This sickness is not unto death." "I am the resurrection and the life." "Lazarus, come forth." He was aware of a rising tide of passion, swelled suddenly as the Archbishop broke into the Creed by the strong voice of Caithness. The tones of the three priests mingled and achieved the Profession, and ceased; and for some minutes Philip again heard only the single voice of the celebrant, with an occasional murmur from the chaplain. Nevertheless, as he knelt listening, the Rite ordered his mind. He forgot to try and reconcile; he was moved by reconciliation. There rose in him a feeling kindred to that with which sometimes he had waited for Rosamond— entire expectation yet mingled with complete repose and certainty. The face of Caithness, when he saw it, had lost its earlier concentration and was filled instead with a profound conviction, a content so deep that he involuntarily looked at the Zulu to see what, if anything, had caused it. But no difference showed in Inkamasi, who still, motionless, glassy-eyed, and lethargic, knelt at the rail, his hands hanging over it. The Archbishop's face visible at moments as he turned and returned, knelt and rose, spread out or closed his hands, was more sombre than that of the other priests, but it was no more strongly moved. Philip had once seen his father the moment before a successful but very dangerous operation, and the look of the celebrant reminded him of Sir Bernard then: it was the look of a man conscious of the gravity of the work before him but conscious also of an entire capacity to deal with it. But was this also then a work of cutting and setting right and binding? was it as possible, if less usual, to restore a man's will as to restore his stomach? The archbishop seemed to be no more agitated than any clergyman delivering a sermon; only as he stood now in the Prayer of Consecration, he suddenly, after the words "in the same night that He was betrayed," paused and repeated them on a more exalted note. "In the same night that *He* was betrayed. . . ." Philip felt himself looking into a different world; a world he had glimpsed once before over the outstretched arm that had been more significant to him than any other experience in his life. To take his part in it, if indeed it really existed, was beyond him; yet he felt that if something was in fact being done there to aid a man he ought to be taking his part in it. He understood the work no more than he understood why Rosamond should be and mean so much. But if the king were really hyp-notized . . . he began to make a wordless effort towards prayer, half absurd though he felt his effort to be. On the in-stant it took him; a sudden warmth leapt within him; his being rested stable upon a rocky basis, and the movements before him became natural and right. He understood them no more than before, but he was assured that they answered to the imperious control that held him. That control was gone again in a moment; he found himself staring only at the ordinary men whom he knew; his mind was undirected, his heart was unwarmed, as before. But as at Hampstead there had opened spaces and distance beyond all dreams, so now there had shown glimpse of a certainty beyond all pledges and promises, a fixity which any after hesitation was powerless to deny. He became conscious of an immense stillness around him; the Archbishop was on his knees before the altar, and the others motionless in their places. The Archbishop's voice sounded: "Almighty and Everlasting God, who alone art the life of all thy creatures and hast made them able to know how in thy eternity they glorify thee, unite them in thy prevailing will, and increase in them that freedom which only is able to bring them to the bondage of the perfect service, through Jesus Christ our Lord." The chaplain and Caithness answered "Amen."

"Almighty God," the Archbishop said again, "make us to know thee through thy Love who hath redeemed us, and bestoweth through the operations of the Church militant upon earth grace and aid upon all that are in adversity. Establish in us, and especially at this time upon our brother here present, a perfect knowledge of thee, overcome all errors and tyrannies, and as thou only art holy, so be thou only the Lord, through Jesus Christ our Saviour."

Before the "Amen" had ceased, he rose, genuflected, turned, and came down the steps of the altar to Inkamasi. He set his hands on the Zulu's head, paused, and went on: "By the power of Immanuel who only is perfect Man, by his power committed unto us, we recall all powers in thee to their natural obedience, making whole all things that are sick, and destroying all things that are contrary to his will. Awake, thou that sleepest, and arise from the dead, and Christ shall give thee life. In the name of the Father and of the Son and of the Holy Ghost."

As his voice sounded through the chapel Philip saw the hands of the king come together, saw them fold themselves, saw his head move, heard him sigh. Caithness moved an arm behind him, but it was not needed. Inkamasi glanced round swiftly, and as he did so the Archbishop as swiftly went back to the altar, genuflected, and returned, bearing the Sacred Gifts. He communicated them to Caithness first, and then, as if in the ritual of his office, to the king; only again his voice lingered on and intensified the formula of two thousand years, the formula by which Christendom has defined, commanded and assisted the resurrection of man in God. As naturally as in any other service of his life, the king received the Mystery; afterwards he moved as if to rise, but Caithness with a smile touched him on the shoulder and made a quiet signal of restraint, and he desisted. They remained in their places till the Rite was done. The Archbishop and the chaplain passed out, and in due time the others also rose and made their way to the door.

The chaplain met them there; he and Caithness exchanged a few murmured sentences, and then the three went back to the car.

There Caithness said: "I'll drive this time; you two get in together." Inkamasi hesitated a moment but he obeyed, and the priest added hastily to Philip. "He knows you; better tell him everything he wants to hear——"

"Yes, but look here," Philip began, a little startled. "I'm not clear what——"

"No, but never mind," Caithness said, rather more like the vicar for the moment than the godfather or even the priest, "you're able to explain what's happened, aren't you? He's met you and he hasn't met me—that's why you'll do it better. In you get."

In accordingly Philip got. But he didn't quite see how to open the conversation. Did one just say engagingly, "You must be surprised to find yourself here?" or apologetically, "I hope you don't mind our having carried you away?" Or could one risk saying, with an air of relief, "That was a near thing?" And then supposing he said, "What?" or "How?" What had it been near to? and how? Philip began to wish that his father was in the car. But before he had found the exact words, the African turned to him and said, "Will you tell me, Mr. Travers, what has been happening?"

Philip tried to, and thought he failed badly. But apparently enough became clear to satisfy Inkamasi, who listened intently, and then said, "You've done me a greater service than I quite know, I think. It's very good of you."

"Not at all," said Philip. "My father didn't like leaving you there. Perhaps we ought to apologize . . . but . . ."

"No," Inkamasi said, "no, I don't think you ought to apologize. If you've made my life clear to me, that doesn't seem a thing to apologize for." He stared in front of him. "But that we shall see," he added, and relapsed into silence.

Philip, looking at him, thought that he wasn't looking very friendly, and that he was looking rather African, in fact rather—savage. Savage was a word which might here, in fact, have a stronger meaning than it generally had. Inkamasi's head was thrust forward, his jaw was set; his hand moved, slowly and relentlessly, along his leg to his knee, as if with purpose, and not a pleasant purpose. "I hope he *isn't* annoyed with us," Philip thought. "My father must have meant it for the best." But before they reached Kensington the king relaxed; only there was still about him something high and strange, something apart and reserved, something almost (but quite impersonally) exalted—in short, something like a chieftain who knows that he is a chieftain and is instinctively living up to his knowledge. When they reached Colindale Square, Philip, being on the near side, got out first, and half-held the car door for the stranger. Inkamasi got out and smiled his thanks. But he didn't utter them, and Philip was suddenly aware that he had expected him to. As it was, Inkamasi seemed to have relegated him to the position of an upper servant, yet without being discourteous. Sir Bernard met them in the hall.

Chapter Seven

THE OPENING OF SCHISM

That evening after dinner they were all in the library. Sir Bernard was sitting on the right of the fireplace, with Caithness next to him; opposite him was Isabel, with Rosamond between her and Philip. Roger lay in a chair next to the priest, and pushed a little back from the circle. In the centre, between Roger and Philip, opposite the fire, was the African. Roger looked at him, looked at the rest, and muttered to Caithness: " 'On him each courtier's eye was bent, to him each lady's look was lent, and Hampstead's refugee was Colindale Square's king'." He looked at Rosamond: "She doesn't look happy, does she?" he said. "Why doesn't she go and plan food for her first dinner-party or practise giving the housemaid notice?" He became aware that Sir Bernard was speaking and stopped.

". . . evidence," Sir Bernard was saying. "It's a silly word in the circumstances, but it's the only one we've got. Is there enough evidence to persuade the authorities—or us either for that matter—that Nigel Considine has anything to do with the High Executive? I've drawn up a statement of what happened last night, and I think I'll read it to you; and if I've forgotten anything or the king can tell us any more——"

They sat silent, and he began. Actually, except for the two women, they all knew the substance of it before, but they were very willing to hear it again compacted after this little lapse of time.

Everything was there—the photograph, the music, the other visitors, the guns, the king's sleep—and against that background ran the summaries of Considine's monologues,

conversation, and claim. As they listened that river of broad
pretension flowed faster and deeper at their feet; they stood on
its brink and wondered. Was the source indeed two hundred
years off in the past? was it flowing towards an ocean of infinite
experience till now undiscovered, unimagined—undiscovered
because unimagined? Across that river their disturbed fancies
saw the African forests, and shapes—both white and black—
emerging and disappearing, and from among those high
palms and falling creepers, that curtain of green profusion,
came the sound of strings and the roar of guns. The dark face
of Inkamasi, whatever he himself might be, grew terrible to
them, not merely because of his negro kindred but because of
the terrifying exaltation which so darkly hinted at itself
in the words they heard, and when suddenly the delicate voice
that was reading ceased, it was of Inkamasi's figure that they
were all chiefly aware, whether they looked towards it as
Caithness did or away from it into the fire at which Rosamond
Murchison stared.

Sir Bernard put down his paper, and looked for a cigarette.
For once, among all his friends, no-one forestalled him. He
found one, lit it, and sat back, reluctant to spoil his story
with any bathos of comment. In a minute Inkamasi moved.

"I've thanked you already, Sir Bernard," he said, and
suddenly Isabel felt Rosamond's arm quiver, as it lay in her
own, "and I'll thank you once more. You and Mr. Caithness
have done a great thing for me. You've set me free from a
power that has been about me since I was a boy."

Roger turned his head. "You mean Considine!" he asked.

"I mean Considine," the African answered. "Something
I can tell you perhaps that you don't know. It's true—what
he says. He is a hundred—two hundred years old—I do not
know how old. He was known to my grandfather as the Deathless, and to his grandfather again, and others before that. He
has been a power among the chieftains and the witch-doctors,
but not always to their liking. For many of them had become

conjurers, debased things, frogs sitting in the swamp, losing knowledge as you of the West have lost knowledge, and these he defeated and sometimes killed, till from the Niger to the Zambesi the rest feared and obeyed him. Sometimes he went away for long periods—then, I suppose, he was in Europe or elsewhere—but he always returned, and his return went before him into the villages and then those who had sold their magic for gifts were very greatly afraid.''

Sir Bernard with the slightest disdain said as the other paused: "Magic! Did Mr. Considine draw circles with a thigh-bone and make love-philtres from banana-trees?"

Inkamasi smiled back at him. "Is there any certain reason why a love-philtre couldn't be made from a banana? But he wasn't concerned with that kind of magic. He desired a greater mastery, and that I think he found. Most men waste their energies, even at their best they waste them, on fantastic dreams and worthless actions. Above all they waste this power which you call love but we have called lordship. It is said among some of us that the high Spring is the time of lordship. This power and lordship Considine and his schools have sought to use. They have sought to restore its strength to the royal imagination from which in the beginning it came. Mysteriously, yet by methods which they say are open to all, they have learnt to arouse and restrain and direct the exaltation of love to such purposes as they choose. They have learnt by the contemplation of beauty in man or woman to fill themselves with a wonderful and delighted excitement, and to turn that excitement to deliberate ends. But the first of these ends is life, that other ends may be reached in turn. Whether any before Considine has done this thing, I do not know; but I believe that he has done it. He has so filled the uttermost reaches of his being with the imagination and consciousness of life that his body, renewed so from time to time, when it is unusually weary, let us say, is impervious to time and decay and sickness. Accident might destroy him.

But this mastery and transformation of love and sex is but a beginning. Have you not asked yourselves what is the death which spreads through creation, so that all things live by the death of others? Men and animals, we live by destruction. But these diverse schools have asked themselves whether indeed this is the whole secret, or whether it is so far but a substitution—a lesser thing taking the place of a greater. If man can descend into death, may he not find that what awaits him is an incredible ecstasy of descent and return? Considine is seeking to find that way. To be the food on which one feeds, to be free from any accident of death, to know the ecstasy of being at once priest and victim—all these ends are in his search."

He paused considering, and Caithness said: "Do you speak of this from your own knowledge?"

The king answered: "Not of my own experience, for my father turned from the ways of his father, and brought me up in the Faith and sent me to England to learn the ways of the mind. Nor would he let me be initiated into the ways of the assemblies, though my grandfather and the other wise men of his generation belonged to them. But when I was only a child the Deathless One came and persuaded my father—I cannot guess with what words—and I was given into his hands. He bound my will and my thought lest a day should come when he should need me. I think he bound all the sons of the kings of Africa. So he would sometimes talk when I was there, because he held me so that I could not speak without leave."

"But you came to England," Sir Bernard said.

"Yes," the king said, "only he knew where I was and what I was doing, and when the time had come he called me and I came."

"What do you think he really wants?" Roger said abruptly. —"Why is he making war?"

"I think he wants what he says," the king answered, "the freedom of Africa. I don't think he minds about destroying or

109

even defeating Europe, he only needs a continent where the schools may flourish, and the gospel of ecstasy be born."

"The defeat of Europe on that scale", Sir Bernard said, "sounds rather like a moment of unusually exalted and not specially reliable imagination."

Inkamasi leant forward with a quick fierce movement.

"Take care," he said, almost angrily, and his eyes burned at them, "take care you don't underrate him or despise him. Ever since he determined to do this he has made his preparations—he has chosen and trained his men and armed them. He has wealth—are aeroplanes and submarines, yes and guns, so difficult to buy and have shipped in parts as provisions or cotton or iron rails or Bibles or machinery to appointed harbours? Then there was the War—who had time to bother about the interior of Africa during the War?——"

"One way and another", Sir Bernard protested, "there are a large number of Europeans in the interior of Africa, watching it and doing things to it."

"Yes," Inkamasi answered, "and how many of your Europeans themselves are in it? How much of the white Administration belongs to the Mysteries? Has no conqueror ever been civilized by the nation he ruled? A white general may lead the attack on London yet; the Devotees themselves are often white."

"The what?" Sir Bernard asked.

"The Devotees," the Zulu answered. "It's a high circle of those who having achieved much choose to render their lives wholly into the will of the Deathless One that he may use them as he pleases. Didn't you see that of the aeronauts in last night's raid the few who lived after they came down shot themselves before they could be taken? They were of the Devotees. Most of them", he added, "are women."

An abrupt movement swept the circle. "Women!" Caithness exclaimed. "Does he depend on the devotion of women?"

"And look here," Philip said rather desperately, "do you mean to say that the white officers could be mixed up in the African armies?"

"As to the women," Sir Bernard said, "the early Church, if I remember rightly, depended largely on women."

"And as to the white officers," Roger said abruptly, "Mr. Caithness will applaud a similar precedent of Jew and Gentile."

Caithness took no notice, except by a nod. He said: "This sleep—is it hypnotic?"

Inkamasi made a movement with his hands. "Call it so if you like," he answered, "but I think rather that hypnotism is a reflection of it. He is able to establish a control on all the consciousness, except the secret centre of a man's being and the mere exterior apprehensions of the world. He can suspend thought and will—until he or a greater than he restores it."

"Well," Sir Bernard said, "the immediate point is—have I enough reasonable (if you can call it reasonable) stuff to send to the Home Secretary or the Public Prosecutor or the Elder Brethren of the Trinity?—who sound the kind of people that ought to be looking after the Deathless One. What do you say, Isabel?"

Isabel was looking at Roger and did not for a moment answer. Then she said, "I think so—yes. Whether they'll believe it. . . ."

"I once put the Prime Minister's stomach right," Sir Bernard said thoughtfully. "Perhaps I'd better go to him. What d'you think?" he added to Inkamasi.

"If you can seize Considine," the king said,—"I say, if you *can*—it will not be easy. For the greatest energy is in him, he and he alone is the centre of all the schools; it is he who holds power, either by the initiation or by the sleep, over the royalties of Africa; he is the union of their armies; without him the energies of the adepts will be divided, the generals will quarrel, the armies will fight. I tell you this, because you have saved me twice, and because I do not think mankind can be saved without intellect and without God."

"It must be almost the first time in the history of the world that those powers have been united," said Sir Bernard. "But what of you?"

The king looked at the floor. "I indeed can do nothing," he said, "for I cannot get to my people: I do not know where they are fighting. And I do not want to help Considine, though I long for Africa to be free. I am neither of one side nor of the other, neither of Europe nor Africa. I am an outcast and an exile."

"You are the citizen of another country," the priest said, "that is, a heavenly."

"Also, I am the king," Inkamasi exclaimed, "and there shall be no peace between this man and me. He laid his power upon me when I was a child, he has made me his puppet since, and for that I will kill him, though my spirit goes down with his into hell."

"It was not for this that Christ redeemed you," Caithness cried to him.

"I am the king," Inkamasi said, "and I will put my foot upon his mouth; I, Inkamasi, the king."

Rosamond gave a little choked cry. Philip leant forward quickly and put his hand on hers, but she pulled it away. "It's all right," she said. "I just felt . . . it's all *right*, Philip."

Sir Bernard got up, an eye on his prospective daughter-in-law. "Well, if you are all agreed——"

Roger pushed his chair back a trifle, and said, more sharply than before, "It won't stop you, but—no, we're not."

There was a dead silence. Roger was looking at his wife; the others looked at him. Philip buried his head in his hands. Sir Bernard began to speak when Caithness broke in: "What d'you mean, Roger? Surely there can't be two opinions about letting the authorities know about this charlatan?"

"It may be your duty," Roger said, "I'm pretty certain it isn't mine. You haven't met him."

"Sir Bernard has and Sir Bernard agrees," Caithness answered.

"Sir Bernard and I don't believe in the same things," Roger said. "I can't stop him but I won't have anything to do with it."

Philip got up—for him violently. "Roger," he cried out, "what are you talking about? Are you on this man's side?"

"Yes, I am," Roger said. "At least I can't go against him. He knows there's something in it, and which of you all does that?"

"I know it very well," Inkamasi said, sitting rigid. "And I will kill him because of it."

"You've a right to do as you please," Roger answered, "but I haven't. I've no right except to follow what I know when I find it." He looked over at his wife. "Aren't I right?" he exclaimed to her.

Isabel also stood up, and met his eyes full. "Yes, darling," she said simply.

"Roger," Sir Bernard said dulcetly, "is it Mr. Considine's feeling about poetry that affects you so much? Because the unfortunate white race has not been entirely silent. Was Dante a Bantu or Shakespeare a Hottentot? A few of us read it still."

"O read it!" Roger said contemptuously. "God knows I don't want to live for ever, but I tell you this fellow *knows*. So do I—a little bit, and I believe it's important. More important than anything else on earth. And I won't help you to shut it up in a refrigerator when I ought to be helping to keep it alive."

"Can't you leave that to God?" Caithness flung out.

"No", said Roger, "I damn well can't, when he's left it to me. I know your argument—it's all been done, death has been conquered, and so as nothing ever dies somewhere else, we needn't worry about it's dying here. Well, thank you very much, but I do. What are you worrying about? I know I can't stop you, but I won't have a hand in it."

"I see", Sir Bernard said, "that the white administration in Africa may easily have been absorbed. I'm sorry, Roger."

"Don't be," Roger said. "It's not a thing to be sorry about." He swept suddenly round. "What about it, Philip?" he cried. "Are you with them?"

Philip, trying to keep his footing, said, "Don't be a fool, Roger, we can't not fight the Africans."

"We can 'not fight' them perfectly well," Roger said, and it seemed to Isabel that his tall insolent figure dominated all the room except for the carven and royal darkness of the seated Zulu, "and you know it. Love and poetry are powers, and these people—will you deny it too?"

"Really, Roger," Sir Bernard put in, "must you dichotomize in this appalling way? It's so barbarian; it went out with the Victorians. If you feel you're betraying the *Ode to the Nightingale* or something by agreeing to my call on the Prime Minister, must you insist that your emotions are universal? Keep them private, my dear boy, or they'll be merely provincial; and the provincial is the ruin of the public and the private at once."

He knew he was talking at random, but the whole room was filled with uncertainty and defiance and distress. A man had come out into the open from behind the fronds and leaves and it was Roger. A trumpet had answered the horns and drums that were crying to the world from the jungle of man's being; and the trumpet was Roger's voice. Was Africa then within? was all the war, were the armies and munitions and the transports but the shadow of the repression by which man held down his more natural energies? but images of the strong refusal which Europe had laid on capacities it had so long ruled that it had nearly forgotten their independent life? But things forgotten could rise; and old things did not always die.

Poland—Ireland—Judah—man. Roger knew something; the voice that had discussed and lectured and gibed and repeated verse now cried its sworn loyalty: a schism was opening in civilization. Sir Bernard looked at Isabel, but she said nothing. She leaned on the mantelpiece and looked into the fire, and her face was very still. Roger relaxed slightly; he liked Sir Bernard, and they had often gently mocked each other. He said, "Yes, I know I can't do anything. I think I'll say good-night and get back to Hampstead. Coming, Isabel?"

She turned her head towards him. "It'll be very awkward, dearest," she said. "The milkman's been told not to call, and what shall we do for breakfast?" She spoke quite seriously, but her lips smiled; only a deeper seriousness and sadness grew in her eyes, and his own were sad as they encountered hers. She stood upright, as if to move, and yet lingered a little on that silent interchange.

"I know, I know," Roger said, answering her smile, "it'll be most inconvenient, but can I stop here?" He looked round at them all and flung out his hands. "O you're charming, you're lovely, all of you, but how much do you care what the great ones are doing? And in these centuries you've nearly killed it, with your appreciations and your fastidious judgements, and your lives of this man and your studies in that. What do you know about 'huge and mighty forms that do not live/Like living men'? Power, power, it's dying in you, and you don't hunger to feel it live. What's Milton, what's Shakespeare, to you?"

"If this is just a literary discussion——" Caithness began.

"What d'you mean—just a literary discussion?" Roger said, his temper leaping. "D'you call Islam a mere theological distinction? Can't you understand any other gospel than your own damned dogmas?"

"Roger, Roger," Sir Bernard murmured.

"I beg your pardon," Roger said, "and yours too, Sir Bernard. But I can't stay here to-night. I know it seems silly, but I can't." He looked back at his wife. "But I shall be all right, darling," he said, "if you'd rather stop. I can even go and buy a bottle of milk!"

Isabel smiled at him. "I think I'll come to-night," she said. "To-night anyhow." She looked down at her sister. "Rosamond, you might as well stop here, mightn't you?"

Rosamond looked up with a jerk. "Stop," she exclaimed. "What, are you going back? O I can't, I can't. I'll come."

They all stared at her. "I wasn't just listening," she went on hastily. "I was thinking of something else. Are you going at once, Isabel? I'll get my things." She was on her feet, when Philip's hand took hold of her arm. She jerked it away. "Let me alone," she cried out. "Aren't you going with them?"

Philip, in spite of his opposition to Roger, hadn't been at all certain; or rather, he was extremely troubled about being certain. He couldn't begin to imagine himself on the side of Considine and the Africans, but he had a curiously empty feeling somewhere when he thought of denying them. It was all so muddled, and he had hitherto thought that moral divisions, though painful, were clear: such as not cheating, and not telling lies except for urgent reasons, and being on your country's side, and being polite to your inferiors, and in short playing the game. But this game was quite unlike any other he'd ever played; what with the piercing music that called him still, and the song Considine's talk of love sent through his blood, and the urgent appeal to him to do what he so much wanted to do, to exult and live. But of course when Rosamond put it like that—no, he wasn't. He was going to be on the side of his country and his duty and his fiancée. He said so.

She said: "I thought not," almost snapping at him. "Then leave me alone. I thought you wouldn't."

The king at this moment stood up. He had been silent, concerned with his own thought of vengeance, while the breach between Roger and the rest had widened, and now he thrust himself up in the midst of them, an ally and yet a hostility, a dark whirlwind of confusion in their thoughts and in their midst. He came to his feet, and Rosamond, as if by the force of his rising, seemed flung against her sister. She clung to Isabel, and Isabel said, speaking of ordinary things in her own extraordinarily lovely voice: "Very well, darling, we'll all go. Perhaps Sir Bernard will give us a loaf of bread."

Sir Bernard, almost disliking Rosamond—he hadn't wanted her there at all, but she'd insisted on coming, and without being rude to Philip he could hardly refuse—said: "Also the jug of wine, if it's any good. The Sahara will no doubt presently serve for Paradise. Ian, will you come with me as far as Downing Street?"

The breach widened indeed, but he was more aware of it than Roger, and as he became aware of it he refused and bridged it in his mind. He had been very nearly irritated, and irritation inflamed all the exquisite contemplative mind: he turned the cool spray of medicinal irony on himself till he was able to smile at Roger and say, "Well, if you will go—But let me be in at the death, won't you? While gospels exist, let's enjoy them as best we can. Good-night."

A little later he and Caithness, having telephoned for an appointment, came to Downing Street, where, parting from the priest, he was after some slight delay carried in to see Raymond Suydler himself; which attention and privilege he owed to the Prime Minister's gratitude for a restored stomach.

It was a long time since Sir Bernard had seen him; his attention to his stomach had been paid during the Prime Minister's first administration, and this was his second. He was a man who had made not merely an opportunity but a political triumph out of the very loss of public belief in politics which afflicted the country. He had carried realism to its extreme, declaring publicly that the best any statesman could do was to guess at the solution of his various problems, and that his guesses had a habit of being right. In private he dropped only the last half of this statement, which left him fifty per cent of sincerity, and thus gave him an almost absurd advantage over most of his colleagues and opponents. It had taken some time certainly for his own party to reconcile themselves to the enormous placards "Guess with Suydler" which at the General Election outflamed the more argumentative shows of the other side. But the country, half mocking, half understanding, had laughed and followed, in that mingling of utter despair and wild faith which conceals itself behind the sedate appearance of the English. Chance, no doubt, had helped him by giving him an occasional opportunity of lowering taxation at home and increasing prestige abroad, but his denial of reason had done more. It was not cynicism; it was, and it was felt to be, truth, as Suydler saw it, and as most of the country did. In any state of things, the facts—all the facts—were unknown; circumstances were continually changing; instability and uncertainty were the only assured things. What was the use of rational discussion or fixed principles or far-sighted demonstrations? "Guess—guess with Suydler." He was reported to have said that the English had only had one inspired fool as Prime Minister—Pitt; and two intelligent men—Melbourne and Disraeli, who were hampered by believing, one in a class, the other in a race. "I would rather guess with Pitt, if you'll guess with me."

Sir Bernard remembered all this as he shook hands, and observed with a slight shock Suydler's large, ungainly form. The one cartoon which had really succeeded against him had been called "The Guessing Gorilla," and Sir Bernard recollected with pleasure that it was not his own obsession with Africa which had remarked the likeness. The ugly face, the long hanging arms, the curled fingers, the lumbering step, had a strange likeness to a great ape plunging about the room. He shook hands, and his visitor was quite glad not to feel those huge arms clutching him. There was, he thought, altogether too much Africa about, and he almost wondered for a moment whether indeed Suydler were preferable to Considine. . . . But he reminded himself that it wasn't personalities but abstract states of existence with which he was concerned, and he took the chair the Prime Minister offered. The huge bulk swelled before him, loomed over him, was talking . . . talking. . . . Sir Bernard felt a great weariness come over him. The excitement, the incredibilities, of the last twenty-four hours had worn him out. And what was the good of trying to defend the intellect in this place of the death of the intellect? Witch-doctors were invading Europe, and he had gone running to an ape for help. . . .

"—absurd talk about possible reasons," the Prime Minister was saying. "The whole thing's an example of the failure of organized thought. No-one can find out the root of the trouble."

"I wonder you ask them," Sir Bernard said.

"I don't; they tell me," Suydler answered. "There was a man yesterday—an ex-Governor—was talking to me. I had a kind of bet with myself how many synonyms he'd use for guess—I think it was about twenty-four. We may assume—not improbable—very likely—may it not be—reasonable assumption—working hypothesis—possible surmise—news suggests—my opinion is—better theory—never a plain straightforward guess. Never used the word once."

"It's not a favourite, except with children; they love it," Sir Bernard said. "Perhaps", he added, struck by a sudden thought, "that's why they're nearer the kingdom of heaven. They're more sincere. However, I came here to say that I'm not certain that I didn't dine yesterday with the High Executive. I mean—I guess I did."

"That's fair, anyhow," Suydler answered. "Who did you guess he was? And—not that I mind, but as a concession to the Permanent Officials—why did you guess him?"

Sir Bernard held out his papers. "It's all there," he said.

Suydler put out an enormous hand—its shadow on the carpet stretched out, black and even more enormous—and took them. "How tidy you are," he said, grinning, "but you always were,

weren't you? Your operations were always miracles of con-
ciseness. If you've extracted the truth now, that'll be another
miracle. Excuse me while I look at them."

He didn't take long over it; then he chuckled, put them down,
and leaned back. "And you've got this Zulu king of yours?"
he asked. "Ready to testify and identify and all that?"

"Certainly," Sir Bernard said.

Suydler linked his fingers and stretched his arms out. "Well,"
he said, "if you like—though I've met Considine a few times—
but if you like to make a pattern with him in, I'm not sure
that I won't go with you. It'll look awfully well. . . . 'Government discover High Executive.' Why, as of minor interest,
didn't you come before?"

"Because, until I'd got the king's opinion—guess, if you
like, I couldn't," Sir Bernard explained. "And he went off
into a real stupor the minute he reached Kensington—as if
he had to get his own faculties into order."

"Two hundred years—" Suydler said. "But what a price
to pay! No women, no fun, no excitements. All, if I've got it
right, squeezed back into yourself." He pressed a bell. "It isn't
fair to let him go on suppressing himself and misleading others,
is it?—'A long life and a dull one'—that's the end of all you
theorists."

Sir Bernard stood up. "Well," he said, "if you think I'm
right I'll go."

A secretary came in, but Suydler kept him waiting. "Right!"
he said, "no, I don't think you're right. I think your mind
and his may have—what shall I say?—coincided by chance.
But there's no such thing as 'right.' It's all a question of
preferring a particular momentary pattern of phenomena.
There's nothing more anywhere. How can there be? At this
moment the past doesn't exist, the future doesn't exist, and
we know nothing much about the present!"

Avoiding any immediate discussion of the nature of existence, Sir Bernard got away. Walking down Downing Street

he considered the Minister. "Considine and he both look into the abyss," he thought, "but Considine sees it beating with passion, and Suydler sees nothing. A chaos or a void? Black men, or men who are no longer white?" He saw the intellect and logical reason of man no longer as a sedate and necessary thing, but rather a narrow silver bridge passing over an immense depth, around the high guarded entrance of which thronged clouds of angry and malign presences. Often mistaking the causes and often misjudging the effects of all mortal sequences, this capacity of knowing cause and effect presented itself nevertheless to him as the last stability of man. Always approaching truth, it could never, he knew, *be* truth, for nothing can be truth till it has become one with its object, and such union it was not given to the intellect to achieve without losing its own nature. But in its divine and abstract reflection of the world, its passionless mirror of the holy law that governed the world, not in experiments or ecstasies or guesses, the supreme perfection of mortality moved. He saluted it as its child and servant, and dedicated himself again to it, for what remained to him of life, praying it to turn the light of its awful integrity upon him, and to preserve him from self-deception and greediness and infidelity and fear. "If A is the same as B," he said, "and B is the same as C, then A is the same as C. Other things may be true; for all I know, they may be different at the same time; but this at least is true. And Considine will have to hypnotize me myself before I deny it. Suydler is wrong—a guess may be true once and twice and a thousand times, for man has known abstraction, and no gorilla of a politician can take it away from him."

Chapter Eight

PASSING THROUGH THE MIDST
OF THEM

There followed a few days of uneasy quiet. The news from Africa was vague, but more cheerfully vague. It was generally understood that organized naval measures were being taken to overcome the submarine forces of the enemy, which had succeeded in making the African coasts so dangerous and had proceeded so far afield that until such measures had been concerted and carried out the landing of fresh troops had become impossible. It was even rumoured that attacks had been made on certain European harbours, but if this were so the Government concerned saw to it that no hint was allowed to appear in the Press. Energetic operations had been planned; the more energetic movements of the enemy seemed to have ceased, though the clearance of white troops from North Africa appeared to be proceeding slowly but systematically.

The financial panic had also been stayed to some extent by Government action. For the Prime Minister had announced that, as the simplest means of meeting the emergency, the Administration had decided to make loans to the federated control of any particular industry which was seriously affected. Conditions of application, examination, payment and re-payment were to be settled by a Commission set up for the purpose; the immediate affair was to steady the markets, and dazed directors of innumerable companies found themselves offered millions in order to buy up shares in their own con-cerns. Unfederated companies rushed to federate; all news-papers, for example, found themselves part of one large business, controlled by a common Board which immediately borrowed or was offered a subsidy of some millions, with which it repurchased the shares which Nehemiah and Ezekiel Rosenberg were throwing before the world. It looked therefore as if these devoted believers would secure their money as well as their jewels; and the coming of Messias or the building of the Temple be prepared for by the English in a general increase of taxation. Sir Bernard, as he contemplated the world, foresaw a possibility that the whole business, military and financial, would gradually expire, having ruined a great number of small shareholders, increased the financial strength of the larger, cost a great deal in armaments, and probably massacred a host of Africans in circumstances of more or less equal fighting.

"I had some expectation," he said to Caithness as they turned into the Square, after an early afternoon walk, "of becoming a travelling doctor in my old age—probably with a donkey cart; and going from village to village, curing indigestion and collecting sixpences. You know the kind of thing—'Travers's Pills make Stomachs Tractable'—'Dainty Digestions Decently Doctored.' You might have joined me, and we would have put stomachs and souls right together. 'Stomachs on the right; souls on the left: Advice free: only real cures paid for.' But I should have stipulated for no miracles."

"Then you'd have wanted an unfair advantage," Caithness said. "I should have to send quite a number of my patients to you; lots of them think it's their conscience when actually it's their stomachs."

"Still on your theory the soul's wrong anyhow," Sir Bernard pointed out.

"Quite," Caithness answered. "But they have to understand that, not merely moan over their pains. However, the question isn't likely to arise. Things do seem to be a bit quieter now."

The exertions of the Government and (presumably) of the police did not, however, succeed in tracing either Nigel

Considine or his friends. Justified by several different kinds of warrants, an examination of the Hampstead house was carried out but with no results. Whatever staff of whatever servants had occupied it had disappeared as completely as its master. Inkamasi was examined and re-examined, but though his story was given in fuller detail, the details did not much help. It was clear that the High Executive had done no more than preserve him in case he should be wanted; the Zulus themselves, who were apparently taking an active part in the war, were (so far as news could be obtained) under the headship of another of their race, a cousin of Inkamasi's, less directly but still closely connected with the great chieftain and hero, Chaka. The king was allowed to remain in seclusion at Sir Bernard's house, where he spent his days reading, brooding, and talking sometimes to his host and to Caithness. Philip rather avoided him.

Philip indeed had his own troubles. Apart from the complete wreck of his purposes which the war had brought about, apart from the agitations which his new experiences had introduced into his inner mind, he suddenly found himself on the most extraordinarily difficult terms with Rosamond. She refused to come near Colindale Square, she occasionally even refused to see him when he went to Hampstead, and when she did see him she was in a nervous and irritable mood which was quite unlike the normal Rosamond. Philip's own meditations on the relations between love and Rosamond were thwarted and upset by the discovery that Rosamond, to all intents and purposes, wasn't there for love to have relations with. She had always kept love in its proper place, and had never displayed any particular interest in its more corporeal manifestations, suggesting by her manner that such things were a trifle silly. If he tried to explain something of the marvel which she seemed to him, she had listened placidly and with good humour, but without much gratification and with no kind of exaltation at all. His own exaltation, however, had not been exactly forbidden to thrive—until now. But now she would not have it; she shrank from and repelled it. She wouldn't be touched; she wouldn't be approached. Isabel told him that her sister was sleeping badly. But what Isabel didn't tell him was the dubious and unhappy cause of that broken sleep.

Roger, coming in early one evening, found his wife alone. He kissed her and flung himself down, and a silence gathered them up. Presently Isabel stirred: "Well, darling?" she said, "what do you think about it all?"

Roger said nothing at first, then he uttered, "I've done what I can. I've thrown over a course on the probable sources of the minor comedies of the early nineteenth century, and where Mrs. Inchbald found her plots—Mrs. Inchbald—I ask you, Isabel! Where did Mrs. Hemans get hers?—and I've talked to them for all I'm worth on the Filial Godhead and mighty forms and encountering darkness and Macbeth. I can't do more—that way. I don't know enough: I'm a baby in it, after all."

Isabel said quietly, "You want to know more?"

Roger answered, "I want—yes, I—the thing that's me wants to know, not like wanting appletart with or without custard, but like wanting breath. There's air outside the windows, and I shall smash them to get it or I shall die. There—you asked me."

She came and stood by him, and he took her hand. "You don't feel it like that?" he said.

"No, not like that," she answered. "But perhaps I can't. I've been thinking, Roger darling, and I've wondered whether perhaps women don't have to do it anyhow. I mean—perhaps it's nothing very new, this power your Mr. Considine talks of— perhaps women have always known it, and that's why they've never made great art. Perhaps they *have* turned everything into themselves. Perhaps they must."

He looked up at her, brooding. "I know," he said, "you live and we talk about it."

125

"No," Isabel said, sitting down by him in front of the fire. "No, dearest, not only that. We only live on what you give us—imaginatively, I mean; you have to find the greater powers. You have to be the hunters and fishers and fighters when all's said and done. So perhaps you ought to go and hunt now. But we turn it more easily into ourselves than you do—for bad and good alike. And we generally do it very badly—but then you've given us so little to do it with."

"I don't believe it," Roger said. "I don't believe in all this sex differentiation. And yet——"

"And yet," she said, "it doesn't matter now. We needn't waste our time on talking abstractions. What do you want to do, sweetheart?"

"I don't know what I can do," he said. "I talk about smashing windows, but that's rather silly. I want to find this power and master it and find what there is to be discovered. I want to live where *they* live."

"They?" she asked.

"Considine and Michael Angelo and Epstein and Beethoven," he answered. "I can feel a bit of what they do, I want to feel more. I've been trying to—don't laugh. All the way home I've been saying things to myself, and trying to see what's the thing to *do*. There's the feeling every element in them first —not just seeing the words, but finding out how one belongs to the words, how one's own self answers to all the different words, like criss-crossing currents. And then there's turning all that deeper into one's own self, into one's desire—and that's so hard because one hasn't a desire, except general comfort!"

"O Roger dear, that's not true! You have," Isabel said.

Roger hesitated—"Well, perhaps!" he allowed. "Anyhow I kept losing hold and just feeling all vague and dithery, so I tried to turn one thrill on to another line—d'you see?—and I do think it might work. But it'll need a lot of doing, and I'm not sure——" he relapsed into silence, and then said abruptly, "Has Philip been along?"

His wife was about to answer when Rosamond came into the room, and the conversation returned hastily to ordinary things. She wasn't looking at all well, Roger thought, and she was getting positively hysterical these days. Curious that she should be Isabel's sister. But of course Isabel was unusual. He reflected gloomily, while the women chatted, that on Considine's showing he probably wouldn't have been married to Isabel—the energy of love would have gone the other way, would have been transmuted or something. Lots of people must have had to do it in their time; lots of people must have been disappointed in love and then—Yes, but most of them just blew along till the worst was over. To use the worst and the best for something that was, as far as ordinary knowledge went, different from both. The abolition of death—the conquest of death.

The unnameable Muriel appeared in the room. She said, "Two gentlemen to see you, sir. They didn't give their names. But one of them sent this——" She passed over a slip of card bearing a word or two—" 'How goes it? N. C.' "

Roger jumped forward. "Here," he exclaimed, "where are they? Bring them—all right. I will." He was out of the room and into the tiny hall. There he saw Considine and Mottreux.

"Good God!" he said. "Come in. I thought you——"

Considine shook hands with a smile. It occurred to Roger that that swift smile was always very near showing with Considine. It danced on the surface of a deeper rapture, as if, to the world, that was all that could be made of something within the world.

"We came", he said, "Mottreux and I, to fill an hour. Do we interrupt?"

"No," Roger said. "Come in." He turned to Isabel. "May I present my wife?" he said. "You've never met Mr. Considine, have you, Isabel? And Colonel Mottreux." His eyes fell on Rosamond. "Miss Murchison—Mr. Considine, Colonel Mottreux."

127

As he found them seats he cursed Rosamond. Who wanted her there? Well, she'd have to lump it. He stood back, and let his look rest on Considine. Then he said, "But I thought Sir Bernard——"

"Certainly Sir Bernard," Considine answered. "But I don't think Sir Bernard or Mr. Suydler either are likely to interfere with me. It isn't from them that my dangers now will ever come—except by literal accident. So, since I was about, and since to-night I shall be busy, and shall leave London—I came to see you."

"Are you going to Africa?" Roger said before he could stop himself.

"I have come to ask you whether—if I go—you also will come," Considine said.

Roger was picking up a box of cigarettes from the table; he put it down again and his face went pale. "I?" he said.

"I know that you believe," Considine said, "and I offer you the possibility."

Roger, with a heroic effort, avoided looking at Isabel. He said in a calm silly voice, "It's awfully kind of you, of course, but I don't see how I can. Not this side of Christmas."

Isabel said, "I think you might. It'll be death if you don't."

He looked up at her, and she added, "It'll be death to you, darling, and then there'll be nothing left for me. If you go, there may. And I can do—what we were talking about."

"But I can't decide all on the moment," Roger protested to Considine, though he still looked at Isabel.

"You have decided," Considine said. "But of course you may not do it."

"And have I decided," Roger said sardonically, "to live for a hundred years and try all sorts of experiments with my unhappy body?"

"'I will encounter darkness as a bride,'" Considine murmured. "Yes."

It was true, and Roger knew it. Chance might thwart him, as (so he understood) it might thwart Considine himself, but the decision was in his blood and bones. He would have to follow this man—as once, he had read, other men had thrown aside their work and their friends to follow another voice. When explosions happened you were just blown. Isabel would be all right as far as money went—and till he had entered into this mystery he could never now serve Isabel rightly. Those other men had followed a voice that went crying how it was not come to send peace but a sword—the peace of the sword perhaps, the reconciliation in a greater state of being which——

He pulled a chair forward. "Tell me about it," he said. He was vaguely aware, as he did so, that Rosamond had slipped from the room, and was grateful. The four of them were left. Roger picked up the cigarettes again and offered them to Isabel who took one, and to Considine and Mottreux who refused. He himself hesitated.

"I don't", he said, "see any reason why I shouldn't smoke, and yet when I'm really concerned I don't. Except by habit."

"It absorbs energy," Considine said. "When it's a dominant habit it absorbs less energy than the refusal demands, so naturally it has its way. But when it's not quite inevitable you're conscious of the energy wasted—of a divided concentration—and you hesitate!"

"Is that why you don't smoke?" Roger asked.

"I don't smoke just as I don't eat—since you ask me," Considine said, the smile breaking out again, "because it doesn't amuse me. Any more than golfing or dancing or reading the newspaper. Certain things drop away as one becomes maturer."

"And eating's one of them?" Roger asked, putting down the cigarettes.

"It's necessary to an extent still," Considine answered. "I suppose a certain minimum of food may be necessary, until—afterwards. Then perhaps not. But it's nothing like as necessary as one thinks. There are so many better things to feed on.

Shall I quote your Messias again?—'I have meat to eat that ye know not of.'"

Isabel said, more suddenly than was her habit, "It was to do the will of Him that sent him."

"What else?" Considine answered. "What else could it be?"

"But you don't claim to be doing that will?" Isabel said. "You're not in obedience, are you?"

"I am in obedience to all laws I have not yet mastered," he answered. "I am in danger of death—until I have mastered it—and therefore in obedience to it, and a little to food and sleep."

"But you said that danger——" Roger began.

"I said that danger will not come from my enemies," Considine answered; "isn't there any other? There are laws that are very deep, and one of them may be that every gospel has a denial within it and every Church a treachery. You—whom I invite to join me—you yourself may be a danger. It isn't for me to fear you because of that chance."

Roger leant forward. "That's it," he cried out, "there's nothing that may not betray."

Isabel said softly, "Can't Mr. Considine transform treachery too?"

"I can guard against it at least," Considine answered; "I can read men's minds, under conditions, but the conditions may fail, and then—could Christ do more?"

Isabel answered still softly, "Mightn't the missionaries you killed have joined with something which was greater than you because it had known defeat? Have *you* known defeat?"

"No," Considine said and stood up. "I've mastered myself from the beginning and all things that I've needed are mine. Why should man know defeat? You teach him to look and expect and wait for it; you teach him to obey and submit; you heal his hurts and soothe his diseases. But I will show him that in his hurts as in his happiness he is greatly and intensely lord; he lives by them. He shall delight in feeling, and his feeling shall

130

be blood within his blood and body in his body; it shall burn through him till that old business of yes-and-no has fallen away from him, and then his diseases will have vanished for they are nothing but the shadow of his wanting this and the other, and when he is those things that he desires, where are the shadows of them? Do I starve without food who do not need food? Do I pine for love who do not need love? Do I doubt victory who am victory? There is but one chance of defeat, and that is that death may strike me before I have dared it in its own place. But even that cannot face me; by ambush or treachery it might take me, but I will neither expect it nor allow for it. It is a habit man yields to, no more; and I will be lord of that customary thing as I am of all, and draw power and delight from it as I do from all. Who follows?"

Isabel, as if from a depth of meditation, answered: "But those that die may be lordlier than you: they are obedient to defeat. Can you live truly till you have been quite defeated? You talk of living by your hurts, but perhaps you avoid the utter hurt that's destruction."

He smiled down at her. "Why, have it as you will," he said. "But it isn't such submission and destruction that man desires."

There was a little silence; then he said again, speaking to Roger: "What then will you do?"

Roger looked down at the floor, and only when a much longer silence had gone by did he say, "Yes; I'll come. You're right—I'd decided already, and I won't go back."

"Then", Considine said, "to-night you will be at Bernard Travers's house, for I shall come there. And don't fear for your wife, whatever happens. I will not destroy London to-night."

Roger looked up again sharply. "But——" he began.

There were voices in the hall; Muriel's, Rosamond's, others'. Roger got up, looking over his shoulder, and turned. Isabel and Mottreux also rose: only Considine stood motionless. The door opened and Rosamond came in. Behind her were uniforms—a police inspector followed, and another, and two or three men. The inspector said: "Mr. Ingram?"

"What's this about?" Roger asked staring.

"We've had information that there's a man here whom we want," the inspector said, looking round, and letting his eyes rest on Considine. "Mr. Nigel Considine?" he asked.

Considine did not speak or move.

"I've a warrant here for your arrest," the inspector said, "on a charge of high treason and conspiracy to murder." He showed a paper and stepped across the room. Mottreux said something, and the inspector glanced at him. But he halted a pace or two away from Considine, it might be to give his men time to come up, it might be from hesitation in the sudden oppression that began to fill the room, as if invisible waters flowed through it. The air weighed on them, stifling them with its rich presence; the inspector put a finger to his collar as he poised watchfully. Rosamond sank heavily on to a chair; Roger drew deep breaths, sighing as he did sometimes in his passion after repeating mighty verses aloud. The air spoke; in the voice of Nigel Considine the element of life, echoing from all around, said: "Whom?"

The inspector struggled forward; it needed labour, so heavily was he oppressed by the depths into which the air had opened. He took a step and staggered as he did so. The eyes fixed on him saw him rock and steady himself; he said, holding himself upright, "Nigel Considine, I——"

"I am Nigel Considine," his great opponent answered, and also moved forward, and the quiver that went through them all answered the laughter in the voice. The inspector reeled again, half-falling sideways, and as he recovered footing a sudden hand went out towards him—whether it touched him or not they could not tell—and he stumbled backward once more. The wind swept into their faces, and on it a ringing laughter came, and in its midst Considine went on towards the the door, with Mottreux by him, sending towards Roger one imperious glance from eyes bright with joy. The uniforms thronged and shifted and were in confusion, and wind swirled in the room as if strength were released through it, and Roger, half-dazed, ran forward and saw the two visitors already in the hall. The inspector came heavily and blindly back; he called out; his men moved uncertainly after Considine who paused, turned, and paused again.

"I am Nigel Considine," he cried out. "Who takes me?"

He flung out his arms as if in derisive submission, and took a step or two towards them. They recoiled; there was renewed confusion, men pressing back and pressing forward, men exclaiming and commanding. Someone slipped and crashed against the doorpost, someone else, thrust backward, tripped over a foot; there was falling and stumbling, and through it Roger saw the wide-armed figure offering itself in laughing scorn. Then, with a motion as if he gathered up the air and cast it against them, so that they blinked and thrust and shielded their eyes, he turned from that struggling mass of fallen and pushing bodies, and went to the front-door. A panting Muriel leaned against it; he laughed at her and signed, and hastily she drew away, opening it, and he and Mottreux went through.

Roger gazed after him "I have lived," he sighed. "I have seen the gods. Phœbus, Phœbus, Python-destroyer, hear and save."

Chapter Nine

THE RIOT AND THE RAID

Philip jumped on to a bus—any bus—the first he saw. He had been walking for ever so long, and he must sit down. But also he must be moving; he couldn't be shut in. Things were worse than he had ever imagined they could be; indeed he couldn't quite imagine what exactly they now were. The Hampstead flat was in a state of acute distress and turmoil; he had arrived that evening innocently enough, to find half a dozen policemen all arguing with Roger, who was glowering at Rosamond, who was crying hysterically in Isabel's arms, who was keeping, not without difficulty, a grave sympathy with all of them. He had naturally hurried to Rosamond, but not with the best effects; the sight of him had seemed to distract her more than ever. Out of the arguments and exclamations he had at last gathered—and more clearly after the police had at last grimly withdrawn—that Considine had been there, and that Rosamond, after she had realized who it really was, had gone through a short period of conflict with herself on the right thing to do. She said it had been conflict, and that only her duty . . . whereas Roger, in a few words, implied that she had been delighted at the chance, and that duty—except to herself—was a thing of which she was entirely unconscious and incapable. Anyhow, after a very short period she had rung up the police-station and explained to the authorities there what was happening. Why the police hadn't arrested Considine Philip couldn't understand. Isabel was concerned with her sister, and Roger wasn't very clear in his account. Somebody had gone through the midst of somebody else; somebody had been like Pythian Apollo. But

he couldn't bother about all that; he was too anxious about
Rosamond. Had he been challenged, he would have had to
admit that for a guest to try and have another visitor arrested
in the host's drawing-room was not perhaps . . . though for
Roger to call it treachery was absurd. If anything, it was
public spirit. He knew nothing—Rosamond had seen to that—
of such an orgy as the episode of the chocolates which Isabel
so clearly and reluctantly remembered; he knew nothing of a
greedy gobbling child, breaking suddenly away from its
ordinary snobbish pretences, giving way to the thrust of its
secret longings and vainly trying to conceal from others' eyes
the force of its desires. She had cheated herself so long, consciously in childhood, with that strange combination of perfect
innocence and deliberate sin which makes childhood so
blameless and so guilty at one and the same moment; less
consciously in youth, as innocence faded and the necessity of
imposing some kind of image of herself on the world grew
stronger, till now in her first womanhood she had forgotten the
cheat, until her outraged flesh rebelled and clamoured from
starvation for food. And even now she would not admit it; she
would neither fight it nor flee from it nor yield to it nor compromise with it. She could hardly even deny that it was there,
for there was no place for it in her mind. She, she of all people,
could never be capable of abominably longing to be near the
dark prince of Africa; she couldn't thrill to the trumpets of
conversion nor glow to the fires of ecstasy. Nor could she hate
herself for refusing them. But she could and inevitably did hate
the things that resembled them—Considine's person and
Roger's verse and Philip, all of Philip, for Philip to her
agonized sense was at once a detestable parody of what she
wanted and a present reminder of what she longed to forget.
And now, like all men and all women who are not masters of
life, she swayed to and fro in her intention and even in her
desire. At Kensington she had shrunk away from Inkamasi and
fled from him; at Hampstead she thought of him and secretly

longed for him. Power was in her and she was terrified of it. She had been self-possessed, but all herself was in the possessing and nothing in the possessed; self-controlled, but she had had only a void to control. And now that nothing and that void were moved with fire and darkness; the shadow of ecstasy lay over her life, and denying the possibility of ecstasy she fled through its shadow as far as its edge, and halted irresolute, and was drawn back by a fascination she loved and hated. She was alive and she hated life; not with a free feeling of judgement but with servile fear. She hated life, and therefore she would hide in Hampstead; she lived, and therefore she would return to Kensington. But neither in Hampstead nor Kensington, in Europe nor Africa, in her vision of her unsubservient self, nor of her monstrous master, was there any place for Philip, much less a Philip aware of the exaltation of love.

But it was not till after, shocked and bewildered by the venom she had flung at him in that dreadful scene, he had at last gone that she began to fear that her relations with Kensington might have been severed. And, not being there, she was determined to get back there. She would run there and then run away, till the strait-jacket of time and place imprisoned her as it imprisons in the end all who suffer from a like madness. It is perhaps why the asylum of material creation was created, and we sit in our separate cells, strapped and comparatively harmless, merely foaming a little and twitching our fingers, while the steps and voices of unknown warders come to us from the infinite corridors. But Rosamond was only beginning to hurl herself against the walls of her cell, and the invisible warders had not yet had occasion to take much notice of her. The jacket waited her; when the paroxysm was done she would no doubt come to regard it as becoming wear and in the latest fashion. Whether such a belief is desirable is a question men have not yet been able to decide.

Since Roger was so cruel to her, so detestably unfair, she would go to Sir Bernard; there was no other friend in London on whom she could descend without notice. Sir Bernard would understand her motives; he'd tried to get that hateful man arrested. Isabel tried her best to prevent her, saying even that Roger might be going away. But this didn't seem to placate Rosamond, and at last Isabel said no more. Roger said nothing at all until Rosamond had left them "to put some of her things together." Isabel said: "I'm not sure that it's a bad thing: Sir Bernard may be able to do something. What she needs is a sleeping-draught."

"What she needs", Roger said, "is prussic acid."

Meanwhile Philip had walked, walked millions of miles, it seemed, till at a sudden last weariness struck him and he got on a bus. The heavens beyond that firmamental arm had been pouring anger and distraction and hatred down on him, and he didn't understand it at all. He had been trying to please Rosamond—which, unlike most people who use similar phrases, he actually had. He sat on the bus and thought so for a long time, until he became aware that someone was speaking to him.

The conductor had come up and was standing by him, peering out through the front of the bus, and saying something. Philip roused himself to attention, and heard him say: "There's something up; can't you hear it, sir?"

Philip listened and looked round. The night was clear and he recognized in a mass that lay on his left Liverpool Street Station. The bus was going slowly, for it was interrupted and hampered by a number of people running down the road in the same direction. There was a sound in the distance which resolved itself, as he listened, into the noise of shouting.

"What the devil is up?" he said.

The conductor—a short rather gloomy fellow—gave a sinister smile. "I shouldn't wonder but what I could guess," he said. "I thought it'd happen sooner or later. I said it was a silly business, letting it be known all over the place that they'd millions and millions worth of jewels in the house. 'Jewels to the Jews,' I called it, when it got about. Everything gets about. And if it wasn't jewels—and some say it wasn't—it was money. Hark at that!"

Another shout, nearer now as the bus moved on, brought Philip to his feet. "Is it the Rosenbergs?" he said. "But they can't have got them here."

The bus, as he spoke, turned into Bishopsgate and was brought almost to a stop by an accumulating crowd. Philip jumped off and allowed himself to be carried in the steady stream that set towards one of the side turnings. He caught fragments of talk: "Say they're going to bribe the negroes"; "know all about those bloody niggers"; "great jewels like turnips, been buying them for months"; "lowsy old Jews"; "Christ Almighty"; "bloody Jews." But what had roused the crowd he wasn't yet at all clear. His coat buttoned, and his collar turned up, his stick firmly grasped, he was carried round one corner after another. In the darkness he was aware of continually changing neighbours, among whom were certainly some of his own class and standing. He saw a brown lean face which he thought he recognized; a large fat face with an open mouth from which issued stridently a continual and monotonous cry of "Dirty Jews!"; a happy excited face— two or three of them all in a knot together. He was thrust backwards, sideways; the crowd lurched diversely and pinned him against some railings. A few feet ahead, it seemed to him, so far as he could judge in the darkness, that the crowd centred before a particular gate and house. There the shouting rose loudest, and sticks were rattled on the railings. He saw the helmets of two policemen within the gate and before the front door. Another call went up: "Come out, you bloody Jews!" "Come out and bring us the jewels!" "Come out and we'll show you what we'll do to the niggers!" He caught fresh fragments of the talk round him. A woman of sixty near by said with a sensuous shudder to her neighbour: "They do say that Jews eat babies." "Ah," said the neighbour, "foreigners'll do anything," and in a minute or two passed the information on in turn. Soon after, someone in front of the house shouted: "When did you eat the last baby?" and though a roar of laughter answered it, it was laughter with a hint of madness. Philip managed to edge a little farther towards the house, in the garden of which he now saw two or three hats and caps as well as the helmets. The police, however, at this made a sudden move, one man was flung sideways into the next narrow garden where he fell with a crash, another scrambled hastily the other way, and a third dropped flat on the ground. In the recoil that followed, Philip achieved the front of the house. "All right," he said hurriedly to the police. "I'm with you. Let me in." They took one comprehensive look at him, decided on the risk, and as the crowd swayed back he slipped through and turned to face it.

"Who the hell are you?" half a dozen asked him. "Another baby-eater?"

"Come to get the jewels," another voice answered. "Come on, there's only three of them." Nevertheless Philip's stick and the truncheons of the police held the front rank yet a little doubtful.

In the pause a window opened over their heads and a voice said: "Why are you here?" A roar of laughter and abuse followed. "Hand out the jewels! Come out and meet us! Who's afraid of the niggers? Who's doing a bunk? Jew! Jew! Jew!"

The voice said coldly: "Sons of abomination, what have we to do with you? Defilers of yourselves, who are you to come against the Holy One of Israel?"

The laughter and abuse grew more violent. "'Ark at him," said a thin hungry-looking man near Philip. "O my Gawd; the 'Oly one of Hisrael!"

"You may destroy the house and all that is within it," Rosenberg said, "and you shall be smitten with fire and pestilence and all the plagues of Egypt. But the jewels, even if they were here, you should not touch or see, for they are holy to the Lord. They are for the Temple of Zion and for Messias that shall be revealed.''

"'Im and 'is Messias,'' said a stout woman. "I 'opes Messias isn't in a 'urry for them jewels!''

A stone flew through the air, and at the same time a huge fellow pushed to the gate, where he looked up and spoke: "Look 'ere,'' he said, "are you Rosenberg?''

"I am Nehemiah Rosenberg,'' the voice said.

"Then you look 'ere. We 'appen to know that you've been in with the Government and the capitalists to get all this money out of the working classes and get away with it to the niggers as like as not. And we don't 'old with it. Now we don't want to 'urt you but we don't let a lot of bloody Sheenies get away with our money to those blasted niggers, not much we don't. Give us them jewels and I'll see they're put in safe keeping: I swear I will. And if you don't I'll damn well put a light to the house myself.''

A roar of applause answered him, though the stout woman, who appeared to Philip to preserve an attitude of detachment worthy of Sir Bernard, said generally: "Ah, I don't 'old with Socialism,'' and one of the policemen added agreeably: "You keep your mouth shut, Mike Cummings.''

"Thank Gawd,'' Mr. Cummings said, "I never could keep my mouth shut while honest men are being put on.''

Rosenberg leaned out of the window. "I tell you,'' he said, "the Lord shall avenge Himself upon His enemies. In the morning you shall say, 'Would God it were night,' and in the evening you shall say, 'Would God it were day'; and His anger shall be with you in your secret chamber. . . .''

Something flew through the air, struck the wall, and dropped at Philip's feet; something smashed the glass of the window above him. He clutched at his stick, and at the same time saw one of the policemen dragged sideways and clubs and belts appearing around him. He was back against the front door, and heard it creaking as the rush of the crowd in a storm of shrieks, curses, and yells came against him. Something hit his shoulder, a large dirty chin came close to his eyes, and an elbow or a stick drove into his side. At the same moment the door gave and they all crashed into the narrow passage together. The first in were past him and up the stairs; the next few in their haste ignored him; and then it was all darkness and pandemonium. He heard a loud voice upstairs, over-whelmed by the louder tumult of the crowd, a sudden silence above, noticeable in a momentary cessation of the uproar without, and then a cry: "Hear, O Israel, the Lord our God, the Lord is One." Chaos beyond anything he had known earlier in the riot broke out again, chaos of voices, but also now chaos of movement—part of the crowd in the house trying to get out, part trying to get upstairs, part uncertain and confused. Shouts of "the police" were heard from the street, the pressure round Philip lightened, and he found one of his former allies next to him again, trying to force a way up-stairs. Exclamations of terror broke out, the crowd thinned, and when at last they entered the upper room, they were only in time to prevent the demonstrative Mr. Cummings from slipping away. Him the constable seized, while Philip, taking in the appearance of the room, with a taut rope stretched across it and out of the window, ran across to join Ezekiel who, torn and bleeding, was leaning out of it. He knew before he looked out what he would find, nor was it till he had helped to pull up the hanging body of Nehemiah that he found time to wonder why the crowd had so swiftly destroyed their prey. But as Ezekiel and he undid the çord, and laid and arranged the body on the table he gathered from Cummings' persistent babble that nothing of the sort had been intended. The Jews were to be frightened into betraying the hiding-place of the money or the jewels, and the rope—meant for one of the packed boxes of luggage that stood by the wall—had been adjusted with that idea. And then Nehemiah had struggled, and the rope had slipped, and so "help me God" no-one was more surprised than he to hear that the Jew was dead.

"Is it likely I'd mean to kill him? Me that's never hurt a canary! It's all a mistake. . . ."

"The Lord gave," Ezekiel said, standing up and looking at the body, "and the Lord hath taken away. Blessed be the name of the Lord."

By this time more police were in the room, some of them with prisoners. Philip explained his presence to the officer in charge, and when this was confirmed by the two original constables and he had given his address it was suggested that he might prefer to make his way home.

But he hesitated as he looked at Ezekiel. "What about Mr. Rosenberg? Hadn't he better come with me? I'm sure my father would be glad," he said, and was permitted to propose it.

Ezekiel nodded gravely. "A burden is laid upon me," he said. "I shall go alone to the land of my fathers."

"If you've got any money or jewels here, Mr. Rosenberg," the Inspector said, "you'd better let us take charge of them."

"We never had any," Ezekiel answered; "they are in safe keeping." He turned again to the body, intoned over it a Hebrew prayer, and, while the last great syllables echoed from the ceiling and walls, indicated to Philip that he was ready. Two constables were to come with them till they had found a taxi; the four went silently downstairs, and, as they came out into the street, heard, remote but unmistakable, the sound of the guns.

In Kensington Sir Bernard and three of his guests were playing bridge—Caithness, Isabel and Roger. The king, as usual, was shut in his room. Rosamond was where Isabel had hardly dared to hope Sir Bernard would succeed in getting her —in bed and asleep. It was a Tuesday evening, and very often on Tuesday evenings, because Roger was generally free then, the Ingrams did visit their friend. Sometimes they played—if Philip or Rosamond or some other visitor would join them; sometimes they talked; sometimes they went to the theatre. Sometimes they even stopped the night; Sir Bernard was very fond of them, and between him and them existed that happy state by which fathers and children who are no relations may enjoy relationship rarely achieved by fathers and children who are. Sir Bernard all but understood Roger; Roger all but envied Sir Bernard. And what they did not understand and envy salted their talk with agreeable mystery. The evening therefore bore a bearable similarity to the past. The tact which Sir Bernard and Isabel possessed in common soothed over the fact of Rosamond's hysteria, and in effect combined in finding her a bed and putting her there. Once in the house indeed, from exhaustion or cunning or content or fear, she grew docile, and was content to be managed. Sir Bernard's forty years of practice had made him an adept at managing people. Roger had begun, from a sense of decency, to try to explain why they were there, or why he was there. But Sir Bernard refused to hear.

"I'm quite sure you don't want to tell me," he said, "and being told things—there's nothing I like better, but a sense of duty destroys the satisfaction. Like the people who refuse to be loved by a sense of duty. At my age one's only too grateful to be loved—*loved*, mark you—at all. Let's pretend nothing ever happened."

Hampered in this by the fact that the guns began almost immediately, they nevertheless did make the evening rather like one of their old enjoyments. It had been announced by Authority, after the last raid, that, in the event of another, official bulletins of the progress of the raid would be delivered to the wireless at regular intervals and announced by that means to the public. Arranged entertainments would, so far as possible, proceed as usual; and it was hoped that all listeners-in would follow their ordinary custom, and lessen the chance of panic, at creating which (as had been discovered in the Great War) all air-raids over such places as London were directed. If the experiment were found unsuccessful it would be discontinued after the trial.

"We shan't want the entertainment," Sir Bernard said, "but we may as well know what's happening, so far as the Government will tell us."

"I'm not sure of that," Isabel said. "Suppose the thing says, 'Great aeroplane dropping fiery bombs directly over Colindale Square'."

"It won't," Caithness said. "I'll bet you a dozen pairs of gloves, Isabel, that if we're all blown to heaven the last thing we hear is: 'No aeroplane has yet reached London; the raid is being effectively repulsed.'"

"Done," said Isabel.

"An anthropomorphic heaven," Sir Bernard said, and picked up the cards.

For some time the game and the entertainment proceeded. Then the first announcement was heard.

"The first Government communiqué has just been received," the loud speaker announced. "'Raiders have attempted to approach London from all sides, but have entirely failed. Four enemy planes have already been brought down. A number of bombs have been dropped, but all in uninhabited districts. The O.C. London Air Defence announces that no losses have been sustained by our forces'."

"I hope they'll use imagination," Sir Bernard said. "One or two planes destroyed on our side would make the bulletins credible."

"I do wish you wouldn't say 'imagination'," Roger complained. "It isn't, you know; only the lowest kind of cunning fancy."

"I've never been clear that Coleridge was right there," Caithness said meditatively. "Surely it's the same faculty— the adaptation of the world to an idea of the world."

144

"Well, if the O.C. London Air Defence *has* an idea of the world," Roger said, "you may be right. But is an idea a pattern?"

"O surely!" Caithness interrupted. "If an idea isn't a pattern what good is it?"

"If we're playing bridge," Isabel said forbearingly, "could you manage to forget your ideas for a moment? Thank you so much."

A new voice, after a quarter of an hour, took up the tale. "Latest communiqué," the loud speaker reported. " 'Enemy planes continue to be sighted. It is supposed that in all some eight hundred are engaged in the raid. None have appeared over London. Five villages have been destroyed. African troops have been landed from giant airships, and have occupied the ridge of Hampstead and Richmond Park. Other airships have appeared on the western side. Posts of Government troops have been overwhelmed in the north and south'."

"The devil they have!" Roger exclaimed.

There was a short pause, then the loud speaker continued, with another variation of tone: " 'In the name of the things that have been and are to be, willed and fated, in the name of the gods many and one . . .' "

Isabel laid down her cards, Caithness jumped to his feet, Roger sat upright in his chair. Sir Bernard, leaning back in his own, said in a voice of considerable interest, "Mr. Considine, I believe."

" '. . . the High Executive of the African Sovereigns warns the English of the folly of defiance. It is reluctant to make a difference in belief a reason for the destruction of London, and it does not propose, even under the provocations of the Government, to endanger the city to-night. But it is compelled to display the ardent and unconquerable forces at its disposal, and from the centre of the white race it seriously warns them that the forces now in action shall be multiplied a thousand times to effect the ends upon which it is determined

—the freedom of the black peoples and the restoration of Africa. It exhibits something of the strength of its armies and the devotion of its martyrs, and it asserts firmly that, if a third raid upon London becomes necessary, then London shall be destroyed. It urges the English to consider carefully what they are fighting, and if any among them believe that in love and art and death rather than in logic and science the kingdom of man lies, it entreats them, not to any transfer of allegiance, for it recognizes in the folly of patriotism a means of obedience to the same passionate imagination, but to a demonstration on behalf of peace. In the name of their own loyalties it appeals to the children of passion and imagination; in the name of a vaster strength than their own it threatens the children of pedantry and reason—in this first proclamation made at London in the first year of the Second Evolution of Man'."

"Then," Sir Bernard said, "with more adequate assurance than Drake had, we can go on with the game."

But Roger and Caithness were both on their feet. Caithness said, "I wouldn't trust him too far."

Isabel, still looking at her cards, murmured, "I don't think you need worry, Mr. Caithness. He told us the same thing this afternoon."

"You've seen him?" Caithness incredulously exclaimed.

"Yes," Isabel said. "In fact, we made a kind of appointment with him."

"*You* did?" Caithness said, still more astonished.

"Well—I did for Roger," Isabel said, and lifted her eyes. "He'd never have done it himself. I hope you didn't mind, Sir Bernard?"

"Almost thou persuadest me to be a monogamist," Sir Bernard said, but there was unusual tenderness in his voice. "Here, do you mean? Because, if so, perhaps that's him."

It was not; it was Philip and the Jew. They came into the room accompanied by Inkamasi who had descended from his to discover the progress of the raid. Philip introduced Ezekiel to Sir Bernard and in a low voice gave him the brief tale of the evening.

"I'm very glad you're here, Mr. Rosenberg," Sir Bernard said, in quite a different tone from his usual placidity. "I'm your servant in everything. You'll use us as you will. Ring, Philip."

But even as Philip's finger touched the bell there was a louder ring in the hall. Sir Bernard paused and glanced swiftly at Isabel, who sat down by the card-table. In the minute that it took the feet of the maid to go to the front door she looked up at Roger and said: "Be good to me, my darling, and find out everything you can." Roger, more shaken than she, did not answer except by his gaze. There were voices and footsteps; then the door was thrown wide open and Considine stood in the entrance of the room. Behind him was Mottreux, and behind him again two or three others—in whose faces, so far as he could see them, Sir Bernard thought he recognized the gentlemen who had waited on them during the dinner at Hampstead. But he had no time to consider; he looked back, where everyone else was looking, at the High Executive who stood in the entrance.

"A good meeting," Considine said, "but I mustn't wait. Who will come with me?"

In the immediate silence Roger heard himself say, "I."

"The king also," Considine said.

"Fool," the Zulu cried. "You've come to me now, and do you think you'll get away? You're mine, you're mine."

He was standing almost on the other side of the room, nine or ten feet away. But as he ended, he crouched low, and in one terrific movement leapt—right across the intervening space, sending himself forward and upward, so that he crashed down on Considine as a thunderbolt might strike from the sky. His hands were at the other's throat, and before that descent of angry vengeance even Considine for a moment staggered and seemed likely to fall. But before he could either fall or recover,

in the second after the onslaught fell, Mottreux sprang
forward. The others saw the revolver in his hand and cried out;
their voices were overwhelmed by the shot. Inkamasi reeled
and crashed, his hand to his thigh where the blood showed.
Considine recovered himself and glanced at his friend.

"Mottreux, Mottreux, is it necessary?" he murmured.
"Am I afraid of his hands? Well, it's done; let Vereker see to
him. It's only a flesh wound."

He moved a step aside, so that another of his companions
could come forward and do what he could with Isabel's help
and with improvised bandages for the wounded man. After a
few minutes Considine went on: "Mr. Ingram and the king;
Mr. Rosenberg, I have your cousin's jewels, and others I
have bought for you. Come with me; there's no place for you
here." He cast a glance around. "Is there any of you beside
for whom that's true?"

"If you take the king you shall take me," Caithness cried
out. "I demand that you——"

"Why demand?" Considine's laugh answered him. "I
invite you, I entreat you, to come. Sir Bernard?"

"No," Sir Bernard said. "We've come out of the jungle and
I for one am not going back."

"The king, Mr. Caithness, Mr. Rosenberg, Mr. Ingram,"
Considine said. "Very well. Mrs. Ingram?"

"No," Isabel said. "Africa's near enough here."

"You are perhaps a wise woman," Considine said, "but if
you are you shall be a centre of our wisdom in London, and
all the women of England shall learn from you what it is they
do. Your husband shall come back to you with victory.
Good-night then. Good-night, Sir Bernard; I leave you to the
sauces that you prefer to food. Come, my friends; come, my
enemies. Mottreux, you and Vereker shall make the king as
comfortable as you can in the first car. The others will come
with me in the second."

He swept them with him out to the door, to the large cars

that waited for them. Roger, obeying a gesture, got in and
sat down with his back to the engine; Caithness sat by him.
Opposite the priest was the Jew. Considine occupied the other
seat. Figures moved about the other car; from the doorway
Isabel and Sir Bernard silently watched. Considine raised a
hand to them, and as the car slid away he said to Roger,
"There is defeat defeated. But you may be at ease; there is
again to-night no danger to them from my people. And to-
morrow, or if not to-morrow then the day after, the Government will ask for peace."

"Surely they won't dare," Roger said. "And if you're not
hurting London, what *are* you doing?"

"I'm teaching London to feel," Considine said, "to feel
terribly. It will know panic to-night such as it has never
known. It will know the depths which it has never dared to
find. Blame its sterile hopelessness for its suffering."

"Is that why you bring the African armies here?" Caithness
asked.

"Armies?" Considine laughed. "O I know I caused that
tale to be spread. But those of my people who are here are
entering into their greatest moment, and I give them the
sacrifice they desire. Wait; you shall see them." He picked up
the speaking-tube and said something to the driver. The car
ran swiftly northward, went round by Regent's Park, into
St. John's Wood, and came out at last round Primrose Hill
on to Haverstock Hill somewhere below Belsize Park Station.
But a few minutes showed that this way was impossible. The
road was full of people pressing downward, less thick below
the station because of the mob that surged round the entrance,
which no vehicle could get through. Beyond and above it the
Hill was a noisy tumult of refugees, and beyond in the midnight sky was a red glare, above which again the useless
searchlights crossed and wavered. Hysterical shrieks, curses,
the noise of many separate scuffles came to them. Near them
two wheelbarrows laden with bundles had come into collision,

149

and the owners were fighting wildly in the midst of their scattered goods. Here and there a woman lay in a dead faint; in places the white robes and black cloaks of the Dominicans of the Priory showed as they laboured to create some sort of order. ("No doubt", Considine murmured to Caithness, "the Anglican clergy are somewhere about too. But of course they haven't the same advantage in dress.") More and more fugitives were hurrying from the side turnings. Even as the car slowed down, to turn down one of these and escape, two young men scrambled on to the driver's seat. "This car is going to take us," one said drunkenly; the other hung on to the wheel. Roger glanced at Considine, who, observant but motionless, was lying back in his corner. The driver abandoned the wheel, and with what seemed but a light blow knocked one sprawling into the road; the other let go the wheel to protect himself, was dexterously flung overboard also, and the car backed a little way down the Hill. Considine took up the tube again. "Go round as far as is necessary," he said. "I must come to the top."

Eventually, after many pauses and very long detours, the thing was done. They came back from the north on to the Hampstead ridge, and heard beyond them a noise quite different to anything that had passed before. "I will have the car opened," Considine said to the driver. "Go slowly till you come near Highgate and then bend away to the stopping-place."

The glare by now had become much stronger, and Roger saw Considine suddenly stand up. Almost at the same moment a great cry in a strange tongue roared out beyond them. A black soldier appeared running and shouting beside the car, and another, and then, rushing towards them, a whole group. He heard the steady beating of drums, and a cry resolving itself into English: "Deathless! Deathless! Glory to the Deathless One!" Considine, raising his right hand, made with it, high in the air, a sudden gesture; the cry beat all round them and ceased and broke out yet more wildly: "Glory to the Master of Love! Glory to the Deathless One!" Negroes ran by the car, rushing up to it, to touch it and fall back exhausted; they leapt and twisted at it.

He felt a sudden lurch and guessed insanely what the obstacle was they had passed over. The cries, now in African, now in English, made an arch of sound: "Death for the Deathless One!" he heard. "Glory to the Lord of Death!" They were passing now between blazing fires each with its own dance of whirling figures, which broke and hurled themselves at the car, or flung themselves prostrate in adoration as it rolled by. Opposite him the figure of Considine seemed to dilate in the red glare; again and again he made the high mysterious gesture with his right hand; every now and then he cried out in a great voice and a strange tongue. Roger tore his eyes away and looked out over the Heath, but beyond the light of the watch-fires it lay in darkness, a darkness which seemed to him to be continually resolving itself into these leaping, shrieking figures. Caithness was leaning back in his corner, his eyes shut, his lips moving in swift murmured prayer.

Roger looked back as the car suddenly stopped and Considine, signing for silence, began to speak. What he said Roger could not tell, but as he ended and the car moved on again, a shout greater than any before went up. He knew instinctively the meaning—it was that whereof the rhythm leapt into the former English: "Death for the Deathless."

But whatever the cries, Death itself began to accompany them on their passage, for there was heard suddenly a revolver shot, and then another, and as Roger, supposing for a moment that the English had begun an attack, looked round him, he saw one of the running foaming figures by the car stabbing at himself with a bayonet, and saw the madness spreading to others, saw the steel glinting and crimson-streaked faces in the light of the fires. Many of the negroes had torn off their tunics, and some were already naked from head to foot; among whom appeared here and there a yet wilder form in skins of various kinds and high plumes of feathers, leading some eddy of the general dance. Close by him two great negroes caught and held and stabbed at each other with broad knives and more shots sounded around them. Again and again he felt a horrid jerk and lurch of the car, and still through it all Considine stood upright opposite him, and with an exalted but unmoved face considered the revelry he had bidden to be.

At last this journey along a ridge of blazing watch-fires between two seas of darkness came to an end. The crowds of negroes began to thin. Considine threw up both hands, made a downward and outward gesture, cried out once more, and sat down. The last negro halted, flung himself on the earth, the car gathered strength, swept on, and after a while issued at last into the darkness and silence of the open country.

Caithness spoke bitterly, "Are you letting that horde of negroes loose on London?" he asked.

"You heard me," Considine answered. "You heard me an hour ago. I have let the English feel panic, panic such as they have not felt since the Vikings raided their coasts and burned their towns a thousand years ago. They have been afraid of their feelings, of ecstasy and riot and savage glee; they have frozen love and hated death. And I have shown them these things wild and possibly triumphant; and what fear of a thousand armies will not do, fear of their own passions will. They will ask for peace. As for my Africans, they ask for death and they shall have death. Most of them will kill themselves or one another to-night; those who survive till to-morrow will die before your soldiers. I do not pity them; they are not the adepts; all that they are capable of I have given them. They die for the Undying. How many martyrs would the Churches offer me of such a strain?"

" They die for your schemes," Caithness said.

"They die for the Master of Death," Considine answered,

"either for me or for another. If I do not achieve, another will. Do you think it is an idle brag to call this year the First of the Second Evolution? It is a truth the story of your Christ darkly foreshadowed. Him that you ignorantly worship declare I unto you. Your martyrs in the past have died, many of them, in such an agony of supreme rapture, and those of many another faith. But I bring you achievement, I bring you the fulfilment of desires, the lordship of love and death."

There was a little silence; then he went on, slowly and almost to himself: "It is a long work, and many have waited for it. My father longed for it and did not see it, though he knew the beginning and taught it to me. This was the beginning of sex when far away in the ages the world divided itself in its primal dark instinct to destroy death which seemed its doom. And when man came he desired immortality, and deceived himself with begetting children and with religion and with art. All these are not ecstasy, but the shadow of ecstasy. Kingship and dynasties he created and cities and monuments and science, and nothing satisfied that hungry desire. And then he created love, and knew that that which existed between a man and a woman was mysterious and powerful, but what to do with it he has not known. Only a few have known, Caesar and a few others, and they have been struck down. I think perhaps Chaka knew, for he was of the initiates. I taught him what to do and how to govern his energies. But he had an irresistible hunger for cruelty and destruction, and when the time came he was destroyed. For the true adepts care for nothing but to discover the secrets, and to enter into communion with ecstasy; and if they shall govern the world, as they shall, they will do it to make known to all men the things they themselves know. Fast and vigil they keep for this, as my father taught me when I was a boy two centuries ago. In trance and in waking they keep the end before them. I beheld in a trance the making of sex, I went down to where in history and in the individual being—which are one, as all the mystics know: inward or backward, it is the same way—to where those high laboratories lie. And there, in trance or in waking I do not know, I myself carried out the great experiment, and I laid my imagination upon all the powers and influences of sex and love and desire. In the adolescence of my life I did this, and I have thriven upon that strength ever since. For first I bent it to my own life. I set before myself three hundred years from that night, and not two hundred have since gone by. I have gathered from many women all that imagination desired, and I have changed it to strength and cunning and length of days. I have never kissed a woman; all that have lived with me have had what lovers they desired. For a kiss also is but the shadow of ecstasy. Then they taught me in the lodge of the initiated how, though death might be far, yet it was certain, and that at death the ghost of man wanders stripped of all powers that it has gained in a place of shadows, and that there remained yet to be found the secret of how man could go into that place armed with passion and high delight and return to this world when and as he would. He that has mastered love has mastered the world, and he that masters death is lord of that other. Also as the delights of mere bodily love are but shadows beside the rich joys of the transforming imagination, so this itself is nothing compared to the revivifying intoxication of the passage from life to death and from death to life. And I set my purpose on this and laboured to achieve it. But, while I brooded, the feet of Europe came nearer, and the blind intelligence of Europe looked into the clear light of the lodges and said: 'It is dark, it is dark,' and smelt wickedness. And the religion of Europe came, and the learning of Europe. Then we the adepts knew that, unless we made Africa free, in a little while Europe would trample over us and we should be gone; and we resolved that Europe must be stayed.''

He paused and looked out over the fields and hedges between which they were passing. Then he went on more sharply and swiftly:

"Not that all the Europeans who came to Africa then had closed themselves to wisdom. Some of the white officers sat in our lodges and were initiated and entered into trance, and made themselves strong men; there have always been some who would do this—Mottreux was one; I met him in Uganda, and there was a French General in Morocco, and in the south Simon Rosenberg's great uncle. And there were others. All of us set to work to unite Africa. We knew the lodges already in various parts of the land, and we drew all these into one. And we spoke with the chiefs and kings; little by little we brought them into our purpose. The witch-doctors and sorcerers were ours already, though they were in the outer circle. They gave us a means of ruling the tribes, and little by little through many years we proposed to ourselves to show the people of Africa the doctrines of freedom and sacrifice and ecstasy, and I determined to strike at Europe by panic and strength."

Roger said abruptly, "Yet you seemed to wish that Mottreux hadn't fired."

"Why, for myself," Considine said, "if men without weapons come against me I'll meet them without weapons, heart to heart and strength to strength. But shall I waste years imposing my will on the Governments of Europe—and spend my energies so? It shall be a shorter business. They proclaim guns and they shall have guns. But for the adepts—— If I wish Mottreux had not fired it was for his sake, not mine."

"Your friends may fire at you one day," the intolerant voice of the priest broke in, "when they want something you can't give them."

"Pieces of silver, for example," Considine said, not turning his head.

The night lay about them; they swept on through it. Roger looked out on the unseen countryside, and remembered the words that had brought about his own meeting with the conquistador who sat opposite him. "I will encounter darkness as a bride"—he was rushing towards that darkness now. The dark closed them in, but they were speeding towards the core of the darkness; the words themselves were swallowing them up. All the miracles of the poets had rent and illumined and charged that night, but the mingling light and dark which was in all easily accepted verse lay far behind them now where the wild rapture of the Africans surged above London. It was as if he had passed from them from something which was himself, to something which was even more himself. His very physical body was being carried in towards the energy which created art. Art . . . the ancient word so often defiled and made stupid stood for a greatness only partially explored. His body felt the energy opposite him—an energy self-restrained, self-shaped. "And hug it in mine arms——" but if the arms could not bear it, if the awful blasting power of that darkness should destroy him as the glory of Zeus destroyed Semele? It was too late now for choice; he was lost and saved at once. Onward and onward, away from the ironic contemplations of the children of the wise world and from the shrieking self-immolating abandonments of the more ignorant sons of rapture; away from young perplexity and young greed; away from Isabel. High-set, as the moon now rising, he saw her, knowing in her daily experiences, her generous heart and her profound womanhood, all that he must compass sea and land to find. This was the separation that had been between man and woman from the beginning; this was fated, and this must be willed. It was the everlasting reconciliation of the everlasting contradiction—to will what was fated, to choose necessity. Perfect for one moment in his heart, he knew the choice taken. He willed necessity. All the poets had done this in their own degree—the very making of their verse was this, their patience and their labour, their silence till the utterance they so long desired rose into being within them. This was the secret of royalty—the solemn anointed figure of government to whom necessary obedience was willed, and so through all orders of hierarchical life, secular or religious, vocational in every kind, trade or profession, ceremonial or actual. Love too was its image, but love and not the beloved was the necessity; to love, and only to the beloved as the sacred means, the honourable toil was given.

Something different was in the air; his nostrils felt, far off, the smell of the sea.

Chapter Ten

LONDON AFTER THE RAID

The wild figures that danced on the outskirts of London that night were but few and scattered representations of the more monstrous forms that filled it within. The serpent skins that clothed some of the leaders of the dance were poor vestments if compared to the mad dragons of escaping multitudes. Considine had indeed loosed but few of his meinie on the hills of the north and the south; he had not cared, it was afterwards discovered, even to justify the announcements of burning villages and destroyed troops which he had caused to be broadcast. A few bombs had been dropped but more for noise and mental horror than to destroy. He had even reassured London, speaking from its centre. But there were many whom the reassurance did not solace, and there were many, many more, who did not hear it, for they were already in flight. It was known in the small streets and the slums of the extremer suburbs that the Africans had landed, and of those who in those crowded buildings heard the news there were few who did not rush out to seek safety. The north fled southwards; the south fled northwards; the west broke away towards the east. Over the east alone no hostile airfleet manœuvred and fought the English planes while its laden airships sank earthward to landing places prepared long since. Many a house with wide grounds had waited for this night; flares summoned the enemy and they came. At most they numbered few enough in comparison with the defenders, and they were not meant for attack. But on all convenient heights their fires blazed, and sacred revels were begun which till now had been hidden in the black night of African swamps. As there the wild animals fled from the drums, the conches, and the screams, so now the terrified population rushed away to what it hoped was safety. The slums poured out their people, and not the slums alone. From many a fine house, lying happily on the outer rim of London, cars issued bearing huddled women and children, while men, both young and old, drove them furiously away. A brother coming back home would bear the news, or a father peering from a window would be aware, dreadfully near him, of the awful barbarian tumult breaking out, and household after household sought by their mechanical inventions to escape from the strange gospel which called to their uncomprehending minds. Considine's voice had hardly ceased its proclamation when opposite Charing Cross a laden car from near the Heath crashed into another similarly laden from the Terrace at Richmond. This was but the first of many similar catastrophes. London became the enemy of London; civil war, chaotic and bloody, surged through the streets. Ealing and Highgate and Streatham, listening to the guns, heard instead the riot roaring through them, hesitated and feared and shrank, and then, as the rumours grew louder, and the panic in the streets spread into the houses, themselves swept out to swell the flood. The spray of the approaching waves of humanity mingled; the first fugitives passed each other and soon began to call out, and heard how they fled not towards safety but towards new danger. And behind those earliest and most timorous souls came the main hurrying processions. They came up towards the centre; stations and tubes were choked, and yet tubes and stations offered no certain refuge from an enemy pursuing on foot. It was not merely death dropped from the skies that threatened but death hastening along on earth. Round about Piccadilly and Pall Mall, clambering over the railings of the parks, trying to rest in Trafalgar Square, surging over the bridges and even running on and falling from their parapets, surging also from the thoroughfares of the north, the mob converged on the central lines of Oxford Street and Holborn and Cheapside, of the Strand and Fleet Street and Ludgate Hill and Cannon Street. There it sought to pause, but still the continual presence thrust it from behind, and now it was driven on not merely to escape death that pursued from afar but death that threatened close at hand. The mere necessity of breath oppressed it, the desire of escape not from Africa but from itself. Ignorant and at odds with itself it swayed and exuded itself, and was magnetized by some slight movement and rushed after in blind despair or even blinder hope. A woman with a baby would take a few steps down a partly deserted turning, and others would follow, and a small eddy would be set up which a mile away was reflected in another insane and multitudinous onrush. A young man would pull his girl into an arch or doorway for rest, and others would see and follow, and a little tumult would break out in that greater tumult, and the first couple were fortunate indeed if they both emerged from that tiny crush alive into the evermoving surges that poured by them. Yet, terrible as the fear was, fear was not present alone; desire and loathing and the cruel darkness of abandoned souls walked in the mist of the crowds and took their pleasure as they could. Abominable things were done, which none saw or seeing stopped to prevent. Shrieks went up in hidden corners, and laughter and sudden silences answered them, silences hardly discernible in the general roar and themselves filled with the never-ceasing sound of the guns. How many devotees of Considine's choosing rode through the air to death that night was never rightly known, but not till the late November dawn was high did the movement of his planes or the efforts of the English gunners cease. There was therefore, for the elements of demented London, no desire of return as there was no chance of return; within and without the passionate terror hurled them on. Farther and farther east they poured; not merely the Thames but great reservoirs and docks and small tributaries of small rivers, swallowed those

who were pushed aside; and there were puddles in the street
which were not water where someone had striven to guard
his belongings, and heaps that were a dreadful hindrance to
those who came behind. A pestilence of the spirit walked in
the night and slew its victims as it went.

It hovered in the streets; it rested in churches and such
public buildings as had been readily and benevolently opened.
For in the early hours of the exodus men had supposed that it
would, however serious and tragic, still be quiet and controlled.
Certain authorities therefore had hoped that the buildings in
their charge would be of use to exhausted fugitives. St. Paul's,
in a holy goodwill, was so opened. The crowd entered, increased, filled it, flowed over the rails of the sanctuary, clam-
bered upon the altars, and within its walls suffered and
inflicted horror. The windows of public-houses, as of eating-
houses and gunsmiths, had been smashed, and bottles of
drink obtained, and the strongest men made use of their
strength. On the High Altar a drunken woman smashed a
bottle over the head of a vociferating assailant, and was shot
by his companion before the victim had died. The kingship
which Inkamasi so proudly held had here its apish rival in
savage might or dextrous cunning; yet that kingship was unstained, as all lovely things are unstained by their detestable
imitations, since beauty cannot be manifested unless the mind
assents. Without that assent, beauty itself must be tyranny;
but with that grave acceptance there is no government that
is not beautiful, for love is not only the fulfilling but the
beginning of the law.

In Kensington all that night Sir Bernard watched, as if
on a rocky island—one of a scattered archipelago of such
islands—a lingering child of a lost race watched the sea over-
whelm his city. After the departure of Considine with his
guests or prisoners—no-one was quite sure which they were—
Sir Bernard had gone back with Isabel and Philip to the library.
He stood there with his back to the fire, suveying the room,

the stains of blood on the carpet and the divan, the empty chairs round the card-table, and the dropped cards, the general disarray that had meant companionship and now meant desertion. He looked at Isabel, now enduring a separation deeper than his own—at least, presumably; everyone would say it was. Even in that moment he found himself wondering whether Isabel or he would miss Roger the most; it was so difficult to compare these things. Isabel had lost her husband; and he had lost—a friend who lived mostly in Yorkshire, and a younger friend whom he saw perhaps three or four times a month for an hour or two, and a barbarian chief whom he'd only known a few days. O and a Jewish mystic whom he didn't know at all. They didn't, all of them put together, sound intimate beside Isabel's loss, and yet . . . It wasn't *whom* you lost; it was *what* you lost, what centre of what concern or quality of yourself was torn away, so that your own capacity moved helplessly in the void. Something very like stability had been torn from under him. He looked at Isabel again and wondered. Was it merely her youth that made her seem, in that house of desertion, the least deserted of them all? He was old; he'd outlived his time; he was living on his memories. There went through him a rare flash of envy; Isabel hadn't to live on her memories, Isabel——

Sir Bernard recaptured a sense of proportion. "No-one who's just in the throes of seeing Considine go off with a Zulu, a Jew, a clergyman, and an expert in the poets ought to talk of living on his memories," he said to himself. He said to Isabel as tenderly as possible: "Why did you tell Roger to go?"

"Because I wanted him to, since he wanted to," she said. "More; for I wanted him to even more than he did, since I hadn't myself to think of and he had."

Sir Bernard blinked. "I see," he said. "But—I only ask— isn't it a little risky . . . deciding what other people want?"

"Dear Sir Bernard, I wasn't *deciding*," she said, "I was wanting. It isn't quite the same thing. I want it—whatever he

wants. I don't want it unselfishly, or so that he may be happy,
or because I ought to, or for any reason at all. I just want it.
And then, since I haven't myself to think of, I'm not divided
or disturbed in wanting, so I *can* save him trouble. That's
all."

"O quite, quite," Sir Bernard said. "That would be all.
And is that what you call quiet affection?"

Isabel looked a trifle perplexed. "I don't call it anything,"
she said. "There isn't anything to call it. It's the way things
happen, if you love anyone."

"Of course," Sir Bernard said. "Too much excitement has
made me dull to-night. Of course, it's the way things happen.
The whole round world has noticed it. So you wanted Roger
to go?"

Isabel said, a little unhappily: "When you put it like that it
sounds somehow as if I didn't really, or only because he wanted
to. Don't you see I couldn't want it *because* of him? He—
somehow *he* wanted it in me. O I don't know. I'm not as
intelligent as you, but I know it was the one thing I had to have
to make me happy."

Sir Bernard looked at her again, very steadily. "And does
it make you happy?"

"Utterly," Isabel said. "O of course it's dreadfully painful,
but—yes, utterly."

On that rich and final word they fell into silence. Irony,
even loving irony, could say no more. The mind accepted a
fact which was a contradiction in terms, and knew itself
defeated by that triumphant contradiction. Sir Bernard wished
he could have heard Considine and Isabel arguing—not that
Isabel would or could have argued. So far as he could see, she
was saying exactly the opposite of Considine, and yet they
curiously agreed. They were both beyond the places of logic
and compromise, even amused compromise. They were both
utterly, utterly—well, they were both utterly, and that was
that. It was no wonder Isabel didn't want to go to Africa.

It was Philip who presently, wandering restlessly about the house, brought them news of the number of fugitives who were beginning to hurry along Kensington High Street. Sir Bernard, hearing, frowned. "This," he said, "if it's happening everywhere, may mean pure hell before long. Let's go and look from upstairs." There was an attic window which commanded the High Street, and from it they surveyed the increasing crowd. A few of the fugitives, turning aside, hurried through the square in which the house stood, but not many; most of them pressed frantically onwards.

"I'd better make sure the front door's fastened up," Philip said suddenly. "We don't want any of them pushing in." He added, more carefully, "I suppose actually there's no danger."

"Of course not," Isabel said. "Mr. Considine said he wasn't going to hurt London."

"I don't really see," Sir Bernard said, "how one can be expected to believe Mr. Considine. You can't refuse your mind and yet have people accept your word, can you?"

"But surely you do believe him?" Isabel said. "He *said* so."

"I know he said so," Sir Bernard patiently explained. "What I'm trying——O very well. Besides, you're right. I do believe him, but I can't think why I should. The Second Evolution of Man, I suppose. Considine at the bottom of a well—and what a well!"

"That man's very tired," Isabel said, watching a party of five; a woman carrying one child, a man with two, who had just turned into the square, and were stopping even in their haste for a necessary minute. "He oughtn't to go on—nor ought she. Sir Bernard, don't you think——"

"Yes," Sir Bernard said. "I suppose you want to rest, too. Good God, you do! And feed?"

"Well," Isabel said, blushing slightly, "I was thinking, if you'd got any milk, the children . . . I could just go and speak to them."

"Then Philip will go too," Sir Bernard said. "Ecstasy has

very curious forms sometimes, especially if it happens to be attacking anyone who isn't."

"Isn't what?" asked Isabel. "I thought you were talking about me."

Sir Bernard took her arm. "Come down," he said. "Philip, go and open the door," and as the young man obeyed, "Is that true?" he asked.

She turned clear eyes upon him. "I'm no good at words," she said, "and I'm a fool at knowing things, but when there's something in you that has its way, and when Roger's doing what he must do, and I too—— O every fibre of me's aching for him and I could sing for joy all through me. Isn't that all the ecstasy that I could bear? Come and let's do something before it breaks my heart to be alive."

Chapter Eleven

THE HOUSE BY THE SEA

It was indeed by the sea that the house stood at which the car eventually arrived. Through the wide porch in front of which it stopped the light shone from the open door; a light in which expectant figures moved and waited. Roger got out, stiff and weary, and as he stretched himself wondered afresh at that strange company of travellers. His fellows seemed less weary than he; the old Jew's movements were slow but not difficult, and Caithness, once out, glanced swiftly round him as if to discover any sign of the king. Oppression lay, Roger thought, on him alone, perhaps because he alone was yet unused to a deliberate co-habitation with belief. The past popularity, the long tradition of religion supported its diverse champions against a present neglect. But art had never been popular, and its lovers in all ages were few and solitary. His own belief was as passionate as that of the Jew or the Christian, but it was more often thwarted and more greatly troubled.

They gathered in a group, waiting for that fourth of their company in whose train they had been brought there, the incarnate epiphany of immortal conquest. He delayed to speak to the driver, and as the others stood they savoured more fully the presence of the ocean. They could hear the faint sound of it in the darkness; they could smell and feel it in the air, as if the secret medium of all their journeys sensibly expressed itself to them. Fresh and everlasting, alien yet alluring, distant and deep yet delicate and close, it drew them together and unified them by its subtle existence. Caithness said unnecessarily: "We must be close to the shore; that's the waves we hear." Neither of the others answered him, and before the words had well died away Considine came up to them. He invited them with a gesture and they followed. In the porch Mottreux met them. He saluted his master and said: "All's well: we've put the king in his room. He's in a slight fever but otherwise he's all right."

Considine nodded. "The captain's not here yet?" he asked. "No; I hardly expected him. To-morrow. My friends will be tired; show them their rooms."

"I should like to see the king," Caithness said, with a sound of challenge.

Roger saw Considine's smile leap out. "Take Mr. Caithness to him then," he said to Mottreux, and then to the priest: "But do remember, Mr. Caithness, that the king, being a Christian, is not yet able to be negligent of material hurt. You and Sir Bernard insisted on his being liable to pain; you'll no doubt teach him to endure pain." He turned to the others. "Good-night, Mr. Rosenberg," he said, "to-morrow we'll talk of your journey. Good-night, Ingram; sleep." His eyes looked into Roger's and sent through him a doctrine of obedience. He and the ocean swept the young man up and away into themselves; Roger saluted and followed the gentleman who waited for him.

They came into a hall which opened round them as if into distances. The walls were hung or covered with some kind of deep grey from which light shone, almost as over a landscape. Its furniture was not merely furniture but natural to it; a chest showed like an antique boulder on a hillside; a table was a table certainly, but it had grown in its place, and had not been set there, a chair or two glowed darkly as if shrubs of glistening leaves reflected the sun. Roger walked after his guide with a sense of perfect proportion such as no room he had ever entered, however admirably decorated, had given him; the best had been but arranged art, pleasant to his judgement, while this was an art which answered his human

167

nature and contented his blood. It communicated peace. He
followed up a staircase, down a corridor, and was shown into
a perfectly ordinary guest-room, where all necessities awaited
him. His companion uttered a few courteous sentences,
smiled, bowed, and left him. Roger went across to the window,
but he could not see outside; the darkness was too deep. He
thought of going back and switching off the light, took a step
that way, and felt all through his body Considine's voice
saying: "Sleep." To oppose that government was too much
for him; he turned to the dressing-table.

As he made ready for sleep he thought once more of
Isabel. The knowledge of her moved him, yet differently.
He had been apt to wonder what he could do for her; now
indeed he wondered what he could do. There was all his
knowledge, all his concern, but it opened up like a mountain
lake from which as yet no irrigating streams ran to the plains
below. The weight and darkness of this power pressed on him;
he himself was the bank which closed those waters in, yet far
away he was also the plain which needed those waters. They
lay silent; they held such mysteries as verse held, and sometimes the surface of them was troubled by a wind which rippled
it into words. "The passion and the life whose fountains are
within . . . ," "felt in the blood and felt along the heart . . ."
(what passion along what blood?), "in embalmèd darkness
guess each sweet" (what hint of what discovery?), "Where
the great vision of the guarded Mount . . . ("the guarded
Mount" . . . what vision?), "fear no more the heat . . . fear no
more . . . " (did that song come from within the vision of the
guarded Mount wherein also the passion and the fountains of
life lay?), "fear no more . . . merrily, merrily, shall I live now."
They did not answer each other; they flowed towards each
other and intermingled, and dissolved each into others,
meaning in sound, sound in meaning, and always fresh
ripples rose and ran on that dark surface, away towards the
bounded infinity, and in and between them all was the vast

power of which they were but gleaming movement momently seen. Between them, as into that vast, received and to be strengthened, he sank to sleep. In the last second of mingling knowledge and dream he had a vision of a wide desolate plain, across which, coming swiftly towards him, ran a tall, young, uncouth, and violent figure, holding in a hand stretched high above his head what, even at that distance which was yet no distance, was known for a curiously tinted and involuted shell. It was running at great speed, and crying out as it came, crying in a great voice, "A god, yea, many gods," and the dreamer suddenly recognized that runner and knew it for the passionate youth of Wordsworth, coming in his own dream of saving poetry from a world's destruction, and crying out in his own divine voice across lands and waters how the shell was poetry and uttered voices, "voices more than all the winds, with power"; and the winds awoke in all the quarters of the vast heavens under which the intense young visionary ran, and roared down towards him and into the shell he was stretching out towards Roger, and they reverberated "power, power," and the shell sang "power," and the visitant with longer and wilder steps was leaping forward, and then darkness swept over all, and the vision lost itself in sleep.

He woke the next morning, and lay for some moments wondering whether Muriel would be bringing the tea in soon, whether perhaps if he opened his eyes he would find that she had already brought it, and even that Isabel had already poured it out. As no-one said anything however, he opened his eyes, and almost immediately realized that his chance of tea was very small. At least, he rather doubted whether Considine's household provided early cups of tea, and the doubt was justified. None appeared. Roger, telling himself that he didn't mind, wondered for a second whether cups of tea at reasonable times weren't actually more important than lines of poetry, or at least whether the two were entirely incompatible. Nobody objected to wine, and if he had to

The House by the Sea

choose for the rest of his life between wine and tea he had no kind of doubt where the choice would rest. Poetry and such things could give him all the wine he wanted, whereas tea was unique, "a thing of beauty and a joy for ever." "That's right, misquote," he said to himself crossly, and repeated the line correctly—"a thing of beauty is a joy for ever." Under the sudden spell the immediate urgency of tea faded. It was silly to want tea so much when he had that power attending him. He said it again, slowly, and, much consoled, got up.

Baths apparently Considine provided; he dressed and, hoping he was doing the right thing—it was close on nine— went downstairs. In the hall he found Mottreux, Caithness, and two or three more of Considine's friends, the young Vereker among them. The hall struck him as being very cold, perhaps because the front door was wide open, and a rather helpless November sun was doing the best it could with a morning mist that lay about the house. He said almost as much to Vereker—Mottreux and Caithness were conducting a stilted conversation upon, so far as he could hear, their various visits to America—and Vereker answered that the door should be shut if he liked. "We don't notice the cold," he said.

"Don't you, indeed?" Roger said, feeling that it was like Vereker's cheek. He was a younger man—he was *apparently* a younger man. Looks were nothing to go by; Considine himself was enough to go by, and at that his momentary irritation passed and he said sincerely: "Don't you?"

"The body, after all, ought to be able to manage that," Vereker said, "to adjust itself, I mean, to whatever temperature it's in and enjoy it; that's why it's the delicate thing it is."

Roger said: "And if you shut the door and turned on a furnace suddenly—then?"

"Yes, *then*," Vereker said laughing. "All this wrapping up and unwrapping—it's so unnecessary. To do without food, that does take longer. But it's the same principle. Here's Nigel."

The House by the Sea

It was by the single Christian name (or the name which he had recovered from the misguided habits of the Christian church), Roger found, that his followers generally referred to him, partly in love, partly in submission, partly in mere recognition of his own unique quality, though they carried themselves to him with all the behaviour of respect possible.

He came in now from the drive with a general word of greeting for his own people, and particular salutations for Roger and Caithness, to the former already intimate, to the latter courteous but distant, as if to some hostile ambassador. After the greetings he said generally: "We shall have news to-day. I've felt it already."

"A premonition?" Caithness asked politely.

"Why do you despise premonitions?" Considine answered. "Let's go to breakfast, shall we? Of course," he went on, as they sat down, "if you mean the stupid blur of untrained sensation, that is, as it sounds, negligible. But if you can feel a country in its air can't you feel its people too? All last night I heard and felt them, the voices of the great towns and the small villages, the talk and the doubt and the terror. Early this morning I felt it all gathering into one, the solitary thoughts of the peasants and the determination of the financiers; it swayed one way and another as it came to me, it veered and shifted as winds do, but it blew against my spirit at last as the wind on my face, and I smelt the news that went on it. Suydler will give way."

"Can you feel a whole nation?" Roger cried.

"Why not?" Considine asked, almost gaily. "Didn't you feel the crowd round your gate when you saved the king? can't you, even in darkness, feel the passion of a crowd? And do you think it isn't possible for me to feel the purpose of a wider, less certain crowd? I can feel England as you can feel English verse. And they'll yield; they'll talk of peace."

"It's less possible than for you to hear them," the priest said. "They won't yield so easily." Roger heard the hostility of his voice, and remembered that to Caithness much more than to him, the figure which sat at the head of the table, breaking a thin piece of toast, was indeed the High Executive of Africa, by whose will the Christian missions had been massacred—priests and converts alike, going down before the rifles of their enemies. The thought shook him; lost in his own concern with what Sir Bernard mocked and he adored as the exalted imagination, he had forgotten of what the executive imagination was capable. It was not only debonair but ruthless. It had spared London, but rather from convenience and scorn, from the grace of its superior power, than from any more tender sentiment. He remembered, without any immediate connexion, that it was Wordsworth—the Wordsworth of his dream—who had exulted over the defeat of the English armies—certainly he had called it a truth most painful to record, but Roger, looking at Considine, excused Wordsworth. It was, certainly it was, a painful truth, but undeniably a truth, if any of the whole mad dream were true, that this was no matter of chat and comfort but of anguish and ecstasy. The quiet house had lulled him, as the sound of the sea in which men are at that moment drowning, and drowned men are furnishing food for shellfish, lulls the sleepy holiday-maker after food. Some other cold than November's touched Roger; he tried to think, and Wordsworth ran through him again, crying "Yea, Carnage is Thy daughter." Carnage . . . carnage . . . the High Executive was presiding over a changing world, and he who was following that summons was accepting the blood shed for that change. He was accepting blood, as all men do by living. But he knew it. He leaned back from the half-eaten breakfast. Considine was speaking.

"I don't say the English are frightened," he said, "they desire what they think rightness for Africa; also they do not willingly oppose ideas; also they—or some of them—desire wealth. They are divided, and Suydler will play for the rich. I can satisfy even the rich; I can buy them out. The Church fortunately has refused the secular arm.''

"Do you mock at it then?" Caithness demanded, he also having ceased to eat.

"It's more purely Christian than ever before," the other answered; "its nature is in complete defeat; there and there only it thrives. Your wife was right, Ingram; that's the choice between defeat and victory. But I've chosen victory and I have it. Will you eat no more? Then," he stood up, "you shall come with me, Ingram; for I've a visit to make. Mr. Caithness may go to his penitent if he chooses, or make his meditations anywhere about the house or the grounds. Presently I'll come to the king. Vereker, do you relieve the wireless man. Mottreux, will you be about in case the captain comes?"

They saluted and rose to their feet, as, taking Roger by the arm, he left the room. They went by corridors and stairs to the left wing of the house stretched backwards towards the sea, corresponding to another wing on the right. Between the two ran a verandah, a wide lawn, and a terrace, from which steps led down to a lower terrace, and so on to the edge of the cliffs. And as they went the young man felt everywhere something of that sense of distance which he had experienced in the hall on the previous night—a distance in which all near things existed in a peculiar natural order. The house might have been one of those mythical buildings which in various legends have been lifted from the earth by music, as Troy rose to Apollo's harping or Pandemonium

> *like an exhalation with the sound*
> *Of dulcet symphonies.*

There were no pictures, so far as he could see; instead, the walls were covered with soft hangings, of different colours, but each colour richer than ever he had seen it before. Here and there these deep tapestries were worked with shapes, mostly, so

173

far as he could discern, symmetrical designs, though occasionally a human or non-human figure showed—a man or a winged monster or even a small complex city thick with houses and crowds. But Roger could not see them very well and he was not allowed to pause to examine them. Considine walked on, humming to himself, and again Roger recollected with a curious shock that this mature easy form, moving so lightly and gaily beside him, was the High Executive of African ecstasies. Suddenly he recognized the words into which Considine had changed his humming and exclaimed, almost stopping—"But that's Shakespeare!"

> "—shall I live now
> Under the blossom that hangs on the bough—

Yes," Considine answered. "D'you think Shakespeare didn't know something of it? Yet you must have lectured on the *Tempest*."

"If you mean that Shakespeare believed in the Second Evolution of Man——" Roger rather desperately began.

"He imagined its nature," Considine answered. "Think of it—and read Ariel's songs. Not that you'll understand them yet. Nor do I. Perhaps no-one will—properly—until after the conquest of death. He is your greatest poet because none but he has so greatly lived and died and lived in his verse. 'On the bat's back'—that's the purity of being. He imagined it. But here"—he paused at the door of a room, and his voice became graver—"is the physical experiment."

He opened it and they went in. It was a large high room, and there moved in it continually a little tender breeze, as of spring, though there were no windows, or, if there were, they were hidden behind the pale yellow hangings which here also hid the walls. They shook, ever so faintly, in the movement of the air, and it seemed to Roger for a few moments as if everywhere great fields of daffodils trembled in that gentle wind.

174

The vague suggestion passed, and left in its stead a thought of a universal sun shedding a golden presence through clear air, and then that again vanished, and he knew they were only wonderfully wrought hangings, and some beautiful light diffused itself over them. In the middle of the room there was a low divan, on which lay a motionless figure. In one corner was a chair on which a man sat, who, as they paused in the entrance, rose and came over to them. Otherwise the room was bare.

Roger looked again at the motionless figure on the divan, gazing at it in a sudden recollection. He knew the face, he had seen it rapt into an ardent intention, offering itself to death and to the High Executive of death. He turned sharply to Considine. "But it's Nielsen," he said.

Considine nodded, and said to the watcher of the dead, "There's no news?"

"None, sir," the man said. "He hasn't stirred or breathed."

"It's seven days," Considine said absently, and walked across the room to the couch where the dead man lay. Roger followed him, his heart beating more quickly than usual. What—what was expected, here and now?

Considine seemed to feel the unspoken question. He said, still looking at Nielsen: "We're waiting for the result."

Roger said: "You're waiting for him to live?"

"If it may be," Considine answered. "He was a strong spirit." He knelt down by the couch and looked intently into the dead man's eyes. Roger waited, growing more troubled every moment with terrible expectation. This man had intended passionately to succeed in his unpreluded task; he had meant to live. Could so high and strong a purpose break laws which only gods and sons of gods had suspended in the past? Lazarus, the tale ran, had been drawn back from death by supernatural grace, but was it also—was it only—in the power of natural man by natural laws to conquer death? Was the old symbolism of the mysteries true in its reversal? was the supernatural itself but a visionary exhalation of the natural, and could it hold nothing but what the natural held? As he stood gazing a shock went through him, for it seemed to him that a quiver passed over the dead man's face. Considine stiffened where he knelt, and threw out a hand to beckon the third watcher who ran quietly and silently to the other side of the couch. He also knelt, and together the two concentrated themselves on the again unchanging figure. It was motionless in the self-closed stillness of the dead; pallor had touched it, and yet a pallor which—and again the smallest quiver seemed to pass through the dead face. Roger thought to himself, "It's a trance, it's epilepsy, it's——" But Considine was there, and he did not believe—even in that wild rational effort to explain away a thing which hadn't happened and wouldn't and couldn't happen he did not believe—that Considine made mistakes of this kind. The man had meant to die; undoubtedly on that evening in Hampstead he had meant to die. This was no booby show, no conjurer's trick; it was man at the extreme point of his powers sending all those powers to the enlargement of his dominion. The master of the adepts kneeled there, seeking to aid the initiate through the experiment which he himself, called to a different duty, had not yet dared, as the Pope aided St. Francis on a more glorious business than his own. Roger steadied himself; if man could attempt this man could watch the attempt. This was his first test and he would not fail. He would open himself to the knowledge, to the experience of the sight, he would fill himself with it; who could tell but one day he, he himself, might lie on such a couch to await and compel such a . . . resurrection?

It was—it was happening. The eyelids flickered. Considine's gaze was fixed on them; he was leaning forward as if to catch the first glimpse of the returning consciousness, to meet and hold it lest it should fail. A ripple—of darkness or light seemed to pass down the body; in the infinitesimal vibration of all its hues none could tell whether it were darkness or light that shook it. The eyelids flickered again; Roger caught himself in the midst of a passionate wish that they should open; they might hold madness or horror; they might strike him and blast him with their power or splendour or ungodly terror. Or they might be gay—gay beyond all dreaming: "merrily, merrily shall I live . . . " No; he couldn't bear such piercing glee—"on a bat's back"—death the bat ridden and flown by a laughing joy. He couldn't bear it; he looked at Considine, and for a brief fraction of a second Considine's eyes flashed at him and away, but in that swift meeting Roger felt command and nourishment and burning expectation, and in its power he set himself again to await revelation.

But for awhile it seemed as if all was done. The body was again rigid and there lay before the straining eyes only the awful barricade of death. Roger thought suddenly how absurd it was—all this abstraction and personification; there was no such thing as death, there were only dead men and dead things. Men tried to make dead men bearable, comprehensible, friendly, by giving to them a general name. Death as an imagined person might be terrifying, but he was, so imagined, human. But Death was nothing of the sort; Death was neither Azrael nor any other immortal shadowy being— it was only dead men and dead things. "Insubstantial Death is amorous"—even the poets pretend; no, not always—"O but to die and go we know not where . . ." and to come back.

It moved. The hand extended along the couch moved, simultaneously with what seemed a breath. Roger strangled a cry. The hand jerked again, so tiny a jerk that only its force made it perceptible. Something was trying to move that rigid organism, and not quite succeeding. But the signs of its presence spasmodically showed. The nostrils quivered slightly; the lips just parted. The fingers twitched.

Considine said: "Help him then," and at once the third

man leapt into activity, and others who had silently entered the room behind Roger, unnoticed by his fascinated attention, ran softly up. He thought afterwards that some bell must have been rung by the other watcher when first the body had stirred, and that these had gathered in readiness. They were about the dead man; they concerned themselves busily with it; they did this and the other, Roger didn't very well know what, for he was trying not to hope they would be unsuccessful. All the time Considine hardly moved, save to put himself in a more convenient position for the workers; all the time his eyes remained fixed on those closed eyes, and his will waited for the moment when it could unite itself with the restored will of the dead.

After so much toil and vigil they failed. What time was spent there Roger hardly knew. But suddenly he knew a difference in the body about which they stood or moved. It changed to a more dreadful pallor; a greyness crept over it. Beyond the knowledge even of the adept it endured withdrawal; the kingdom so nearly grasped fell away. The neophyte of death was swallowed up in death; beyond all earlier semblance, and before their eyes, he died indeed. Considine signed to the workers to cease; he said to them: "Look," and they obeyed. He said again: "Look, look as masters. Don't lose a moment; change this into victory within you. Death here shall be life in you; feel it, imagine it, draw it into yourselves; as with all experience, so with this. Live by it; feed on it and live."

But he himself rose to his feet, and with a sign to Roger to accompany him went out of the room. In silence they went back to the hall, then Considine spoke. "Now you shall rest," he said. "It's failed this time, but we shall succeed yet, and you'll see it or hear of it. Meanwhile, do what you can to make this sight part of you and make it part of your will to immortality and victory. If you want food it's here. Presently I'll come to you again; we're hardly likely to move to-day. But now I must go to the king."

He nodded and moved off, and presently Caithness, sitting in talk by the king's bed in an upper room, heard the door open, and looking round saw him in the entrance. The priest stood up abruptly and Inkamasi stirred.

"How is our guest?" Considine asked. "Have you convinced him how wasteful vengeance is, Mr. Caithness? and therefore what folly?"

Caithness said, with almost a sneer, "It's fitting for *you* to talk of folly and waste—you who spend the blood of the martyrs for your own foolishness. Why have you come here?"

"For a better reason than you came to Hampstead not so long ago," Considine answered. "It wasn't a wise night, that, for because of that the king must choose his future to-day. You should have kept to your pupils, Mr. Caithness, to the morals you understand and the dogmas that you don't. But you must leave us now for I must talk to the king."

Caithness looked at Inkamasi. "If you want me to stay," he began but the other shook his head. "Go, if you will," he said; "it's best that he and I should understand each other. I'll remember better this time."

Considine held the door for the priest, closed it, and came to the chair by the bed. He paused there and smiled down at Inkamasi. "Have I your permission to sit down, sir?" he asked, and his voice was moved with strength such as the king never remembered in all their strange intercourse.

"Is this another insult?" he asked, restraining anger.

"It isn't anything of an insult," Considine said, "and you should know it. Haven't I made you what you are, and could I insult the thing I've restored? Therefore I will have an answer —have I your permission to sit?"

The king made a movement with his hand. "I think you've only fooled me," he answered bitterly, "but you can play with me as you choose—only I know it now. Sit or stand, do what you will, I can only watch you and at bottom defy you."

Considine sat down and looked with serious and friendly eyes at the man he called his guest. There was a little silence, then with equal gravity and friendliness he began to speak.

"Don't think," he said, "that in speaking to you by royal titles I do anything out of accord with what I've done in the past. I have always, so far as I could, done according to the gospel which moves in me and my friends, the doctrine of transmutation of energy, of the conscious turning of joy and anguish alike into strength and will, and of that passionate strength and will into the exploration of all the capacities of man. Such men as the priest who was with you just now will tell you to endure or enjoy because this and that is the will of God—at best but a few of them will tell you to use experience as a way of uniting yourself with God. In all the generations of Christendom how many have done that? But I do not turn men to any such remote end; I tell them that they are themselves gods, if they will, and the ecstasy of that knowledge is their victory. Your grandfather in his degree believed in that doctrine though he was an old man when he heard of it and the great triumphs were not for him. But he knew that if Africa was to be held up as a torch to the races that sat in cold and darkness it was necessary that they should be gathered into peace between themselves other than that which the Northern invaders imposed upon them. Therefore we drew those of the chiefs who did not believe, or their sons, into the potential power of the hypnotic sleep; it was so done with the heirs of all the thrones of Africa. It was never the intention of the High Executive—of us who execute the power of the fiery imagination among men—to use that compulsion if those royalties should seem naturally to accept our purpose. But you remember, sir, that your father and you desired Europe rather than Africa, and sooner than attempt to turn your whole nature into a state and process alien to it I proposed to myself only to keep in touch with you and to use you if necessary to keep the Zulus who obey you in peace and alliance with the other African races. I do not conceive that such an action needs defence. My alternative was to destroy you and to let your cousin who now leads your people, holding the sceptre of Chaka and passionately devoted to our cause, be the inheritor of your royalty. But because you in fact were that royalty, because the tradition of royalty is one of the admirable and passionate imaginations of mankind, I was unwilling to do this. If necessary I would bind the king outwardly, but I would neither slay him nor attempt to govern his mind."

"I would rather you had slain me," Inkamasi said, "than held me in such bondage."

"The cords have not been strained," Considine answered. "Save for those few days in my own house, and for my knowledge of your ways, you have been always free. But now, not, I grant, by my will you are free indeed. You belong wholly to yourself, and I who am the son of the interior knowledge of rapture salute the rapture of kingship, the incarnation of government and order and immortality."

"You talk vainly," the king said, "for my cousin leads my people, and there is no place for me on earth. Will you remove my cousin and set me at the head of the Zulus?"

"I will not prevent your return to them," the other answered again, "but I think you know that the rifles of his guard await you. And if not, if you are greeted again with the royal salute, and your armies follow you, will you set them for your sake against all the Powers of Africa? For I do not think you believe in the schools or in the exploration of love and wonder and death."

"I am a Christian," Inkamasi said. "I believe that love and death are at the feet of Jesus who is called Christ."

"Believe what you will," said Considine. "You know what we declare to the initiates of Africa. Will you join us to seek the way by which man descends living into the grave and returns?"

"I will not seek it," the other replied. "It has been opened once and it is enough. And you—are you sure that man can conquer till he has been wholly defeated? are you sure that he can find plenitude till he has known utter despair? You will not let him despair of himself, but it may be that only in such a complete despair he finds that which cannot despair and is something other than man."

"There are many reasons for avoiding the work, and all religions have excused man," the other's voice said. "Despair if you will, and hope that despair may save you. Entreat the gods; I do not refuse you your prayer."

"There's a submission we're slow to understand," Inkamasi cried out, "a place where divinity triumphed—I believe in that."

"Be it so," the answer came; "but tell me then what you will do."

There was a long pause before the king said: "I know there is no place for me upon earth."

"There is place and enough for Inkamasi," Considine answered. "There is no place in Africa for Inkamasi the king. You best know whether there is a place in Europe. You know whether your friends downstairs and in London receive that royalty as I receive it."

"They have all courtesy and good will, but they have forgotten the Crown," Inkamasi said. "They do not mock me but they do not believe."

"They are sons without a mother," Considine went on, "for they know neither the Crown nor the Republic. Royalty is a shade and Equality not yet born. What is the difference between these traditions to me so long as either is held and is a passion? But most men are empty of both. And if I must choose I will choose the king and not the State, for the king is flesh and blood and yet undying, and is a symbol of that we seek."

"Am I left," Inkamasi asked, "to find my only servants in my enemies?"

"It seems," Considine answered, "even so, that I and I only am the friend of the king."

"And what will the king's friend offer the king in his superfluousness?" Inkamasi asked again.

"I have only two things to give," Considine said; "let the royalty of the king choose which he will take from a believer in him. I will offer a house and servants and money, all that he needs, and he may live contented with his knowledge of his own inheritance. Or I will give the king a royal death."

"There will be none to hamper you then," Inkamasi said with a sudden smile.

"There is none to hamper me now," Considine answered gravely. "For the majesty of the king is in my care and on my side, and if the king choose to live without his majesty, though the choice is his own, he will choose to live in a dream. I am the keeper of the strength of royalty; what is outside me is Europe, and that the king knows."

"Yet I thought Europe would aid me to aid my people," Inkamasi meditated aloud—"law and medicine and science."

"They are good in their place, but the question is whether these things can take the place of greater," Considine answered. "But the choice is for the king. Only it must be to-day. To-morrow the submarine returns to Africa, and there are three ways in which the king may go in her. I will have him taken to his people and set among them, that he may try the fates between himself and the man who now rules them, and who inherits royalty if Inkamasi dies. Or I will send him as my friend till peace is signed and he may live a private man wherever he chooses on the face of the earth."

"And the third way?" Inkamasi asked.

"He shall go clothed with royalty and death," Considine said. "I will come when night falls to know the king's mind."

He stood up and went down on one knee, and then moved backwards to the door. There in silence he waited a moment, opened it, and went out.

Inkamasi lay through the afternoon considering all that had been said. The suggestion which had been made to him not only received additional force from the fact that it had been presented as one among several possibilities, but drew its chief strength from the tendencies of his own mind. He knew very well that, of all those by whom he was, or was likely to be surrounded, Considine alone had such intense appreciation of royalty as he himself had. Nor did his own bitter dislike blind him to the fact that his first attempt upon the other had failed, and that to concentrate the rest of his life upon remedying that failure would be not only undignified but treasonable. The king might hate, but his duty was to his own kingship first and always. How to save and serve that must be the first thing in his mind. But for this a life in England among his new circle of friends seemed useless enough. He had a sudden vision of himself growing old, harping upon the tradition which was his, regarded at best as a feeble sentimental survival, at worst as a mere bore. All his profound romanticism rejected the prospect. But to live as Considine proposed would be little better. He would be pitied by himself instead of by others; he would dig his own pit of sentimentality instead of having it dug for him, but the pit would be as deep and fatal.

There was a course Considine had not named, to try and forget that he was the king, to settle down to ordinary work, here or abroad, and submit himself to the idea of the Government, whatever it might be, under which he might find himself: accepting his dispossession simply and sincerely. And this, had there been no alternative, he might have done. But once that alternative had been suggested the colour of the thought of it tinged all his attempts to choose. For though the man Inkamasi might not kill himself—so his creed taught—yet the king had a duty to his kingship. So far as might be, it must never be surrendered; and here was a way by which it might be surrendered in a beauty and greatness equal to its own. Examining himself for the last time, Inkamasi knew that

in turning to Europe he had desired Europe for the sake of
Africa; that he had studied logic and medicine and law for the
sake of the king and his people, and that the king might the
better benefit and govern and be one with his people. He did
not care for the high abstractions of thought; when he talked
of them it was when he took his ease in his private circle and
amused himself as other kings had amused themselves with
jest or hunt or song. And now, the child of unknown things, he
set his face to go up to Jerusalem, that the king's crown might
be properly received by the unvestmenting hands of Death.
Peace entered in on him and he lay looking out of the window,
watching the November twilight gather, and uniting within
himself, not in such a twilight but in a more wonderful union
of opposites, the day of his own individual being and the
mysterious night of his holy and awful office.

Chapter Twelve

THE JEWELS OF MESSIAS

For some time after Considine had left him Roger did nothing. He sat on the verandah and looked out over the grass lawn and the terrace at the sea which lay beyond. And he thought to himself that never in his life had he felt so much, so idiotically, like a baby as he did now. Apart from that recurrent thought he couldn't think. "It's the shock," he said, half-aloud from time to time, but without convincing himself of anything whatsoever, without indeed particularly wanting to convince himself.

A movement or two of a dead hand, of the hand of a man whom even Considine had now abandoned. It had failed, but it had come very near to succeeding. Roger—product of at least a semi-culture of education and intellect—sat there and felt that culture and education and intellect had all vanished together, all but the very simplest intellect. Even his passion for literature had disappeared; he simply wasn't up to it—he had no more wish or capacity for Milton or Shakespeare than a small child, who might laugh if some of the lines were mouthed at him but would be lost and vacant-eyed if anyone tried to explain them or quoted them seriously. That dead hand moving had abolished the whole edifice of his mind; he sat and stared at the sea. In London things had been different; he had been thrilled and romanticized. In London there was no sea, and no golden-hung rooms with a couch on which a dead man lay. In London these things didn't happen. He had heard and believed, but here belief was abolished; he was confronted with the simple fact. It had to be accepted, and its acceptance was what reduced him to a state of infancy.

The Jewels of Messias

The sea—he couldn't look at the shore from where he sat; only at the terrace and the sea beyond—the sea was different. He wondered, vaguely, whether it was Africa, or whether both sea and Africa were names for something else, a full power, an irresistible mass: irresistible if it moved, but then it didn't move. Or hadn't. Hadn't was a better word, because it might. All that mass of waters might gather itself up and surge forward—surge or creep, swiftly or slowly, anyhow irresistible. But he, sitting there, with the memory of that dead hand jerking—as if a sudden wave had flopped forward out of the sea over the green lawn, and then retreated again, and the whole vast mass had swung silent and removed once more. If the mass followed after a while, followed the wave? He would live in it, he would be changed so as to breathe and bear it; he would see what other inhabitants peopled it—there might be one chief thing, a fish of sorts, a swift phosphorescent fish which was called Considine on earth before the sea came. Or if the sea were merely a flat plain for something else to slide over, a huge Africa in the shape he knew from maps sliding over the water—only of course *not* sliding, but marching, millions on millions of black manikins, so small, so very small, but so many, marching forward, yet keeping that mapped shape, and he would be just their size and be marching with them—left, right; left, right. Whether they were alive or dead he couldn't say; the fellow who was marching either opposite him or alongside him—it wasn't clear which—kept quivering and jerking his hand. Hosts of them—Lord of hosts; he had known the Lord of hosts when he was called Considine, and rode on a bat's back; these were the bats. Why was he here among this crowd of bats with negro faces that rose out of that ocean, now throbbing free from the ties which had so long held it? And all the bats were singing—"Fathom five, fathom five; rich and strange." There they were, all coming on; he himself had called them and they were coming.

He heard, but did not notice, a step beside him. Then a

voice he half-recognized said: "Here you are!" It was Caithness's voice, and with the recognition Roger's trance broke. He shifted, looked round, realized that he was cold, stood up, stamped once or twice, and said: "Yes, here I am. But don't," he added, as his mind came more to itself, "ask me where."

"It's a strange place," Caithness said. "He must have many of them, scattered about. Near London, for the airships to land. How's he kept himself hidden all these years?"

"I suppose," Roger said flippantly, "the exalted imagination suggested it. Shakespeare was a good business man."

He found a certain relief in talking to the priest, however different their views of Considine, as an ordinary Christian might find it easier to talk to an atheist than to a saint. It wouldn't last, but just for a little it was pleasant and easy.

But Caithness, not having gone so far, was not so desirous of reaction. He said, looking gloomily at the young man: "I don't know what you find in him. Where did he take you?"

Roger looked out to sea again, and half-unconsciously said, "There." The sea should give up its dead, out of the sea of universal shipwreck the dead sailors of humanity should rise again, their bodies purified by the salt of that ocean, running up to a land which perhaps then they would feel and know for the first time in its full perfection: matter made purely sensitive to matter, and all the secrets of the passion of life revealed. Who could tell what wonders waited then, when emotion was full and strong and sufficient, no longer greedy and grasping, when the senses could take in colour and essence and respond to all the delicate vibrations which now their clumsy dullness missed, when deprivation itself should be an intense means of experiencing both the deprived self and the thing of which it was deprived, when—O when space and time were no more hindrances, when (for all one could tell) the body itself might multiply itself, as certain magicians had been said to do, and truly be here and there at once, or—

"Come then," he prayed, but did not know to whom, "master of life, come quickly."

"It's cold out here," he heard Caithness say abruptly, "let's go in. Have you seen Rosenberg?"

Roger, as he half-reluctantly turned to follow, thought of the Jew with a shock. "No," he said. "I'd forgotten him."

"I wonder what this man means to do with him," the priest went on. "Colonel Mottreux has brought the famous jewels." There was a light sneer in his voice, and Roger knew that the desire and delight of the late Simon Rosenberg was utterly incomprehensible to Caithness. Yet it should not have been so, he thought, for was there after all so much difference between minds that longed to see their own natures made manifest, the one in converted and beautiful souls adorned with virtues, the other in a chosen and beautiful body adorned with jewels? Certainly Caithness thought it was for the good of the souls, but no doubt Rosenberg thought that his wife enjoyed wearing the jewels, and very likely she did. Certainly, also, on Caithness's hypothesis, the souls were likely to enjoy their kind of beauty for a much longer time than Mrs. Rosenberg, even if she hadn't died when she did, could possibly have enjoyed hers. So that Caithness was actually likely to get more satisfaction out of his externalized desire than Rosenberg. But for that you must have a supernatural hypothesis, and the fact that a supernatural hypothesis had quite definite advantages didn't make it true. The fact that man wanted a thing very much never did make it true—or the body that lay within would now perhaps be walking in the house and even coming up to speak to him. . . . He shuddered involuntarily, no more in servile than in holy fear, and to escape from that hovering awe said: "Have they been given to Rosenberg yet?"

"No," Caithness answered. "I don't fancy Considine's all that anxious to part with them."

Roger looked at him in surprise. They had come into the room where they had breakfasted, from which doors of an exquisitely clear glass led on to the lawn in front of the house. The priest walked across and looked out. Roger said, rather coldly: "That's utterly unnecessary. Do you hate him so much?"

"I don't hate him," Caithness said, "except that he's set himself against God, like Antichrist which is to come."

"O don't be silly," Roger said crossly. "Antichrist indeed! What on earth has he done to make you think he'd steal a lot of jewels?"

"What's he done," the priest said over his shoulder, "to make *you* think he wouldn't? Hasn't he put many men to death and stolen the minds of others? If he wants the jewels he'll take them."

"But he *won't* want them," Roger exclaimed; "that's the whole point. I may, or for all I know Mottreux may, but he's no more likely to want them than you are, to be fair to you," he added with a half-humorous admission of Caithness's own integrity.

The door opened, and Mottreux and Rosenberg came into the room. The old Jew looked at them for a moment and then went across to the other side of the room and sat down. Mottreux paused by the door, seeming not to have expected to find the other two there. His dark and hungry eyes rested on Roger and moving towards him, he said in a low voice, "I hear Nielsen has really died."

The sentence itself seemed fatal; in its note of hopelessness it conveyed death. Roger, not finding words to answer, nodded. Mottreux walked slowly over to Rosenberg, to whom he began to talk in a low voice. Caithness, after a minute or so, went over to join them. Roger considered doing the same thing and decided not to. He didn't want to chat, and he couldn't see what, besides mere chat, Mottreux and Rosenberg could have to say to each other. Mottreux, he remembered, was supposed to be waiting for the captain, whoever the captain was. His mind went back to the sea, and he thought suddenly

of submarines. Perhaps that was what Considine had meant
by "moving." It was all such a mad mixture, purple rhetoric
and precise realism, doctrines of transmutation and babble
about African witch-doctors and airships and submarines. He
wondered what Isabel was doing, and whether perhaps after
all he would have been wiser to stop . . . but he couldn't, he
couldn't; the thing that for years had torn at his heart and
brain had to be satisfied. He and she had alike to choose
necessity. But if his necessity could have lain with hers. . . . And
Sir Bernard—what would he have made of this house where
servants of impossibilities talked by the hearth, and he himself
waited for the next moment of explication? Staring at his toes,
Roger thought that that was all he did seem to be doing—
waiting. Was he wasting his time? had Considine meant him
to be doing something all this while? He ought to have been
working, to have imagined intensely the . . .

Considine was in the room. To Roger's preoccupied mind
he might have materialized out of the air, but apparently he
hadn't. He said, "There's no message yet. Mottreux, I'll
dictate the alternative dispositions for the generals, if you will
come. These gentlemen will be able to amuse themselves a
little." He came over to Roger and looked into his eyes, then
he said, smiling, "You've been running after your fancies,
Ingram; you've not been driving even their faint power
through you. Do you think it will happen by itself?"

"I know," Roger said. "I was thinking so—'They heard
and were abashed and up they sprang.' "

"So," Considine answered. "Turn on to that all your heart;
and then turn that on to yourself. Don't let yourself grow
too tired, but never quite let go. We'll talk again soon."
He turned.

"Mottreux?"

The other joined him and they went across the hall into
another room, where a case stood on the table. "There are
Rosenberg's jewels," Considine said. "We'll give them to him

presently; let's look at them once." He took a key from his
pocket and opened the case as he spoke, and then poured upon
the table a glowing heap of jewels. They shone and sparkled;
they gleamed and glinted—some set, many unset; stones of
every kind revealing the life of stone, colour revealing the
power of colour. Considine stood and looked at them, and
if Roger had been there he might have thought that the heap of
jewels and the human figure reflected each other, and that
intense life leapt and re-leapt between them. The man's form
seemed to hold in itself depths of mysterious tint; so clear and
mysterious was the corporeal presence, disciplined and purged
and nourished through many decades by supreme passion.
The deep smile broke out again as he gazed, exulting in the
joy of beauty, absorbing it, and almost visibly transmuting it
into his own dominating awareness of it. He stretched out his
hand and picked up one or two, and a whole diadem of
splendour faded by the unparalleled delicacy of consum-
mated mortality which held it. He laid them down and
laughed softly as he did so, humming again to himself,
" 'Under the blossom that hangs on the bough.' All this," he
added aloud, "but one blossom under which we live for a
moment. Yet they are almost worthy Messias."

But Mottreux leant nearer them, and turned an agonized
face towards his master.

"You are giving them back," he whispered. "You won't
surely?" His hands trembled forward towards the heap. "It's
. . . it's life," he said grasping, and fell on his knees by the table.

Considine looking down at him laid a hand on his shoulder.
"Do you feel them so?" he asked, and felt the answer shudder
through the kneeling man's limbs as he turned his face
upwards.

"Don't give them back," he moaned, "don't shut them up!
they're breath, they're everything, they're me! Don't keep
them in a box—unless I keep it! Give them to me! You don't
want them. You don't care for their life, you've got all the

life you want. I tell you they're like woman, they're more than woman: who ever saw a woman quiver like that? quiver and be so still? I want to grow to them, don't take them away. I haven't asked you much, I'll do anything you want. Tell me someone to kill. I'll give you his blood for these stones. I'll give you my blood for them—only let me love them a little, let me hold them while you kill me. O they'll kill me themselves, they're so merciless. Can't you feel them? Can't you feel them melting into you? Or is it that I'm melting? I . . .I . . . " His voice choked with his passion and stopped.

Considine leant over him. "Now, Mottreux, now," he said, "remember the end of the experiment. Be master of love, be master of death! Change delight that is agony into that agony that is delight. Not for possession, not for yourself, achieve and transmute desire." Standing behind him he pressed his hands on the other's shoulders, till Mottreux crouched under the weight. "Not for a dream like the poor wretch who died but for the power and glory of life, for the marriage of death and love, and for the dominion that comes from them. Mottreux, Mottreux! you that live to beauty, die to beauty!"

But Mottreux, as the pressure relaxed, sprang to his feet and leant half over the table with a snarl.

"They are my life," he said, "who touches them touches me."

"Remember those who have failed on the threshold of achievement," Considine answered. "You seek a deeper thing than these stones hold—you seek the mastery of death. Destroy them then, and enter farther into the chambers of death. But if you touch one to keep or to destroy, for greed or desire, or lest others should gain, you are lost, Mottreux. If you possess you are lost."

"It's not true," the tormented creature exclaimed, and went on hurriedly. "Don't you possess—money and houses and lands? Don't you say that a man can grow by the ecstasy which the things he possesses give him? a miser by gold, and a lover by woman?"

"If the chance of the world throws things into his hands, let him take them," Considine answered; "if it tears them from him let him forsake them. It need make no difference to him. As for me, I use what I have for the purpose of the schools. But if it were all caught away to-morrow what change would it cause in me? The man who prefers possession to abandonment is lost. You've come far, Mottreux, by experience of hunting and war; you've grown and thriven on that rapture. Thrive now on this; all this pain is but your power seeking its proper end."

"Nielsen sought it and he's dead," the other cried out. "It can't be done; it's wilder than all dreams. Haven't others in Uganda and Nigeria tried it and failed?"

"And Jersey and London," Considine said. "More than you'll ever know. Will you disbelieve because a million have failed? One shall succeed and others and their children shall have it in their blood. Leave Nielsen; leave all. Leave this."

He moved to face the other and meeting his eyes held them with so strong a power that Mottreux turned his own eyes away.

But he moaned desperately, "I can't—not this. Anything else—not this."

"Are you a fool?" Considine said, "it's always anything else, and it's always *this*. How will you die indeed if you daren't die now? There's not a man in all this world who doesn't have to relinquish; it's given to us to do it willingly and make our profit from it. Strike and live in the wound."

"But you won't give them back?" Mottreux cried. "At least keep them yourself; don't give them away."

"Certainly I shall give them," Considine answered, "for it's better that they should serve a myth than a man, and if I were to keep them now I should take the kingdom of man away from you——"

As he paused, there was a sharp knock at the door. Considine thrust Mottreux round so that the tormented face was hidden, and cried a word over his shoulder. Vereker came into the room. "Sir, the message is here," he said.

"I'll come," Considine answered, and as Vereker went out he gathered the jewels in his hands and poured them back into the case. Mottreux leaned against the table; he could not speak; he gazed as the traveller whose camel has just fallen might stare after the vanished mirage or as a young boy might when the beloved of his heart gives her sacred hand into another's charge. Considine locked the case, dropped it back on the table, slipped his hand into Mottreux's arm, and drew him from the room.

Meanwhile the three guests, centrifugally repulsed by the very ardour which united them, remained for some time in the one room. They were aware, as they sat there, of increased movement in the house; new voices came to them, and the occasional sound of cars arriving or departing. The expectancy of crisis was heightened, and Caithness who was the most open to external impressions, was the first to give way. Ezekiel still sat, lost in meditation on antique words, by the fireplace; brooding over the manner in which the High and Holy One had in the secret story of Joseph or of David, in the hidden sayings of Ruth or Esther, signified the return of Israel to His pardon. Roger, concerned with other texts, sought to bring into his memory of them the emotion awakened by the sight he had endured; he attempted to realize the august periods of time and space which exist in and are measured by the mastery of poetry. Lines came to him from a distance, but it was not exterior distance; it was himself whose leagues lay between himself and their origin, and all that space of self was no longer void but tremulous with unapprehended life. He had always, it seemed, been too close to them; he understood how small his feeble little understanding was. They rose from an abyss —they had always said so—"the mind's abyss"—"that awful Power rose from the mind's abyss"—his mind's abyss—it would lead him into the abyss—it would define the abyss for him—the powers that inhabited it were his powers——O how little, how little, did the most ardent reader know what mysteries lay in "the mystery of words"——

> *There darkness makes abode, and all the host*
> *Of shadowy things work endless changes; there*
> *As in a mansion like their proper home—*

he wondered for a fantastic instant if it were this house which was indeed their home.

But Caithness's mind was not on such exploration. The nature of his intellect and the necessities of his office had directed his attention always not towards things in themselves but towards things in immediate action. He defined men by morality; it was perhaps inevitable that he should define God in the same way. The most difficult texts for him to explain away had always been those which obscurely hint at the origin of evil itself in the Unnameable, "the lying spirit" of Zedekiah, the dark question of Isaiah—"Shall there be evil in the city and I the Lord have not done it?" He was always trying to avoid Dualism, and falling back on the statement that Omniscience might permit what it did not and could not originate, yet other origin (outside Omniscience) there be none. It is true he always added that it was a mystery, but a safer line was to insist that good and evil were facts, whatever the explanation was. True as this might be, it had the slight disadvantage that he saw everything in terms of his own good and evil, and so imperceptibly to resist evil rather than to follow good became the chief concern of his exhortations. So perhaps the great energies are wasted; so perhaps even evil is not sufficiently resisted. His mind now was full of Inkamasi's defiance; his own pet miracle seemed to justify him, and he thought of himself in relation to the king as the chief champion of Christendom against Antichrist. It was also a little annoying to be treated as if he were in an elementary stage of his own religion, and a personal rancour unconsciously reinforced the devotion of his soul to its hypothesis.

He went out of the room, intending to go back to the Zulu, and saw that the house was indeed more populated than it had been. He saw several new faces in the hall; there were two or three officers in a strange dark-green uniform. One man had a face like an Arab; there was another who might be an Italian. He heard a voice say "Feisul Pasha," and saw a third cross the hall from the front door. He turned abruptly, ran up the stairs, and on the first landing met Mottreux.

The colonel was coming slowly along; his face was pale and wrenched. As he saw Caithness he paused, and the priest instinctively stood still also. So for a few moments they waited, duellists uncertain of what was to come. Mottreux said at last—as if it were not what he meant: "You're going to the king?"

"And if so?" Caithness asked. Something in Mottreux's voice puzzled him. It seemed to wish to delay him; it hesitated; he could have believed that it inquired about something which had not been mentioned.

Mottreux said abruptly: "I suppose you think we're all wrong?"

Caithness very shortly said he did, but the other did not step away. He added: "I suppose you—want us to fail?"

Caithness, again shortly, agreed. Mottreux came close up to him, looked round, began to whisper, and was suddenly taken by a spasmodic shudder. He caught the priest's arm and then let it go sharply, as if he had touched something hateful. He said in a low voice, "If one could . . ." and his voice died away.

In the tone of a director of souls Caithness said:"Could?"

"If one could—make peace," Mottreux whispered. "Would there—would there be room for a man who could make peace?"

He was close up against Caithness, and the priest, feeling

his agitation and shaken by it, dropped his voice to an equal whisper, "But how can—we shan't take his terms."

Mottreux said, "But without his terms?"

"How can you make peace without him?" Caithness asked.

"He isn't human," Mottreux jerked out. "If . . . if one caught a mad ape. . . ."

The truth flashed into Caithness's mind—the possible truth, and the possibility possessed him. In this strange house, amid strange inhabitants, had come the strangest whisper of all, a whisper of antagonism in the very heart of the enemy. His brain ran before him, forgetting everything but this impossible chance. He leaned a little closer yet, and said, "If you can't cage it——"

Mottreux answered, "You know the Prime Minister?"

"My friend does," Caithness said.

"If the ape were chained and caged?" Mottreux said. "If he were quite helpless?"

"If one were very sure," Caithness said, and dared not stop to ask what he meant.

There was an almost breathless stillness, then Mottreux said again, "He's not human; he's monstrous. He robs us of everything—of our souls!"

"He robs you of everything, of your souls most of all," the priest said, not knowing after what mingled mass of colour the other's spirit panted. Mottreux's face took on a sudden cunning, as if he plunged that secret deeper into his heart and veiled it there more securely. He said, "If anything should happen——"

"It would be a fortunate thing for the world," the priest said. "But," he added, "that's in the hands of God."

"Aye—God," the other answered. "But he behaves like God. If anything happened, would your friend——"

Caithness paused. He thought of Sir Bernard, and ironically with the thought there came the memory of his own visit to London, of his talk with the Archbishop, of his insistence that the Church must not use the secular arm. Yes—but he wasn't then in this house, so close against this mad dreamer; he hadn't seen the African horde dancing round the upright figure whom it worshipped, he hadn't heard of this blasphemy of the conquest of death. Never as an ordinary rule—never but when—never but, for this once, *now*—never afterwards, for this couldn't happen twice. And even now it wasn't he or his friends or the Church; it was the man's own follower. And the Zulu Christian would be saved from captivity, and Roger from delusion, and men from a lie. Now—just now—if this whisperer so close to him chose. . . .

"Anyone who saved England," he said, "anyone who did would be a friend to all men."

"You'd see that he was safe?" Mottreux urged. "You'd speak to Suydler? you'd keep me secret till it was right to have it known?"

"Of course," Caithness answered. "You should be with me till all was agreed; it would be easy. . . ."

There was a voice in the hall below; a door opened and shut. Someone came to the foot of the stairs. Mottreux nodded and stepped away, breathing only "Be ready then. I can't tell when it may be." He disappeared down the staircase, and Caithness after a few moments went slowly on to join the king.

Chapter Thirteen

THE MEETING OF THE ADEPTS

It was already dark. The sea was lost, and the drive in front of the house. Roger was alone, for Caithness had not returned from the king, and Rosenberg, though it was but late afternoon, had with a few muttered words gone back to his own room. No-one of the others had come in. Roger had read a little in one or other of the books scattered about—they were mostly what are called the "classics" of various times and languages. They were all in "privately printed" editions, exquisitely done with types he did not recognize and bindings whose colours were strange and beautiful combinations. There was one volume of the fragments of Sappho, another of the Song of Solomon, an Æschylus, a *Gallic War*, a *Macbeth*; there were one or two Chinese texts, and one or two which Roger supposed must be African—at least, the characters were altogether strange to him. There was a manuscript book, half filled with delicate mysterious writing, also in strange characters. He had read in some and looked at others; he had tried to search in them for the power which reposed there, and of which those Greek or English or unknown characters were sacramental symbols. And when he ceased and for a while half abandoned the search he was aware that he did not abandon it, as so often before, to return to an outer world of things different from the secret paths he had been following. Sometimes when he had been reading at home he had looked up to feel the rooms, the furniture—tolerable and even pleasant as it all was—in some sense alien to the sacred syllables. His own writing-table, comfortable and useful, blinked rather awkwardly at him when he returned from the visit of Satan to Eden or the nightingale in the embalmèd darkness. But here there was no such difficulty or distinction; all was natural. As a result of that most fortunate combination of mental and visible or audible things, the tiredness which often seized him in those moments was absent. For it was never great things in their own medium which wearied him; they—he had always known and now more than ever knew—were strength and refreshment; it was the change from one medium to another, the passing from their clear darkness to the fog of daily experience. But here there was no need to return; all was one.

He walked to the window, and looked out. But he could see nothing except the lights of a car standing in front of the door; he turned back into the room, and after hesitating for a minute or two went across it and out into the hall. There he saw a group of men, gathered round Considine. They were breaking up even while he glanced; each of them went off as on separate business. Considine stood alone. He stretched himself easily, smiled at Roger, and walked towards him.

"All's done," he said. "They've communicated from Africa. Your people are in touch with mine. I knew they would begin soon."

Roger, still struggling with a scepticism in political things which he had abandoned in spiritual, said: "It can't be possible that . . ."

"It's certain," Considine answered. "Suydler—what can Suydler do against us? He won't trust himself to flog the English on, nor to cheat the Powers that will want to cheat him. South Africa I will leave for fifty years or so; at the end of that time they'll be begging to come in. Let's go outside, shall we?"

They went out on to the verandah, and, as the coldness of the evening took them, veils seemed to fall away from Considine. Roger felt himself in the presence of maturity and power beyond his thought, perhaps something of that power into which he had been experimentally searching. The man by his side threw off the habitual disguise of years and behaviour which he wore; he moved like a "giant form," and though his eyes, when they rested on Roger, were friendly, their friend-liness was tremendous and wise and, as it might have been, archangelic. He walked lightly, pacing the verandah, and seemed not to depend on the floor to support him; Roger felt clumsy and awkward beside him, earth and a child of earth beside earth purified, infused and transmuted.

Considine said: "We shall go to-night. I've got one more thing to do here, and there's time enough for that."

"You always seem to have time to spare," Roger answered.

"Why not?" the other asked. "Every second is an infinity, once you can enter it. But man's mind sits outside its doors moaning, and leaves his activity to run about the world in a fever of excitement. You will leave that presently."

"How did you set out on this?" Roger asked diffidently. The impetuous angry Roger of London had disappeared; he walked as a child and as a child referred to his adults.

In the darkness Considine smiled. "This morning," he said, "a girl jilted a boy, and the boy said, 'Why do I suffer help-lessly? This also is I—all this unutterable pain is I, and I grow everywhere through it into myself.' I could show you the street where it happened—they haven't yet pulled it down—where the boy said, 'If this pain were itself power . . .'" So he imagined it as himself and himself as it, and because it was greater than himself he knew that he also was greater than himself, and as old and as strong as he chose. The girl's dead long ago; she was a pretty baby."

"But then?" Roger asked.

"Then—a little later—before noon," the voice answered, "the boy found another girl and loved her. But as that love spread through him he remembered the vastness of his pain and what had seemed to him possible because of it, and he asked himself whether love were not meant for something more than wantonness and child-bearing and the future that closes in death. He taught himself how this also was to charge his knowledge of what man could be, and he poured physical desire and mental passion into his determination of life. Then he was free."

Roger said: "But why Africa?"

"My father was a surgeon," the other answered, "though not a poor man, and he went on a ship, taking me with him. The ship was wrecked—it wasn't unusual then—but he and I were saved, and came to shore. I've told you that my father knew something of the old magical traditions—things I haven't much concerned myself with; such as are of value are natural properties of the developing and unstunted nature of man, and the rest are of no value—but by such tricks he made himself feared by the sorcerers. We went far into the inland before he died, and there I found that things which I'd discovered with pain were taught to the priestly initiates. But they held them secret and were afraid of them, and I knew they were for the world when the time should come. And now it has come."

"And the end," Roger cried out in a sudden access of desperation and hope, "what is the end?"

The other turned to confront him, but in the darkness Roger, full of cloudy memories and fiery prophecies, was uncertain what he faced. There had been in the movement something of Isabel, but it was not Isabel; he wondered whether it were not rather the lofty head of Milton, doctrinal yet mysterious, at which he was looking, but the eyes were not Milton's, for Milton was blind, and these eyes were shining at him in the night. It was rather—this figure—something that had to do with the sea the sound of which came to him still, the sea that had come up from its borders and been talking with him though he had not known it for what it was. So it was not eyes, it was light under the sea which he saw, and he was being swept away from human beings into the ocean gulfs and currents. He struck out as if he were swimming, but that did not ease the choking in his throat and nostrils nor the clamour in his ears. With all his power he drove upwards, and it seemed that his head broke out from the waves and beheld not very far off a shore on which his friends walked. He saw Sir Bernard looking ironically out over the waters in which he struggled, looking ironically at him, as if with a smile to see how the rash fool who has sailed on such a voyage now agonized for one plank to cling to. He saw Rosamond, her arm in Philip's, bending him away from the foam, and drawing him safely towards the highroads beyond. He saw Isabel, and her dress was drenched with spray, her dress and her hair, and she had stretched one firm arm towards the sea, and stood on the extreme edge of the land; but her eyes did not see him, and he could not tread water—he was whirled down again as if into the noise of a roaring dance, and again he choked and agonized and sprang upward through a thousand fathoms of water and emerged to see them again, but small, very small. As he gazed a tiny distant bell rang in his ears and called him— a bell far, far below: "ding dong bell, ding dong bell." Hark! now he heard it. It was not now those on the shore who neglected him; it was he who had to leave them on their shore. "Ding dong bell"; they were ringing for him, a knell and a summons at once. Because there was no other hope, he obeyed; he forced himself to cease from struggling, and from feet to lifted hands one direct line he shot downwards, down, down, to where the dead men lay. The noise in his ears might have been the shouting of many voices, crowds and armies, about their lord, or it might have been the sea uttering itself, its voice heard not in its own words but in a tremendous echo, sovereign for those who heard it, shaped into words: "Thus the Filial Godhead answering spake." The thunder of the speech crashed through him as he, assenting to it and to the sea which spoke it, dropped down through the speed of the depth. It was agony to let himself sink so, to release all that he loved, to fall through this alien element by which they

walked; it was pain, indescribable . . . indescribable . . . what?
—not pain but something else, an exquisiteness of pain which
was, now he realized it, not pain at all but delight. How many
there were, far away on that shore beyond him, who fancied
themselves in pain, and, could they know it, carried all delight
in their hearts! Man, through most of his poor ignorant
years, did not truly know what he felt; he was so habituated to
the past that he sighed when he should have laughed and
laughed when he should have sighed. The great passions
swept through him unrecognized till far off he saw the glory of
their departure, and cried out, "That was I." But in rare
moments he knew, and then what power was his! And, could
a man's body be always impregnated with this salt, as his
own was now, and infiltrated with this sea, he might always
know! His experience would always be new, for newness was
the quality of this everlasting and universal life. He knew
delight and named it; unafraid, he summoned it, and it came.
He rejoiced in an ecstasy that controlled itself in great tidal
breaths. He was no longer sinking but walking on the sand at
the great sea's bottom, only the sea was no longer there; he
was himself the sea and he walked in the sun over the yellow
sands. "Come unto these yellow sands." He himself—ocean
calling to ocean; to other seas that danced in a flooding
splendour. Ecstasy was no more a bewilderment; only those
who had not known it were afraid of it, for it was man's
natural life. In the stormy waters of the surface there was
danger and death, but, for those who would not fly from the
depths and the distances, those very depths and distances were
found to be part of their nature. Every step that he took was
delight; he sent out the cry of the released spirit: "Merrily,
merrily shall I live now."

Something lay on his forehead, obstructing him, as if it
were a hand; he laboured under it. It pressed on him, or he
against it, as if alien limitation controlled him; he stumbled
in his walk because it lay over his eyes and blinded him. A

great fear of blindness, of losing this most happy life, filled him. He threw up his hands to tear the obstruction away, and they too were caught and prisoned. He tore them loose; he flung back his head; he was convulsed with a spasm of agony, and he was standing in the darkness of a cold night under a wooden roof, and opposite him was the tall watchful figure of Nigel Considine.

There was a long silence; then Considine said, "It may be known and believed, it can't be lived thus. But it can be found and lived. Let us go in."

In the hall there were a group of some half-dozen; away from them, standing together, were Caithness and Rosenberg. Mottreux was moving about from one place to another. Roger joined his friends. Considine stood still and gathered their eyes and thoughts to himself; when that concentration was sufficient he spoke.

"All's ready," he said, "and you know your offices. All of us, except Mottreux, leave to-night. He remains here. But there are two things yet to be done. Mr. Rosenberg, I present to you the jewels which your cousin left to you." Mottreux came forward slowly and gave him the case, which he offered to the Jew who took it silently. Mottreux fell back a pace or two so that he stood behind his master. His face was livid, and he rubbed one hand backward and forward over his forehead. But he stood, horribly eyeing the Jew, while Considine went on: "I invite you to come with me if you choose, and I will see that you reach Jerusalem. There you may wait in peace the coming of your Messias. If you choose to stay here, you shall be taken to London to-night or to-morrow to any place that you name."

"I will do as you have said," Rosenberg answered. "The Lord shall reward you, and I will rest in Jerusalem."

"But for us, lords and princes, my companions," Considine said, and his tone sank from conversational ease to direction and control, "before we take up again the work that is before us, there remains one ceremony to fulfil. Initiates of love and death, I invite you to a sacrifice of death, by virtue of that hope and determination which shall make you masters of death as you are in your degree masters of love. There is in this house another guest, a child of royalty and an inheritor of one of the great and passionate imaginations of mankind, Inkamasi the Zulu. He is not with us, but we are with him. Shadow though it be of the true ecstasy and fiery life into which we shall enter, it is yet an heritage worthy of honour. To us has been committed the care of these vast and antique dreams; it is ours to see, so far as in us lies, that those who are possessed by them are entertained mightily and dismissed royally. Love and poetry and royalty are adored as the channels whereby the passion and imagination of man's heart become revealed to him, and knowing his own greatness he moves to the final accomplishment, the ending in his own person of all the accidents of place and time. This man is not with us, but in an hour when, superseded in Africa and undesired in Europe, he looks for a throne on which to perish, it must be we who offer him that throne. By no compulsion and no persuasion the King Inkamasi turns to the throne we offer and awaits immolation there. He is driven by the might of his own royalty which demands of him no lesser conclusion; he is received by us as, beyond his purpose, a meet and acceptable sacrifice. Put away from you the desires of your hearts, save the one last desire. I exhort you to come with hands of devotion and a single heart; who knows but this very night the work may be accomplished and there may descend upon one of us that ecstasy which shall drive him into death and in death to resurrection?"

Roger heard and realized what was conveyed by phrase and accent. Appalled by the understanding he took a half-step forward, but Caithness was before him. With a supernatural insolence as high as Considine's own, the priest cried out and confronted his enemy. "You dare not touch him," he said.

"This man is in your care, and his blood is on your head if you hurt him. God shall require it of you; I charge you to let him go——"

Considine had paused to let him speak, but now with a gesture he stopped him, and as the priest panted for words the other's voice set him aside.

"If that time which you and he accept and serve were at your disposal," he said, "I would not prevent your seeking to turn him from his assent. But it cannot be now. You will not encourage him to seek victory in death; and the king cannot fail from his royalty. What we do we do quickly. It is permitted, if you choose, that you shall be with him at his end; console, direct him as you will. But see that you do not interfere now with his and our choice, or you shall be taken from him. The offering which he makes and which we, with vaster purposes, accept is beyond the humble vision of your creed. He dies for the sake of his kingship; we experience his death for the sake of making it a part of our imaginations. Man shall conquer death, not by submitting to it as you teach, and not by avoiding it in a mere prolongation of life, as certain wise yet erring masters have taught, though this may be a necessary step towards conquest, but by entering into and annulling it."

"Antichrist," the priest exclaimed, "is the day of your dominion here?"

"Neither Christ nor Antichrist," the voice of the other answered him, "but I bring a gospel of redemption, and the ends of the world hear it: whom do men say that I, a son of man, am?"

He flung out a hand towards the group of his servants and disciples; he turned his eyes upon them and they answered, Arab and Egyptian, negro and white: "The end of mirage, the palm in the desert," "The last of the Imams, the Shadow of Allah," "The lord of sorcerers and kings," "The bearer of keys, the interpreter of tongues," and, as the mingled voices ceased, Considine's own answered them:

"I am all these and yet I am no more than any of you, for all of you shall be as I. That which I have known I have not known of myself. I am the child of the initiates; their servant and the servant of the mighty imagination which is in man. Any of you shall conclude his kingdom before me; purify yourselves, know, exult, and live. I call to you again, lords of the spirit, postulants of infinity, put away all desire but to be fulfilled in yourselves. The sacrifice of kingship is for the single of heart."

He swept his arms upward and inward in one compelling gesture. "Come, see the death of a man. Come you too," he added to his guests, "if you so will. But if not, then remain here until we come for you again, to accompany the body of the King Inkamasi to the sepulchre in the ocean which awaits him."

He went forward and his servants after him. Vereker signed to Caithness to precede him, and Roger accompanied the priest. Mottreux looked after them; then he went swiftly to Rosenberg and laid his hand on the casket.

"Do you really mean to go with these to Jerusalem?" he said.

"I am determined," the old man answered. "I will make haste to the city of our God."

Mottreux turned sharply away; he went after the others.

They were going to the room where that morning Roger had seen the attempt at revivification, but the last of the disciples did not quite catch them up. Very softly he went after them; when Vereker had entered the room he paused by the door, and as softly moved a key from within to without. Then he pulled the door nearly but not quite shut after him and waited.

The body of Nielsen had been removed; on the low couch, supported by cushions, the Zulu lay. Considine genuflected as he entered, and moving to one side made a sign to Caithness. The priest ran forward, threw something round his neck, and drew a crucifix from near his heart. He kneeled by the couch; Inkamasi leaned his head towards him and they murmured between themselves. Considine, waiting, looked round, and made a sign to Roger to come to his side. He slipped his arm into the young man's and said: "This is a gift of the universe to you; deal wisely with it. Be strong, exult, and live."

The two of them were together, a little distance from the head of the couch; opposite them, at a greater distance from the foot, four others had gathered. Mottreux was by the door with a clear space between him and the Zulu. So set, they waited till the speech between the priest and the king died; while the two yet remained in close and silent prayer Considine said in a low voice to the others: "Enlarge in you the imagination by which man lives; this is perhaps the moment of fulfilment. The work shall be accomplished to-night without ritual or ceremony such as we are used to, in your contemplation alone." He took a step towards Caithness and touched him on the shoulder, saying: "Have you spoken with the king?"

"You're committing wickedness," the priest exclaimed and ceased, broken either by his own passion or by the concentration of the other's power.

"Back, then," Considine gently said, and when Caithness had risen and moved a step or two away, he in turn knelt by the couch.

"Majesty," he said, "are you willing to restore your kingship through us to that of which it is a shadow?"

"Yes," Inkamasi said, "for though I hold you for my own enemies and for misguided men I think you are the only servants of the kingship that is more than the king."

"Majesty," Considine said again, "we are the king's servants and his greatest friends. Farewell." He touched Inkamasi's hand with his lips and rising signed to Roger to follow him. The young man went forward, knelt, and said, "I'm sorry if this happened through me."

"Don't be," Inkamasi said; "it's better to die here than

under the feet of a London crowd—if there's any difference. Thank you, and good-bye."

Roger touched his hand with his lips and went back. The rest, one by one, followed him, ending with Mottreux and Vereker. As Mottreux in turn moved back towards the door Caithness felt a hand press his arm and heard a soft whisper, "Come back and wait by me." The order reached him in his anguish; with a hope that even now something might interpose, he obeyed and slowly withdrew till he also stood by the door.

Meanwhile, his obeisance done, Vereker had brought to Considine a chalice that had been standing, filled with wine, on a carved table at the side of the room. His master poured into it the contents of a small phial; then he took the chalice in his hands, and turned towards the couch. The silence in the room grew so deep, the absorbed attention of the watchers so intense, that Roger felt as if the terrific moment must break in some new astonishing revelation. Regret and sorrow, bewilderment and antagonism, which had mingled in his heart, were swept away; an awful harmony began to exist. So, in other far-off lives, lesser or greater he could not tell, he had waited for Isabel when they were young and happy, and indeed he had chosen necessity; so he had submitted his obedience to the authority of Milton or Wordsworth, waiting for the august plenitude of their poetry to be manifested within him. Till now he had believed that sense of harmony to be all they— Isabel or *Paradise Lost*—had to offer, but he had begun to learn that to pause there was to be too easily content. The harmony itself was but a prelude to some enrichment of his whole being, which in its turn must be experienced in every detail—made familiar that new powers might arise. He gave himself, freely and wholly, to the moment; he was to live the more completely through the king's death. It was no good being distressed or ashamed; his business was to live by it, as if necessary it would be the business of others to live by his death. He gave himself to the moment, and in the moment to the whole charged imagination of man. It was no lie; the mind of man—not his mind or Inkamasi's but man's—was exalted above all the power of things, "of quality and fabric more divine," and yet his own was never nearer or more useful to man's than when he was most intensely aware of all things in himself. He gave himself to the moment.

"Drink, Majesty," Considine said, and gave the chalice into Inkamasi's hands. The king took it, raised it to his lips, and drank. Even as it left his lips, his grip relaxed, his face changed, he sank heavily on to the cushions behind him.

But before the dropped chalice reached the floor, before the sound of its fall could strike their ears, a violent explosion shattered them. Roger, fixed in his surrender, saw Considine jerk his arms up and fall crashing across the litter. Almost before the king's body had sunk lifeless his destroyer lay slain over him. For they saw, as soon as their startled senses acted, that two lives, not one, had been taken. The violence against which Considine had never pretended to be secure, but which had avoided him so long, had struck him at last. The bullet had pierced his skull; the blood streamed over the dead Zulu. And Mottreux dragged Caithness from the room, and shut and locked the door. He held the priest's arm; he rushed him through the house, making for the hall. Caithness ran, and listened to hasty orders: "Go straight to the car in front of the door . . . get in . . . I'll come. Can you drive?"

"Yes," he gasped.

"Get in the driver's seat." They reached the hall; Mottreux looking frantically round rushed him to the front door, paused less than a second to see that the priest was actually scrambling into the car, pushed the door almost shut, lest by chance the other should see him, and sent another mad glance around the hall.

By so small a chance he was defeated. The old Jew, when he was left alone with the casket, had, by some trick of the mind, gone back to the room where he and his companions had spent most of the day. He was sitting there, lost in his meditations, when Mottreux broke in on him, and in one wild dash caught the case in one hand. But Rosenberg held to the trust which the God of his fathers had imposed on him. He was dragged violently from his chair, but he clung to the sacred treasure; he heard a voice yelling oaths, but though he was shaken to and fro he said nothing. His face, as he lifted it, was full of a scorn deeper than time, the scorn of his God for the spoilers of the holy places. He saw the distorted face of a greedy Gentile above him, and before the bullet searched his brain he spat at it once.

But by now the revolvers of the other servants of the Deathless One had blown the lock of their prison from the door, and the momentary prisoners had already nearly reached the hall. In a wild confusion and anger they came; Mottreux heard them, and ran to the glass doors on to the drive. These were fastened, and he was again delayed. By the time he had got them open and was outside, Vereker and the Egyptian were out by the car. He was seen; he fired once and ran along the wall of the house. The shot probably saved Caithness's life, for none of the pursuers were in a state to distinguish between the responsibility of the fugitives for the crime. But Vereker was unarmed, and the Egyptian was distracted by Mottreux's appearance. He left the priest to his companion, and ran after Mottreux, circling widely out so as to command the corner as he approached it. In the darkness it could only dimly be seen.

Voices were calling from doors and windows. There were men in the room where the dead Jew lay. Roger, borne along in the general rush, was there also. He wondered afterwards why no-one had shot him down out of hand, and attributed his salvation to the fact that Considine had treated him familiarly. He tried to order his thoughts, but they only repeated themselves: "Considine is dead; is he dead?" Was he dead? or would he, first again in the great experiment, achieve the work he had desired? The question beat at his brain as he ran. He saw the body of the Jew as he came into the room, and paused by it. Without, from the darkness, there came more shots. Roger pulled himself together; he'd better look for Caithness. If Considine were dead, the two of them would be in a very dubious position; he went as far as the glass doors. There he listened; presently, away round the side of the house, he heard another shot. He slipped out and along to the car, whose lights shone steadily as they had done when last he looked at it before he had walked in the verandah and talked. This was the kind of thing that remained; the imagination of man was blown out in a moment but the light of his mechanical invention remained. He cursed deeply, and saw Caithness, who in a restless uncertainty had got out of the car. Roger walked up to him, but for a few seconds neither of them spoke.

At last Caithness said: "What had we better do?"

Roger answered: "I should think you'd better get away. Inkamasi's dead, so I don't see much point in your staying."

Caithness looked round, and tried to see something in the darkness. He failed, and presently asked, "What's happened to Mottreux?"

"How the hell do I know?" Roger asked. "Why did you bolt with him?" A sudden thought struck him, and he added: "Did you—by God, did you arrange for him to shoot?"

"No," the priest answered, "but I promised to do what I could for him if . . . if he needed it."

"I see," Roger said, and walked a few steps away. He couldn't trust himself to speak. That this dreamer, this master of vision should have been destroyed by—by a traitor and a clergyman. He walked back abruptly and said: "I hope you paid him better than Caiaphas did? Even at half-crowns it would only come to three pounds fifteen."

Caithness began quietly, "Don't be unfair, Ingram——"
but Roger pursued his own thoughts. "And did you promise
him as much for Rosenberg?"

"Rosenberg!" Caithness cried out, startled. "He can't have
killed Rosenberg?"

"Can't he?" Roger said. "What do you think he wanted?
Go and look; Rosenberg's dead and the jewels are gone."

The priest stared at him in something like horror. He had
believed Mottreux to be sincere, and yet now—words over-
heard between the traitor and Rosenberg rushed back, the
likelihood that so great a personal desire rather than a conversion of thought should have alienated him, his turning
away at the last moment, the shot heard in the room close at
hand, the old man slain (for he believed Roger at once), the
seizure of the jewels by a covetous hand. Roger saw him
flinch and said, with a touch of pity out of his own distress,
"You didn't know?"

"God help me!" Caithness said. "I didn't know." He
hadn't known; he hadn't, if it were blameworthy, been to
blame; if he were partly responsible for Considine's death, it
was a noble responsibility, and he would bear it. Out of evil,
God brought forth good. He added, "Then there's the less
reason to say."

Yet they did not move. Behind the house, between it and
the sea, in the darkness, armed men sought one another in
hate and fear, abandoning themselves to a passion which their
master would have bidden them use for the sole purpose of
interior enlargement and further victory. Their strength was
turned to greed of treasure or greed of vengeance; the accident
which had struck Considine down had released their too little
mastered frenzies. The two strangers delayed, reluctant alike
to go or stay in the stillness. And, while they delayed, the stillness burst into tumult. There were shots and voices calling,
Mottreux's voice challenging, a chaos of sound, and breaking
out of it and over it a high terrific shriek.

The shriek terrified them as they stood there; it was a death-call. It scattered their disputes and their dogmas, for, whether he who uttered it was slaying or being slain, it was the cry of an intenser death than that of an ordinary man. One of those experimenting spirits had broken into that cry; it swept out to them from the passion of a nature beyond theirs, and its sound pierced them with fear of death, of that greater life, and of the greater death in that life. The lord of the adepts was dead, and enmity was abroad among them as the dead Zulu had prophesied days before. The cry came to Roger as a blast that drove him away. Nigel Considine was dead; the treachery he had despised had taken him; the final dereliction had swallowed him. If he returned—but Roger fled from that return. His nerve broke; he shrank back against the car, and said to Caithness, "Let's go; let's go."

The priest himself, trembling, turned. "Shall we——" he began, laying his hand on the car.

"No, for God's sake," Roger exclaimed. "Let's leave it all, if we're leaving it. If it isn't for us, let's get away from it. Come; we'll get somewhere."

Caithness silently assented. "But let's get our coats at least!" he said. "They'll be just in there."

"I'm not going in there again," Roger said, "unless Considine himself calls me."

"Then I will," Caithness said. He sprang back into the hall, and in a couple of minutes returned. "We shall want them if we're walking all night," he said, and so, in a mingling of terror and despair, and hope and the commonplace, they went down to the gates and out into the darkness beyond. Once the priest said, "Mrs. Ingram'll be glad to see you back."

"Yes," Roger answered. "Isabel . . ." and said no more.

Chapter Fourteen

SEA-CHANGE

Some time next morning, after wandering long on foot and finding at last in an unknown town a small garage where they hired a car that took them to Winchester, and coming thence by train to London, they reached again the house in Kensington, from which less than forty-eight hours earlier they had been swept away. The streets were still full of wanderers, though it had been known for hours that safety had returned, and the wild intrusion been destroyed. The mob by then had fallen into a waking stupor, not unlike the sleep in which Rosamond still lay; it moved somnambulistically, and the civil authorities, by the use of police and military, by commandeering transport, by supplying food and drink as best they could, managed at last to control and direct it. Laden motor-buses carried the fugitives back towards their houses; taxis, lorries, and all other possible vehicles were put in service for the same purpose. Roger and Caithness made a slow way by the Tubes, now gradually freeing themselves from their invasion, to Colindale Square. They came to it shivering in the bleak noon—as chilled bathers might stumble up a stony beach, while behind them a deserted and disconsolate sea moaned. Sir Bernard came hastily to meet them, deserting for the time being the medley of fugitives who filled his kitchen and overflowed into the other rooms, and for whom conveyances had not yet been found. Roger nodded to him but could not speak; he left explanations to Caithness. In a moment Isabel came also; to her he turned, and with her he shut himself away. Once safe he said to her with no accent in his voice: "He's dead."

217

"Dead!" she exclaimed. "Roger, my dear!"

He had perhaps never entirely trusted her before, for all their sweet friendship. But his defences were down, and he lay exposed, terribly sensitive to her looks and words. She neither sympathized nor condoled; in the deep practice of her love her heart was struck equally with his. She suffered his desolation as she had his desire; the trust of his spiritual necessity with which she had charged herself knew this union also. He realized at that moment the vast experience of love which she had undergone, and accepted it. But he only said with a faint smile, implicitly recognizing her vicarious grief, "Yet you didn't believe in him."

She sat down, wide eyes on his, and ignoring the comment, said in a hushed voice of awe, "Tell me. Can he be——?"

He told her as clearly as he could, what had happened. And at the end she said, "But, Roger, mightn't he . . ." She couldn't finish; her own personal nature fainted before the intensity with which it felt another's hope.

"I don't know," he answered. "If so . . . It may be, but I daren't think of it. Isabel, Isabel, to think what killed him!"

At that moment Caithness was talking swiftly to Sir Bernard downstairs. "So, when I went back for our coats, I saw them," he said; "they were all ready there, all three packets and I brought them with me." He pointed at the table on which three thick envelopes lay which he had extracted from his coat-pocket. "He must have meant to take them with him, or else they were directions for the others. They were on a chest in the hall, waiting till we—till he—came back. Don't you think they ought to go to the Prime Minister?"

"I hate telling the Prime Minister anything," Sir Bernard said. "It's like feeding a gorilla without a body; he can't digest words. I don't know which is worse for civilized man, Suydler or Considine."

"Considine's dead," Caithness said.

Sir Bernard lifted a packet distastefully. "I wish I were a

Christian," he murmured, "then I should feel I ought to. As it is—I suppose Considine *is* dead?"

"Of course he is," Caithness said impatiently. "Mottreux shot him; I've just told you. I'd no notion he wanted the jewels. And even if he weren't—Considine, I mean—that would only make it more urgent that Suydler should have the papers. They may be of use or they mayn't. But he ought to have them."

"They'll all be in cipher, I should think," Sir Bernard said, with a good deal of satisfaction. "Suydler can have a jolly time guessing it. But I don't like it, in spite of Mr. Considine's obscene and pernicious gospel. I don't like giving *any* gospel to Suydler. Yes, all right, I suppose I must. Portrait of Gallio presenting the manuscript of the Evangelists to the Missing Link. You'll have to come too; then you can tell him all about the house."

When as a consequence the house by the sea was approached, late the same day, with great force and much circumspection, the results were a little disappointing. The body of Inkamasi still lay on its royal couch, but the body of the master of the adepts had disappeared. No living person was there; no car in the drive nor submarine in the bay. But behind the house lay Mottreux, a knife-wound in his throat, and sprawled over him, a bullet in his chest, the body of a negro, whom Caithness recognized as one of those that had followed Considine to the king's death. Further away lay the Egyptian, also shot. Vereker and the Arab were not to be found.

But the extent of the catastrophe which the traitor had brought upon the headship of the cause became clear, as the days passed. Considine and three of the closest members of his personal staff had been destroyed, and the great movement was checked. There were no more messages from the High Executive. What tale reached the various headquarters of the African armies the European Governments never knew. But the labouring and anxious generals of their forces began to telegraph the most cheering news. In one or two districts something like panic broke out among the enemy, a great noise of wailing and disorderly firing and then flight. In others the negro forces began to retire, and as they were pressed by the pursuit gave way and were overwhelmed.

The papers Caithness had seized, which after a great deal of trouble were at least partially decoded—only partially; some of them remained mysteries even to the most ingenious cipher-expert—contained sufficient allusions in detail to make the task of the uncovering of Considine's bases—houses in Europe and headquarters in Africa—a much easier business than had been feared. An encouraging but slightly vague account appeared in the Press of how a British patriot, who preferred his Imperial citizenship to his Zulu birthright, had shot Considine while being pressed to join him. It was understood that he had deliberately sacrificed himself in order to help England, and a good deal of quiet (and not too quiet) pride was felt that it was an English subject, or at least a Dominion subject, who had acted so. No Senegalese had done as much, nor the native of any district administered by other European countries. Such was the spirit produced by the British occupation. A rather acrimonious correspondence opened between the British Government and the other Powers on the subject of Considine's own nationality. The French, Italian, Spanish, and Belgian ambassadors presented Notes which pointed out that the late Nigel Considine being a British subject the respective Governments had in equity a claim to be indemnified by his Britannic Majesty's Government for the expense to which they had been put. His Britannic Majesty replied through the High Executive of Mr. Raymond Suydler's Foreign Minister (the Earl of Basingstoke) to the effect that—there were nine mutually destructive reasons why the claim should either not be admitted or should be set against still heavier amounts due to his Britannic Majesty for damage suffered. Mr. Suydler made a great speech at an Albert Hall

Meeting, and was cheered wildly when he announced that the
European Governments had determined to sign no formal
terms of peace with an enemy who had no business to be there
at all, but to hold a conference in Madeira to decide on the
future settlement of Africa, the terms of which would afterwards be submitted to the League of Nations, thus confirming
the passionate belief of the Powers in democratic control.
Mr. Suydler was also loudly applauded in the course of his
witty and brilliant remarks upon the attempts of the madman
who had been responsible for all the trouble to turn his
megalomaniac nonsense into philosophical nonsense. "Guess:
what can you do but guess? We guessed—*and we guessed
right!*" Terrific cheers.

Sir Bernard read it and smiled a little sadly. Philip read it
and let it slip by; he was engaged with a recovered Rosamond
and his career. Roger did not read it. Sir Bernard asked Philip
whether, at a pinch, he would vote for Suydler or Considine.
Philip read it, and for almost the first time in his life startled
his father into real admiration by saying that he should vote
for Ian Caithness. But Sir Bernard's mind illumined the
answer with a drier light than Philip's. He wrote of it to the
priest: "I congratulate you, my dear Ian, on your proselyte—
you can instruct him further when you come up to marry
him. There's a notion grown up that since his career'll have
to be postponed or reorganized or reborn or something, it
would be only reasonable ("reasonable!" I also have my
martyrdoms) that I should make financial arrangements for
him to be married at once. Rosamond's still recuperating at
the cottage in Dorset, she sent me a pretty note of thanks the
other day in which she asked whether you didn't know the
Archbishop fairly well. You'll guess—as Suydler would say—
what she meant. I leave it to you to decide whether you do—
well enough, I mean. If he should be shot by a deacon who
wanted to wear the vestments of the See at a fancy dress ball
I fancy Suydler would be willing to offer you the Archiepiscopal

mitre; he's touchingly grateful to someone, and went so far
as to ask me if there was anything I wanted. I told him I
wanted justice and proportion which is the daughter of justice,
knowledge and abstraction which is the daughter of knowledge. This dreadful tendency to personify and (therefore)
mythologize I attribute to you and the late Mr. Considine,
who was an entire mythology about himself. From Considine
to you (excuse me), from you to Philip, from Philip to
Rosamond—behold the history of religion! The High
Executive disappears under the sea, and leaves its brother of
Canterbury to add a touch of richness to my daughter-in-law's
wedding. If I had indulged myself in irony as long as Provi-
dence, I should be a little tired of it by now, but I suppose he
has infinite patience with himself as well as with us. But
mightn't he occasionally try a new note?"

Of Roger Sir Bernard said nothing, though he thought of
him as he wrote "the High Executive disappears under the
sea." For he was aware that that was all that they knew, and
even that they only surmised, and he thought Roger was
intensely aware of it too. But he did not know how acutely,
and Isabel did not tell him.

Nor had she told him of how much younger and older at
once Roger had seemed since his return. She missed in him
something of warfare and much of scorn. If he was arrogant
still it was a more airy arrogance than of old; if he mocked he
mocked more tenderly. But she wondered whether in his heart
he—and she also—secretly awaited a return.

Roger himself could not have told her. He shut himself
away from the noisy European victories, from the talk and
the congratulations. He took up his work again, but as he
made notes for a special address on *The Antithetical Couplet from
Dryden to Johnson* he was humbly aware that this work was
part of a greater work. It would be his fault if he so touched the
least detail of the divine art as to leave himself or others less
sensitive to its central passion—his fault, his most grievous

fault, his sad incompetence. But even sad incompetence might recognize the Power it could hardly name. He would never cease any more to acknowledge it, to search in it and for it, to believe in it, to wait for it. Other people had their ways; this was his. What more——

What indeed had chanced? Had the submarine, plunging away from that house of mingled death and life, carried with it but the dead body of its lord? and had men somewhere far off, seen that body change beneath inexorable corruption and committed it to the waters of the sea or to the African earth? Did it there undergo the final doom of mortality in slow change, or had some fiercer destruction, the shark or the tiger, seized on it? He had dreams sometimes of sharks fighting round the sinking body of Nigel Considine, and sometimes he had other dreams. He saw the body carried to the submarine, he saw it carried off far into the ocean, and then, sometimes in the vessel, sometimes out of it, he saw it change. Sometimes he saw men in a narrow room watching by it, crying out, hurrying to it, adoring it. But more often—though the dream itself was not often—he saw it floating alone in the middle of the sea, far away, far down, and he saw the eyes open and the hands move, and the whole body stir. Life was rushing back into it; power, spirit, imagination, whatever name sad incompetence found for it, was re-animating the willing flesh. He saw it walking in the waters and heard it calling through them. The creatures of the deep, octopus and shark, greed and ferocity, fled before it. Behind it, as it came, there was no more sea; in front of it the waters flowed into it and became the man who moved in them. Back from the shore they swept, out towards that advancing humanity, and all their mysteries were swallowed up in his shining lucidity. This was the vast of experience, currents and tides, streams and whirlpools, restless waves and fathomless depths, absorbed by man. The salt that tinctured it, as the salt of Sir Bernard's amusement tinctured life, was absorbed also. Valuable as that preservative salt was, in the end it was infinitely less than the elements of which it was part, and to prefer it to the renewed body would be to prefer the means to the end, detachment to union. Irony might sustain the swimmer in the sea; it could not master the sea. A greater than Sir Bernard did that now, if indeed now, up the African sand or the English beach, that conqueror returned.

If he returned. If he carried out the experiment of his vision, the purpose of his labours. If, first among his peers, when all believed him lost, he thrust himself from the place of shades back into immortal and transmuted life, if he held death at his disposal, if he knew how the vivid ecstasy of experience dominated all shapes and forms, all accidents of time and place. If he came now, humming those last songs which the greatest of the poets had made from his own vision of Ariel flying free, smiling at the blindness of extreme pain and the paralysis of extreme possession, guardian of myths and expositor of power . . . if he returned. If now, while the world shouted over the defeat of his allies and subjects, while it drove its terror back into its own unmapped jungles, and subdued its fiercer desires to an alien government of sterile sayings, if now he came once more to threaten and deliver it. If—ah beyond, beyond belief!—but if he returned. . . .